Praise for Wendy Corsi Staub's *The Other Family*

"Great psychological suspense with a wallop of a twist."
—#1 *New York Times* bestselling author Harlan Coben

"A twisty ride steeped in betrayal. The perfect winter read!"
—J.D. Barker, *New York Times* bestselling
author of *A Caller's Game*

"Creepy families, big secrets, and lingering questions come together in this twisty page-turner that will have you speed-reading to try to figure it out."
—#1 internationally bestselling author Darby Kane

"Wendy Corsi Staub has always been one of my favorite writers, but she surpasses even her best work with *The Other Family*. A chilling and addictive novel of suspense, it also speaks deep truths about family ties—and how they can support or destroy us. I really loved this book."
—Alison Gaylin, author of *The Collective*

"Dark, twisty, and irresistible, *The Other Family* is domestic suspense turned up to 11, the gripping tale of one family's cross-country move to Brooklyn—and the explosive revelations that follow when one woman is finally forced to reckon with her past. From her pitch-perfect characterizations to her unerring sense of plot and pace, Wendy Corsi Staub displays a command of the form that's not merely masterful—it's practically diabolical."
—Elizabeth Little, *Los Angeles Times* bestselling
author of *Dear Daughter* and *Pretty as a Picture*

THE OTHER FAMILY

Also by Wendy Corsi Staub

THE FOUNDLINGS SERIES
The Butcher's Daughter
Dead Silence
Little Girl Lost

MUNDY'S LANDING SERIES
Bone White
Blue Moon
Blood Red

SOCIAL MEDIA THRILLERS
The Black Widow
The Perfect Stranger
The Good Sister

NIGHTWATCHER TRILOGY
Shadowkiller
Sleepwalker
Nightwatcher

LIVE TO TELL TRILOGY
Hell to Pay
Scared to Death
Live to Tell

THE
OTHER
FAMILY

A Novel

WENDY CORSI STAUB

wm
WILLIAM MORROW
An Imprint of HarperCollins*Publishers*

THE OTHER FAMILY. Copyright © 2022 by Wendy Corsi Staub. All rights reserved. Printed in the United States of America. No part of this book may be used or reproduced in any manner whatsoever without written permission except in the case of brief quotations embodied in critical articles and reviews. For information, address HarperCollins Publishers, 195 Broadway, New York, NY 10007.

HarperCollins books may be purchased for educational, business, or sales promotional use. For information, please email the Special Markets Department at SPsales@harpercollins.com.

FIRST EDITION

Designed by Diahann Sturge

Library of Congress Cataloging-in-Publication Data has been applied for.

ISBN 978-0-06-308460-5

22 23 24 25 26 BRR 10 9 8 7 6 5 4 3 2 1

Acknowledgments

With gratitude to Lucia Macro, Liate Stehlik, Lyssa Keusch, Emily Krump, Asanté Simons, Amy Halperin, and the team at William Morrow; Laura Blake Peterson, Holly Frederick, James Farrell, and the team at Curtis Brown, Limited; copy editor Gina Macedo; Carol and Greg Fitzgerald and the team at The Book Report Network; those who read the manuscript in various stages, helped me answer questions large and small, or otherwise lent support: Jackie Brilliant, Kyle Cadley, Greg Herren, Maureen Martin, Suzanne Schmidt, Mark Staub, and Veronica Taglia. Especially to Alison Gaylin, who read the earliest draft and buoyed me to keep going, and Brody Staub, who when I told him the premise, tilted his head and said, "What if you twist it so that . . . ?"

Monsters are real, and ghosts are real, too. They live inside us, and sometimes they win.

—Stephen King, *The Shining*

Part One

Nora

The Howell family moves into 104 Glover Street in Brooklyn on the Friday before Labor Day.

Overnight storms have scoured summer stagnancy from the air and the sky begs contemplation, no matter how fatigued one might be from a sleepless red-eye cross-country flight in the middle coach seat.

And so Nora pauses on the stoop with her neck arched, taking in the cloudless swath above neighboring rooftops.

As descriptions go, mere *blue* won't suffice. Nor *cobalt, cerulean, sapphire* . . .

Crayola colors.

She closes her eyes, seeing the delicate blue blooms that grew wild in Teddy's California garden, hearing Teddy's voice. "*These?* You like *these?* Pick all you want. They're an invasive species."

"What do you mean?"

"They're insidious. They creep in and take over. I don't know how they got here, but they don't belong, and I can't get rid of them."

"But they're so pretty," Nora said. "What are they?"

"The botanical name is *Myosotis scorpioides*. Regular people call them scorpion grass. Or forget-me-nots."

Teddy is not a regular person.

Teddy, unlike so many people in Nora's life, is unforgettable.

And Teddy, who believes everything happens for a reason, is certain that this move, even if it's only a temporary corporate transfer, is a dangerous mistake.

"Mom?"

Nora turns away from the forget-me-not sky.

Seventeen-year-old Stacey is crouched just inside the low iron gate beside the dog's crate, petting him through the bars. Though she recently got contacts, she's wearing glasses today because of the long flight. Behind the thick lenses, her brown eyes are underscored with dark circles and blinking up into the sun. Her dark hair is frizzy, bedhead-matted at the back. She's wearing a shapeless hoodie and yoga pants that have never been worn for yoga.

"Can I walk Kato?"

Nora looks to the curb. Her square-jawed, fair-haired husband is talking to the moving van driver who'd pulled up right behind their airport taxi. Keith would say no to sending their teenage daughter out into the city alone minutes after arrival. Keith says no to a lot of things. That's why Stacey's asking Nora.

"Sure, go ahead. There's a dog run that way." She points toward Edgemont Boulevard. "In the park, three blocks down on the left."

"Thanks." Stacey turns to her fourteen-year-old sister

perched on the bottom step, digging through her carry-on bag like she's searching for a lifesaving serum.

Ah, a hairbrush. Same thing, in Piper's corner of the world. She plucks it out and runs it through her hair. It's long and straight and blond, like Nora's. But Piper's isn't pulled back into a practical ponytail, and hers is natural, courtesy of Keith.

"Hey, can you bring my bag in for me while I walk Kato?" Stacey asks her.

"Don't you want to see our new house first?"

"Nah."

"Wait, where are you going?" Keith calls as Stacey drops a black nylon backpack beside her sister and takes off with the pug.

"To the dog run. Mom said it's fine."

"But—" Too late. Stacey and Kato disappear around the corner. He looks up at Nora. "What dog run?"

"There's one in the park."

"What park?"

"The one off Edgemont."

"And you know this because . . ."

"Because I did my homework on the neighborhood, Keith."

"Do you really think it's a good idea to just let her roam around?"

"If I didn't think it was a good idea, would I have let her go? We live here now. She's going to be on her own in the city. Piper, too."

"We've been here five minutes. What if she gets lost? Does she even know this address?"

"She has her phone. We have our phones. It'll be fine."

He doesn't look convinced, but the movers are out of the van, opening the back and setting up a ramp. It won't take long to unload. They're only in New York for a year, and the house is fully furnished, complete with curtains, bedding, and cookware.

"Piper, come on, let's go in," Nora calls.

"One second." She's traded her hairbrush for her phone, scrolling the screen.

Keith slings his leather satchel over his shoulder and starts for the stoop, then turns back and grabs the empty dog crate. "Guess we'd better not leave anything lying around on the street. Come on, Pipe. Let's check out the house. You're going to love it."

Those were the precise words Nora had said to him weeks ago when they'd flown in from LA to find a place to live.

They'd spent a fruitless day slogging in and out of a warm August rain looking at potential apartments and systematically ruled them all out. Most were too inconvenient or too small, and they couldn't afford the ones that weren't. Over dinner, Keith scrolled through Manhattan real estate listings, looking for something they might have missed and could see before they caught their flight home the next afternoon.

"Here, check out this one, Nora. It has outdoor space. You can have your garden."

She peered at his screen. "That looks like a fire escape."

"It *is* a fire escape. But you can put plants on it, and there's an East River view between the buildings, see?"

"A view won't matter to the girls as much as having a *house*. They aren't used to elevators and laundry rooms and strangers on the other sides of us."

She showed him a listing on her own phone—a bargain of a Brooklyn row house. "It has a backyard, basement, stairways, even a front porch."

"That's just a stoop," Keith informed her, as if she didn't know. "Anyway, that row house is no bargain. The rent is as high as the places we saw today."

"Those were shoeboxes."

"Because it was Manhattan. Trust me, you don't want to live in a borough."

"Trust *me*—I don't want to live in a shoebox. I guess we'd better check out the suburbs. New Jersey, or Connecticut, maybe—"

"No way. We're moving to New York to live in New York."

"Brooklyn *is* New York." Seeing him waver, she touched his arm. "Come on, Keith. We need to find something if we're going to do this. Let's check out the house. You're going to love it."

"I doubt that."

"Please?"

"Fine, Goldilocks. Guess it can't hurt to look."

Oh, but it could.

The next day, they took a cab to 104 Glover, the second address from the corner on a block lined with tidy and welcoming redbrick nineteenth-century row houses. All had three tall windows on the top floor; two alongside the front door a level above the street, and smaller, iron-barred basement windows. All had corniced roofs and stone stoops atop twelve steep stairs bordered by ornate black grillwork. They were indistinguishable from each other save a few small details. At 104, the white trim was freshly painted and the stone planters flanking the bottom step were spiked with red fountain grass and trailing blue lobelia.

The property manager, Deborah, greeted them with a warning that it was brand-new to the rental market and they'd have to jump on it if they wanted it. Nora already knew that she did, but she wanted Keith to want it, too. She *needed* him to want it.

After Deborah's tour and some wheedling on Nora's part, he grudgingly agreed.

Flash forward a month and he's acting as though it was all his idea, eager to show off the house to Piper, hustling her along as she dallies over texts to her friends back home.

"They're not even awake at this hour, Pipe! Let's go!"

"Okay, okay, just let me send this last one, Dad!" She presses a button, tucks the phone away, and picks up her own bag, then her sister's, with a grunt. "What's in here, boulders?"

"Books," Nora tells her, "and I'm sure they're all about Lizzie Borden. That's her latest thing."

Keith takes the heavy bag from Piper. "You know Stacey. She's always obsessed over one thing or another. Too bad it's never anything like—I don't know—kittens, baking, yoga . . ."

"Who's Lizzie Borden?"

Keith answers with a casual shrug. "Axe murderess who killed her parents back in the 1800s."

"Ew. Why does Stacey like gory death stuff?"

"A lot of people are interested in true crime," Nora points out.

"Well, I'm not."

Piper is such an agreeable teenager, just as she was an easy baby, toddler, and child.

She was spared colic, terrible twos *and* threes, tantrums, baby fat, acne, adolescent angst, bullying. Spared everything that tormented her sister, and thus Keith and Nora, as they saw their firstborn through each stage. By the time Stacey was in preschool, they'd revised their plan to have a large family. Two children would be more than enough, and parenting was so all-consuming that Nora stopped toying with the idea of eventually going back to work.

They're in the homestretch now. Next year at this time, Stacey will be preparing to head off to college. Until then, Nora hopes that things will go better for her here in New York than back in California; that she'll find friends and fit in.

For her sake, she assures herself. *Not for mine.*

"Got the key, Nora?"

"Right here." Her hand trembles as she fits it into the lock and turns it.

She opens the door, steps over the threshold, and takes a deep breath scented with furniture polish and something vaguely fruity.

The house is dim and shadowed, tall windows shrouded in shades and draperies. She feels along the wall beside the door, presses an old-fashioned button switch, and light floods from the vintage fixture high overhead.

"Nice, isn't it?" Keith asks Piper.

She takes in the ornate oak staircase, polished hardwoods, and antique furniture, and points at a wall niche, where a glass case holds a coppery black orb the size of a cantaloupe. "What's that?"

"Revolutionary War cannonball. It was dug up right here in the backyard. That doesn't happen in California, right?"

"I guess not. What's that?" She's zeroed in on the cast-iron radiator tucked alongside the steep staircase, and Keith explains that it will heat the house when the weather cools.

Piper indicates the sepia Victorian family portrait on the wall above the stairs. "Who are they?"

"They lived here back in the olden days. See the carved mantel behind them? It's the same one that's on the living room fireplace. Here, I'll show you."

Keith leads Piper through the archway like a listing agent.

Remembering how reluctant he'd been to even consider this house, Nora marvels at his proprietary air now. She might find it sweet, or amusing, if she weren't so numb.

The move was exhausting, and she hasn't slept in so long, and . . .

And now that they're here, emotion is swelling in her throat, threatening to spill over.

She closes her eyes.

Just breathe. It's going to be good here. Everything's going to be all right now.

When she opens her eyes, she spots the fruity scent's source: a vase filled with spiky bright red blooms on the marble console table by the door.

Salvia elegans—pineapple sage.

"It symbolizes healing," Teddy's voice whispers in her head.

Nora smiles. It's a perfect welcoming touch for their new lives in the perfect house for a perfect family . . .

On the surface, anyway.

Let the healing begin.

Jacob

ven now, a quarter of a century later, he visits the house.
Sometimes, it's on the way to wherever he's going, or
just a slight detour—walk down one block instead of
another. More often, it's out of his way, yet he's compelled
to go.

He doesn't linger and stare; nothing like that. Not the way
people did back in 1994, after the murders. A triple family
homicide—father, mother, daughter—drew attention, even in
New York, even in those violent days, with the homicide rate
at record highs amid the crack epidemic. The story made all
the papers.

The crime faded from public awareness, but the killer
who'd slaughtered the family at 104 Glover was never ap-
prehended. According to the press, there were no suspects.
Investigation coverage was minimal, and quickly dropped.

He wonders whether Anna had known what was happening as she drew her last breath on that January night,
whether she'd suffered.

Some days, good days, he convinces himself that she
hadn't.

A few weeks before the murders, Jacob's grandmother

had gone to bed on Christmas Eve and failed to wake up on Christmas morning. Such a shame that it happened on the holiday, and without warning, people had said at the funeral.

Yet according to his grandfather, she'd died an easy death. "Berta was always tossing and turning, up and down, up and down. Me, I hear every little thing. That night, nothing. Best sleep I had in sixty years. And Berta—she just slipped away, peacefully."

But there's a difference between dying in your sleep of natural causes and being bullet-blasted in the brain.

On bad days, walking past 104 Glover and remembering the young woman who'd lived and died there, Jacob wonders whether Anna was awake in that last instant. Perhaps she'd been stirred from sleep by a footstep in the hall, or sensed someone standing over her bed.

He pictures her rolling over to face her executioner; sees those big brown eyes of hers widening in dread just before the gunshot.

But of course, it hadn't happened that way. She'd been double-tapped in the back of the head while sleeping on her stomach.

On this sun-dappled late summer morning, he rounds the corner and sees a familiar SUV with an oval *LBI* sticker on the rear window—Long Beach Island, down the Jersey Shore.

The vehicle belongs to the couple who live diagonally across the street from 104 Glover. Luggage is heaped in the back. The owner, dressed in shorts and a Rip Curl T-shirt, stands on the running board, securing surfboards to the top. His wife has just joined him, in a broad-brimmed straw hat and sunglasses with a beach bag over her shoulder. Their voices carry.

"All locked up and ready to go?" he asks.

"Yes. Did you put my wine in the cooler?"

"Crap. I knew I forgot something."

"Blake! Go back and get it. I need it!"

"There's wine down the shore."

"Not the kind I like," she whines.

Some people these days are so entitled, Jacob thinks, moving on past the bickering couple. When he was their age, he wouldn't have—

Stopping short, he gapes at 104 Glover.

No one has lived there since the murders.

Now the front door is propped wide open and a moving van sits at the curb.

Nora

The morning passed in a flurry of cleaning and unpacking, transforming the stagnant, shuttered house into a home filled with sunlight and voices. Now the scents of furniture polish and take-out pizza mingle with the pineapple sage in the front hall.

Passing the vase on her way up the stairs after lunch, Nora again thinks of healing. Of Teddy.

Time to sneak away and make a furtive phone call.

Keith is in the living room with his laptop, working from home to get a head start on the new job. The girls retreated to their rooms, Stacey's in the middle of the hall across from the bathroom, Piper's at the far end. Their doors are closed, and all is silent beyond.

Back home, they have their own suites, with walk-in closets and bathrooms. Here, their rooms are smaller than their closets. There's one full bath for four people, unless you count the rust-stained shower stall in the basement, a 1960s rec room remnant.

But this is New York, and it's only for a year.

In the sunlit master bedroom at the top of the stairs, Nora changes out of the jeans and white T-shirt she'd donned yesterday morning on the opposite coast. Yesterday, yesterday's *life*, might as well have been lived by a stranger.

She puts on another pair of jeans, darker and more fitted, and another T-shirt, this one black. She releases her long blond hair from its tight ponytail and with it, the last of a tension headache she didn't even realize she had.

Better. So much better, she assures the woman in the mirror.

Everything will be better from now on. You can do this. You're doing it. You did it. You're here.

The woman starts to smile, but her blue eyes widen as a faint snatch of music box melody tinkles into the room, and the summer breeze chills.

Nora stands poised, head tilted, not sure whether she really heard it. Was it a ghost? Her imagination?

She steps closer to the billowing curtains and leans toward the open screen, peering down at parallel lines of redbrick row houses and parked cars. She hears only street noise— distant sirens, traffic, a radio, men shouting, kids playing, and then . . .

There it is again. She's relieved to see an old-time ice cream truck trundle into view like an aging crooner taking the stage, timeworn and playing a nostalgic tune. Not a ghost, not her imagination, no reason to be uneasy. But there's something . . .

"I told you so, Nora," Teddy's voice whispers. *"I told you this move wouldn't make anything better. I told you it was dangerous."*

"No," she says aloud. "You're wrong, Teddy."

She shoves her feet into sneakers, grabs her phone, and descends the stairs beneath the Victorian family portrait.

A rigidly posed young mother in a high-collared dress and father in a three-piece suit rest their hands on their seated teenage daughter's shoulders. Her eyes are fixed on something behind the photographer and she's clutching a nosegay of delicate flowers Nora's pretty sure are forget-me-nots, even without the evocative blue.

These people are a part of 104 Glover's history, like the Howells, and all who came between.

Nora peeks through the archway into the living room. The ornate carved mantel in the photo's background remains intact above the marble fireplace.

Keith is in a cushy leather recliner, phone in hand, laptop open, head thrown back, snoring. Yeah, so much for that head start, but Nora is relieved. He won't ask any questions until she's back; might not even realize she's gone.

She grabs the leash draped over the newel post and crosses the wide archway into the dining room. It's formal, with built-in corner cabinetry, another fireplace, and a polished oval table. Beyond tall windows, the brick patio is lush with green foliage and abundant summer blooms. Flowering vines crawl along trellises and arbors, and a thick, thorny border of roses and berries provides a living privacy screen.

Nora's eye lingers on faded blossoms that need deadheading and unruly brambles that need pruning. But first things first.

In the kitchen, she finds Kato snoozing in a sunny patch on the back doormat.

Her voice echoes off the subway-tiled walls, polished stone countertops, and slate floor as she asks, "Hey, want to go for a walk?"

The pug opens one eye and closes it again.

Nora fastens the leash to his collar and gives it a little tug. "Come on. Let's get out of here. Just you and me."

He gets to his feet with an agreeable wag of his tail, though he'd have been content to doze the afternoon away like Keith. Kato's on the lazy side even for a pug, and this morning's walk with Stacey filled his daily quota, and then some. But if Keith asks where she went, she'll say the dog wanted to go out.

She half expects him to appear and call after her as she heads down the steps onto the sidewalk, and holds her breath until she rounds the corner onto Edgemont Boulevard.

Safe.

The ice cream truck has moved on, but the song is stuck in her head.

All around the mulberry bush, the monkey chased the weasel . . .

With the holiday weekend looming, honking traffic snakes toward airports and beaches. Helmeted cyclists whiz along the bike lane, veering around potholes and double-parked vehicles. Kids on skateboards weave around curbside lines at food trucks, deliverymen with loaded dollies, pedestrians pushing baby strollers and wire grocery carts, and fellow dog walkers, some of them professionals with several per leash.

Vinyl-sided houses and brick apartment buildings are interspersed with small shops, ethnic restaurants, and bodegas bordered by buckets of cut flowers. Their perfume is lost in air thick with hot tar, hot food, and hot sun, directly overhead now in a sky that's faded to the soft shade of frayed denim. A dozen different songs blast from car speakers and open windows. Nora recognizes none of them, but they effectively banish "Pop Goes the Weasel."

As she passes a plywood-barricaded construction site, orange-vested workers greet her with wolf whistles and catcalls.

"Yo, Blondie!"

"Lookin' fine!"

Nora clenches her jaw and looks straight ahead, glad she's wearing sunglasses. She isn't used to this. Back home she doesn't often find herself in such close proximity to strangers.

She crosses the street and makes her way into the park, a shade-dappled oasis beyond a low stone wall, looking for a private spot. The street din fades as she follows a winding gravel path lined with ancient trees and colorful perennials in full bloom. Keeping an eye out for leering men and potential muggers, she sees only joggers and strolling families, senior citizens congregating on benches and teenagers shooting hoops on a basketball court.

The park might be different after dark, but right now, it's idyllic. Coiled tension unfurls like fiddlehead fronds as she sits on a vacant bench and dials Teddy's number.

It rings right into voice mail.

"It's me. I know you're traveling, but I just wanted to let you know that we made it. We're here, all moved in, and everything's okay. I'll try you again over the weekend if I can get away, or next week for sure. I love you."

She hangs up and watches a hummingbird dart among a blazing star's bottlebrush purple spires. Kato noses along the path, then appears to be settling in for a nap. He'd be content to skip the dog run, but she isn't ready to head back yet.

She tugs the leash and they move on, past a fountain, an ice cream stand, and a baseball field populated by adolescent girls, bases loaded.

Nora thinks of Piper, who inherited Keith's athletic prowess and played soccer and softball back home. Of Stacey, who did not.

The large fenced-in dog run is crowded. A few owners are playing with their pups while others are congregated and chatting like old friends. All the benches are occupied. Nora unleashes Kato and he trots toward the water fountain, tongue hanging out.

"Aw, somebody's thirsty," a female voice comments.

She turns to see a striking woman. Her lipstick is that ideal shade of red that's always eluded Nora—not so bright it's clownish, not so dark it's closer to maroon. The rest of her face is masked by enormous black sunglasses. Her dark hair is pulled back in a sleek chignon. She's wearing a black sleeveless turtleneck, trim cropped black pants, and black flats—Audrey Hepburn in *Breakfast at Tiffany's*, Nora thinks, returning her smile.

"What's your dog's name?" She bends to pet him.

"Kato."

"Wow, he's adorable. You're adorable, aren't you, guy?" He licks her hand, and she laughs. "Is he always this friendly, or am I special?"

Nora smiles and shakes her head. "Not that you're not special, but . . ."

"Way to burst my bubble. He's like this with everyone, huh?"

"Pretty much. He showed up at our house one day and just kind of stuck around like he belonged there."

"Oh, so he's named after Kato Kaelin? The guy who lived in OJ Simpson's guesthouse?"

"Exactly. At the time, my daughter was reading a book about that case—she's kind of a true crime buff," Nora adds quickly, lest this woman get the wrong idea.

Which is . . . what? That something's wrong with a teenage girl who enjoys reading about murder and mayhem?

The woman nods and moves on. "So, I'm Heather, and those guys"—she points at an enormous, shaggy mixed breed and a small corgi—"are Mutt and Geoffrey. With a *G*."

"I'm Nora. With an *N*."

Heather grins. "Where do you live?"

"Glover Street. We just moved in."

"Wait . . . today? Do you mean 104?"

"Yes, how did you—"

"We live at 128 Glover. My wife saw a moving van this morning. That house has been empty forever. The owner is a foreign businessman, I think in Spain or something?"

She pauses as if Nora might know, and at her shrug, continues, "Well, anyway . . . he had the whole house renovated and I guess he must have been planning to sell it, but he obviously changed his mind and decided to rent it. Yay for you. Welcome to the neighborhood."

"Thanks. Wow—it's kind of crazy that you live a few doors down from us."

"Yeah, Brooklyn is the biggest small world in the world. You'll see. Where are you from?"

"LA."

"No. *Way!* Same!"

"Really? Where?"

"Encino. How about you?"

"We just moved from Woodland Hills."

"Well, LA's not as small a world as Brooklyn, but— Sorry, my phone is buzzing." Heather digs it out of her huge black shoulder bag, glances at it, and deftly answers a text, not missing a conversational beat. "So, when you say *we* . . . you have a family?"

"Husband and two daughters."

"How old?"

"Forty-five but if you ask he'll claim thirty-nine." The quip is rewarded with a broad smile. "The girls are fourteen and seventeen."

"No. *Way,*" Heather says again, as though she's just been told that Nora's kids are her own long-lost children. "*Our* daughter is fourteen, and our son turns eighteen in October."

"So they're around the same age."

"I bet you and I are, too. Forty-four?"

"I will be in December."

"I just celebrated my birthday! And my wife turned fifty the same week. Too bad you missed her birthday bash. Are you into seafood?"

"Uh, sure."

Talking to Heather is like popping popcorn in hot oil without a lid, kernels flying in every direction.

"You would have loved this party. We did a backyard clambake. No sand—you've seen our yard—I mean, not *our* actual yard, but you've seen yours, and it's the same, right? So anyway, I can give you the name of the place that catered it if you're interested. But wait, you probably don't know anyone here yet, do you? You don't. We'll hang out. Our kids can get to know each other. Are they excited about the move?"

"The girls? One is. The other isn't."

"They sound like our two. What are you doing Sunday? It's not a school night or a work night, with the holiday. How about dinner at our place?"

"Um . . . sure. That would be fun."

"Great. What's your number?"

Heather dials the digits as she recites them, and a moment later, Nora's phone buzzes in her pocket.

"That's me. Add me to your contacts. Last name's Tamura." She spells it, asks for Nora's last name, and saves it in her phone. "What don't you eat? Not just *you*, all of you."

"What don't we . . ." Nora shakes her head. "Sorry. Cross-country move, red-eye flight. I'm a little slow today."

"I just meant, is anyone gluten-free? Vegan? Pescatarian? Allergic? Lactose intolerant? We've got it all in our household, so I want to make sure we've got you covered."

"Oh! We eat pretty much anything."

"Well, that's easy." Heather's phone buzzes again, and she looks at it. "Sorry. I should get back. Technically, I'm working."

"What do you do?"

"I'm in marketing."

"So is my husband."

"Where?"

"Cooper-McGovern. It's a West Coast firm and they're opening a New York office. That's why we're here. How about you?"

"Until a few months ago, I worked at the Met."

"The opera?"

"No, my wife's the musician in the family—though not that kind of music, and she rarely performs anymore, but she was pretty amazing back in the day. Anyway, I was in marketing for the Metropolitan Museum of Art for years. God, I loved it. I love art—but who doesn't, right? Now I'm at a start-up that recruited me away with gobs of money, otherwise I would never have left. Sorry—does that sound crass? I swear I'm not crass, but—you know, I'm sure you're wondering why anyone would leave the Met. But we've got college tuition looming so . . . you get it, right?"

She pauses, expecting a response.

Nora nods—presumably at all of the above.

"Do you work?" Heather asks.

"Not anymore, but I'm—I used to be a horticulturalist before I got married and had kids."

"You didn't want to be a working mom, huh?"

She shrugs. "That was the decision my husband and I made. He was doing well enough that I didn't have to work."

"And you didn't want to?"

"I was happy to be at home, especially when the girls were little."

"I get it. But if you want to get back into it just for something to do and to meet people here, you should volunteer with our urban farm."

"What is it?"

"A green space where food is grown for people in need. It's on the roof of an empty warehouse over by the river. Jules will tell you about it Sunday night."

"Jules?"

"My wife."

Right, Jules. Musician, newly fifty, fun party.

Heather brandishes two dog leashes. "Okay, so, seven o'clock, and we're seven doors down. Two-story brick row house, white trim, black iron fence out front. Can't miss it." At Nora's raised eyebrow, she says, "Hey, I'm kidding. Obviously, they all look alike, but the good thing is, we'll know our way around each other's houses. No asking directions to the bathroom when we visit—it's like we're old friends. See you Sunday!"

She leashes her dogs and walks off at a fast clip, phone to her ear.

Nora looks down at her own phone, wishing Teddy would return her call.

"I already made a friend!" she'll say. *"She lives just a few doors down, with age-appropriate kids!"*

What will Teddy say?

"That's great! I'm so happy for you!"

No.

More likely: *"Careful, Nora . . . Careful who you trust . . . You know better than anyone . . ."*

Nora puts her phone back into her pocket.

I know, Teddy. I know.

Jacob

He returns to Glover Street under cover of darkness, armed with binoculars.

Anna's house is lit from basement to eaves, inside and out. The drapes are parted, shades pulled up, windows open with screens in place.

How dare they?

He thinks of Anna, so shy and fiercely private. She wouldn't have wanted strangers living in her house. They don't belong here.

Tobacco smoke puffs from his nostrils like dragon fury as he stalks on past and around the corner onto Edgemont.

It's late, but the boulevard is always busy. Traffic, pedestrians, bodegas, restaurants. At the far end of the block, a police car chirps as it rolls up alongside a group of young men gathered beneath a streetlamp.

Jacob eyes a familiar brownstone. The windows are dark. It had been a private residence in January 1994. Now professional placards are mounted beside the door. He climbs the steps as if he belongs there and scans the lineup. A dentist, an accountant, a financial adviser—all offices now closed.

He glances around. No one in the vicinity is paying any

attention to him. Those who aren't minding their own business are watching the opposite end of the block, where rippling red light bathes the guys being questioned by NYPD.

He quickly climbs over the stoop railing onto the adjacent flat roof of the low shed behind 102 Glover Street and walks to the edge, overlooking 104's back garden. Twenty-five years ago, it had been barren as a prison yard. Now there's a wide bramble hedge below the shed roof, running the length and width of 104's property perimeter, effective as a crocodile moat.

He looks at Anna's bedroom in the upper left corner. Someone is there.

His pulse quickens.

A female figure throws shadows on the walls as she moves around the room, then begins to bend and stretch in a rhythmic pattern. He trains the binoculars on the windows, spinning the lenses into focus.

She's brunette.

She's taking books from the floor and aligning them on the shelves.

Anna's bookshelves, Anna's room, Anna's house . . .

Amid distant sirens and chirping crickets, he hears squealing brakes and the crunch of metal on metal. Somewhere on Edgemont, a car alarm begins to wail.

In Anna's room, the figure turns toward the window.

He glimpses her face.

The impossible image sears his brain, and his limbs go limp. The binoculars fall from his hand and land with a rustle and thud in the tangle of briars below, lost.

Nora

K eith? Girls? You've got fifteen minutes," Nora calls up the stairs at a quarter to seven Sunday evening.

She opens the powder room door to check her reflection in the mirror. Channeling her own inner Holly Golightly, she's wearing a trim black skirt, sleeveless top, and flats. Her makeup is understated, her hair pulled back in a simple headband, and she's accessorized only by sapphire stud earrings that match her eyes. Their expression reflects jitteriness that wavers between happy anticipation and foreboding.

The weekend, spent settling in and exploring the area with Keith and the girls, has gone well. Almost too well, considering they've spent more time together as a family than they have since . . .

Well, they've never spent this much time together. Back in LA, even when they're all home, they're scattered. Here, the bedrooms are small and lack sitting areas and televisions. And the house may be large by New York standards but it offers no bonus rooms, no home gym, no pool.

Nora assumes they'll all crave more distance and private space when the novelty wears off, but for this first weekend, togetherness isn't such a bad thing.

In the kitchen, she cuts a large piece of clear cellophane and centers it around the flowers she's bringing as a hostess gift for Heather and her family.

"You're making a mistake, Nora," Teddy's voice whispers. *"You shouldn't do this."*

It's the last thing she needs to hear right now, so it's probably for the best that Teddy hasn't gotten back to her.

She isn't being reckless, accepting a stranger's dinner invitation. She's being proactive, hoping New York might offer the one thing she'd lacked in California: friendship.

She had a social circle there—the girls' pals' parents, Keith's colleagues' spouses, workout buddies, neighbors. There were plenty of people she could count on for a favor, people with whom she'd shared meals and celebrations and even vacations over the years. But they weren't true confidants, and she won't miss any of them.

Anyway, Heather no longer seems like a stranger. They've been texting back and forth ever since Friday evening, when Nora sent a message asking about neighborhood restaurants. Heather recommended the local Moroccan place where the Howells dined that first evening, and the Asian-Cuban one in Manhattan where they'd had a late dinner last night. Both were excellent, as promised.

If you ask Heather about best places to eat—or buy school supplies, or open a bank account, all questions Nora posed to her—she's the kind of person who shares interesting or funny anecdotes along with an efficient, comprehensive list of options.

Keith comes into the kitchen wearing khaki shorts and a light blue linen button-down, sleeves rolled up. He's freshly shaven, not one to let stubble linger if there's a razor avail-able. Nora has always found his clean-cut good looks appeal-ing, though here in New York, he could do with a little more edge.

"Turned out pretty," he comments, indicating the arrange-ment of roses, sunflowers, and Peruvian lilies in splashy shades of scarlet, orange, and yellow. She'd cut the blooms from the garden, bought the wrap and ribbon at a stationer's on Edgemont, and the turquoise Fiestaware vase at an adja-cent vintage store.

"Thanks."

She ties a fat symmetrical red satin bow around the cel-lophane and fluffs out the loops, conscious of his eyes on her.

"What?" she asks, not looking up.

"What?"

"Why are you just standing there watching me?"

"Can't I admire your handiwork? And you?"

It's the kind of thing he'd have said before things changed, and she'd have found it sweet. Now the words don't ring true. Now she's certain it wasn't admiration: it was scrutiny.

She hears footsteps on the stairs, heavy and methodical. Not Piper, who tends to prance down.

Stacey appears in the doorway. Like Nora, she's dressed all in black, from her bulky hooded sweatshirt to her sneakers.

"Okay, I guess I missed the death notice," Keith says. "Are we going to a funeral?"

Stacey rolls her eyes.

Nora notices that her hair is brushed, brunette kinks tamed into a low ponytail. She's wearing her contacts, and she appears to have helped herself to Nora's cosmetics. It's an expensive brand, but the foundation is a shade too dark for her untanned skin, casting her in sallow shadow. The amethyst liner was meant for blue eyes, not brown, and was applied with a heavy hand.

She just doesn't know what to do. I should help her.

But before Nora settles on a tactful way to phrase the offer, the floor creaks directly overhead: Piper, on the move.

She bounces in like a sunbeam, face glowing and blond hair flowing beneath oversize burnished metallic sunglasses propped on her head. A yellow romper bares her tanned limbs and matching sandals reveal coral-polished toes. Delicate gold jewelry glints at her ears, neck, wrists, and one ankle.

"Are we going?"

Nora smiles. "We are. Is that the outfit you bought last week on Melrose, Pipe?"

"Uh-huh." Piper twirls around. "How does it look? Too short?"

"No, it's perfect."

"Thanks."

Piper's gaze flits to Stacey, taking in her sister's appearance. She looks as though she wants to say something—searching for a compliment, maybe, and then realizing it would come across as perfunctory, same as anything Nora herself might say.

Nora picks up the vase. "Hey, Stace, can you carry this?"

"Let Piper. The flowers match her *ensemble*." She emphasizes the last word with an exaggerated French accent.

Piper laughs as though it was intended as a sweet little joke. "They do! Here, I'll take it, Mom."

"Thanks, but I asked your sister."

"And *my* sister offered," Stacey shoots back.

"I don't mind. Really. No big deal." Piper holds out her hands and Nora gives her the vase.

Keith catches her eye and she shrugs. He doesn't know what it's like to be a girl like Stacey, at that age. So many things he doesn't know . . .

Nora turns away and pulls on her sunglasses before stepping out into the warm summer evening.

Jacob

Jacob had returned to Glover Street on Saturday, confident that the owners of the row house across from Anna's were spending the weekend on Long Beach Island. He'd lounged on their bottom step for an hour, armed with cover stories in case someone came along, recognized that he didn't belong, and confronted him.

He'd correctly guessed that wouldn't happen in a city populated by hurried, harried residents who mind their own business. The few neighbors passing by had failed to give him a second glance.

Across the street at 104, all was quiet. The front windows were closed, curtains and shades drawn, and he wondered if he'd imagined what he'd seen on Friday. Not just the moving van, but *her*.

When night fell, he walked around the block and accessed the rear shed roof again, thinking of the binoculars buried in the thorny hedge below. It didn't matter. There was nothing to see at 104. The shades were drawn and Anna's room was dark.

Back home in bed, he'd dreamed about Anna. It wasn't the first time, but she was so vivid, alive again.

"Do you believe in ghosts, Jacob?" she kept asking him

in his dream, as she had in real life so many years ago. "Do you? Do you believe in ghosts?"

He reached for her, expecting her to vanish, but his hands touched warm flesh. She was really there. He held her close and wept into her soft brown hair.

"I'm so sorry. Please forgive me . . ."

The dream stayed with him today. As shadows filtered the fading sun, he bought a thick Sunday *New York Times* and returned to the stoop across from 104 Glover.

Now he watches the house over the top of the open Sports section, chain-smoking and slapping flying insects that stick to his sweat-dampened skin in the humid dusk.

He should leave, and yet . . .

The shades are open. Maybe someone is there. Maybe Anna . . .

Do you believe in ghosts?

She'd asked him that question after his grandmother's death, not long before her own.

"No," he'd said. "Do you?"

"Yes."

"Have you ever seen one?"

"No. But . . ."

She murmured something that sounded like *I've been one*.

When he asked her if that was what she'd said, she shook her head. "What? No! Why would I say that?"

"Then what did you say?"

He doesn't remember her answer now. It hadn't stuck with him the way *I've been one* had. She claimed she hadn't said it. Maybe she hadn't. She wasn't a ghost; she was still alive back then.

She can't be one now, because there's no such—

Across the street, the front door opens.

He sits up.

A woman emerges.

She isn't the person he'd seen in Anna's room Friday night. She isn't Anna, or Anna's look-alike, or Anna's ghost.

She's a stranger with long blond hair and movie star sunglasses.

She isn't alone. There's another one, another blond stranger, a teenage girl who trails behind the woman, carrying a large bouquet.

Red-hot rage sweeps over him.

Who are they? What are they doing in Anna's house?

A third person emerges, a man. He, too, is blond and attractive. He lingers on the threshold, holding the door open for . . .

Anna.

Twenty-five years mourning her; two days reminding himself that she's long gone; an hour convincing himself that there's no such thing as ghosts . . .

Yet there she is.

She looks around as she descends the steps, glancing up and down the street and then across. Her gaze drops on Jacob like a coin in a slot.

He opens his mouth to call out to her, but her name is mired in his throat.

She looks away, walks away, following the trio of blond strangers.

Move! Run! Go after her!

His legs refuse the command to chase her down.

What if he did? Would he grab her shoulders, spin her around, and . . . what?

Simply hold her in a fervent embrace? Demand to know what she's doing here, why she's with these people, how she can be alive again?

He watches her drift away with the others, this fake, perfect family that looks nothing like her, nothing like her own. But of course not. Anna's family died together, the three of them, in this house.

He bows his head, eyes squeezed shut.

When he regains his composure and looks up again at last, searching for her, the street is empty. She's vanished once more.

Nora

The house at 128 Glover is in the middle of the block, shadowed by the leafy branches of a tall London plane tree growing at the curb. Ascending the front steps, Nora notes the planter filled with bedraggled, leggy geraniums. They should have been planted in full sun, desperately need to be deadheaded, and the pink shade clashes with the red brick. Her fingers itch to snap off the faded, skimpy blossoms. Better yet, just scrap the whole thing and start fresh.

If things go well this evening, maybe she'll offer some friendly botanical advice. She can volunteer to help choose fall plantings that will thrive in this shady spot—coleus would be ideal, and coral bells . . .

Heather must have seen them coming and is waiting in the doorway, gracious and smiling. She's wearing a sleeveless black shift, and Nora congratulates herself on her own wardrobe choice.

Heather introduces herself to Keith and the girls and exclaims over the flower arrangement, "Ooh! Where did you get this? It's gorgeous!"

"Mom made it," Piper says proudly.

"Oh, right, Nora, you did say you were . . . was it a horticulturalist?"

"Yes, but not in years. Now it's just more of a hobby."

"Might want to rethink that. People around here would pay a fortune for something like this. Including me. Oh, here come Mutt and Geoffrey."

The dogs trot in with tails wagging and tags jangling. Piper lights up and bends to pet them.

Stacey is subdued, darting a glance over her shoulder as if she's longing to go back home. Nora is tempted to hiss, *Why can't you behave like your sister, just this once?*

But every mother knows better than to compare her children—at least not aloud, in their presence.

Heather invites them in. Nora notices that she's barefoot, with delicate feet, a shiny red pedicure, and a toe ring. "Do you want us to take off our shoes?"

"Nah. I grew up in a traditional Japanese household. Old habits die hard, but everyone else wears shoes around here."

The house might be identical to 104 on the outside, but inside, the only similarity is the floor plan.

After setting the flower arrangement on a lime green pedestal table in an entrance hall painted the color of grape jam, Heather ushers them into a stark white living room. It looks like a museum gallery, filled with monochromatic geometric furniture and modern art. A dangling metal sculpture hangs where the light fixture should be, whirling in a breeze from a strategically mounted industrial fan. The fireplace is obscured by a massive painting featuring what appear to be oranges and a single bloodshot eyeball.

The house smells of incense and pungent spices. Nora

hears familiar music blasting from the rear of the house—the wailing rock guitar, thumping rhythm, and haunting male vocals of Radiohead's "Creep."

The song was popular during a time in her life she'd rather forget. Still, it beats "Pop Goes the Weasel." It's been looping through her brain the past few days, though she hasn't encountered the ice cream truck since Friday.

Keith gestures at half a dozen stands that hold acoustic and electric guitars and asks Heather if she plays.

"Gawd, no. Our son does, and Jules, of course—she's a musician."

"Professionally?"

"Yes. She's also a chef—not professionally, but she's making one of her specialties, Thai chickpea curry with kale, and it tastes as good as it smells." Heather raises her voice and calls, "Hey, babe? They're here! Babe!"

The music's volume drops a notch in the kitchen. Pans rattle, water runs, and a female voice returns, "Be right there!"

"Have a seat, and I'll go round up the kids." Heather scoots out of the room and up the stairs.

"She's a whole lot of energy," Keith comments, low, in Nora's ear.

"*Good* energy."

As opposed to Stacey, gazing, or more likely glaring, out the window at the street as if she wants to escape.

"I guess we should sit." Keith starts to settle on a low bench.

Piper gasps. "Dad! That's a table!"

Seeing the four mats arranged on the floor around it like chairs, he leaps up again.

Someone gives a robust laugh. "Sit anywhere you like. We never eat at that one."

Nora turns to see a tall Black woman coming in from the kitchen. Her hair is long and braided, and she's wearing white denim shorts and a vintage black concert T-shirt, the print too washed-out to read.

"I'm Jules, and let's see . . . Nora, Keith, Piper, and Stacey." She points to them each in turn. "Heather told me all about you. Not that she knows *all* about you. But what she knows, she mentioned. And *you*." Jules whirls a finger in the air and then aims it at Stacey, peering at her face. "Did we meet?"

"Uh . . . I don't think so. But, I mean, I've been around the neighborhood the last few days. Walking the dog in the park . . ."

Jules peers at her, then shrugs. "Yeah, that must be it. I had a bad head injury years ago so I forget a lot of stuff, but not faces. Or lyrics. *Nor* lyrics?" She pauses, weighing the grammar, and settles on "*Or* lyrics. Especially if I wrote them."

"You write lyrics?" Even Stacey can't maintain glum apathy.

Jules is the kind of person who takes a room like a storm and whose presence likely lingers like receding thunder after she's moved on.

"A long time ago. What can I get you all to drink? Beer, seltzer, red, white, pink?"

"Pink?" Piper echoes. "I love pink. I'll try that."

Again, Jules laughs heartily. "Sorry, baby girl, it's wine. Rosé."

"Oh . . . I thought it was seltzer."

"And now *she's* pink," Jules says as Piper blushes.

Heather is back, so light on her bare feet that she didn't make a sound descending the stairs.

A young teenage girl slips into the room just behind her.

Courtney is a fair and freckled strawberry blonde who resembles neither of her mothers. She does, however, share their good-natured confidence, greeting the visitors with an easygoing grin and firm handshakes all around and asking the girls which schools they'll be attending.

"We're both going to Notre Dame. It's in Greenwich Village." Piper's pronunciation is self-conscious, but she says it like a local, as Keith had taught her—not "green-which" but "gren-itch."

"Nobody calls it that," a male voice says, and a young man enters the room.

Lanky and towering over even six-foot-tall Keith, he has an angular face, intense eyes, and a pile of shaggy dark hair. He, too, is dressed in black, more mood than fashion statement.

"Nobody calls it Gren-itch?" Piper echoes. "Wait, so it *is* Green-witch?"

"No! Geez. It's just the Village, unless you're a tourist. Which you are, so I guess . . ."

"She's not a tourist, she lives here now," Courtney says. "And *you're* a jackass."

"Guys! Cut it out!" Jules snaps. "Lennon, introduce yourself!"

He shakes hands all around as politely as his sister had, but without smiling.

Nora's hand feels clammy in his cold, firm grasp, and she pushes back the memory of a young man she'd once known. He'd looked nothing like Lennon. But there's something about this kid, an intensity to his presence, that throws her back to an interlude she's spent all of her adult life trying to forget.

Jules asks, "How did you guys pull off this amazing feat—landing two daughters in a decent high school at the last minute?"

"It wasn't easy," Keith says. "My old college roommate is married to a woman with friends in high places. I called him the second we knew we were moving, and she pulled some strings."

"And waved a magic wand, apparently," Heather says. "Wow. Do you know how lucky you are?"

They do. Some New York City parents begin laying the groundwork for secondary education while their children are in diapers. Public high schools depend not on neighborhoods, but on entrance exams and advance applications. Acceptance decisions are made long before the previous school year ends, and the best schools have long waiting lists. The same is true of private schools, and they come with an astronomical price tag.

"We were on pins and needles for about a month, but it all worked out," Nora says, and turns to Lennon and Courtney. "Where do you go to school?"

Heather answers for them, like a passenger grabbing the wheel to avoid a swerve. "Courtney's at Brooklyn Friends, and Lennon goes to Collegiate. That's in Manhattan, so he can take the subway with your girls."

"Um, they're in the Village, and I'm on the Upper West Side." His response isn't a blatant protest, but the message is clear, and received.

Stacey lifts her chin. "No worries. We know how to get there."

"Yeah, we practiced yesterday with our dad."

Piper's comment brings a glint of amusement to Lennon's eyes, but he says nothing.

After silence that goes on a split second too long, Jules says, "Let's go into the kitchen."

They follow her through the archway into a dining room painted in high-gloss rainbow stripes and clearly not used for dining. There's no table, and the corner hutch is filled with books instead of dishes. They're arranged in haphazard fashion, some sideways, others vertical, many with bookmarks poking above the pages as if no one has ever bothered to finish reading them. A large electronic keyboard and full percussion set take up most of the room, along with an enormous tank filled with tropical fish that match the walls.

"Is that a gold record?" Keith indicates a large plaque propped on the mantel.

"Uh-huh. Mine."

"Congratulations! That's amazing!"

"I know, right?" Jules grins.

Heather rolls her eyes. "No false modesty there."

"Hey, if I had one of those, you'd have heard about it the second we met," Keith says.

"Oh, I'll be happy to tell you *all* about it, and then some. Come on into the kitchen."

Trailing Jules over the threshold, Nora stops short, and Heather bumps her from behind. "Sorry—you okay?"

"Yes, just . . . wow. I was expecting it to be . . . uh, modern, I guess, like the rest of the house."

Like her own kitchen, completely renovated in neutral shades with glass-fronted cabinets and sleek modern appliances.

Here, the Formica counters and ceramic tile floor are speckled beige, the stove and fridge olive green. The busy wallpaper isn't just citrus fruit colored, it depicts them. The cabinets are knotty pine, with vintage monkey figurines on an open triangular shelf tucked alongside the sink window.

All around the mulberry bush, the monkey chased the weasel . . .

The ice cream truck tune dribbles into Nora's head as Jules lowers the volume on a Bluetooth speaker tucked beside a row of old-fashioned ceramic cannisters. A memory flutters at the edges of Nora's mind like curtains in a gusty chill.

Jules is talking. "Every time we think about remodeling, we decide the retro look is still kind of cool. That, and we're always too broke to do it right."

"I like it. It looks exactly like my parents' kitchen in Kansas when I was growing up," Keith tells her.

"This *is* my parents' kitchen when I was growing up."

"I think everyone had this kitchen," Nora murmurs, running a fingertip over a familiar black iron drawer pull.

"No, Jules means that literally," Heather says. "She grew up here. We bought it from her parents when they retired. She was pregnant with Lennon at the time."

Her son cracks a grin at last, and it's a sardonic one, aimed at her. "Hey, Nora? News bulletin—a woman doesn't need a husband to have a baby."

Jules, stirring a bubbling pot on the stove, tosses the metal spoon aside with a clatter and spatter. "Lennon!"

"Look at her! She's acting all shell-shocked, like someone just told her I was hatched out of a giant dinosaur egg."

Nora tries to explain. "That's not what I was surprised about. I . . . I was just caught off guard by the kitchen—that it's so retro. But I'm sorry if it seemed like I was—"

"Whoa, no apologies necessary from you," Heather assures her, and levels a look at her son. "Lennon?"

"Sorry. I didn't realize that people in Kansas don't know about the miracles of modern medicine."

"Maybe *they* don't," Stacey speaks up, "but *we're* from LA."

He turns to her. "Yeah? That's cool. I thought I heard something about Kansas, so . . ."

"My dad grew up there. The rest of us are from California. So we are actually aware of, you know . . . miracles and modern medicine, and stuff."

He offers a two-fingered salute and one-word response. "Respect."

After a moment of silence, Jules hands him a long-tipped lighter. "Go out back and light the candles for me."

"Are you going to say please?"

"Please. And thank you. And, Stacey, if you wouldn't mind carrying this stuff out?"

"Sure." She accepts a napkin-lined basket and bag of chips from Jules and follows Lennon out the door.

Jules turns to them. "Sorry. He's a piece of work."

Nora could say that he's met his match in Stacey, but abstains. Tonight, her daughter has done just fine so far.

"You want some seltzer?" Courtney asks Piper.

"Is it pink?"

"What?"

Piper catches Jules's eye. They laugh. "Never mind," she tells Courtney. "Sure, I'll have some."

"Out back, ladies, in the big blue cooler." Jules dispatches them to the patio, armed with tortillas and kimchi queso.

Heather turns to Nora and Keith. "Really, I'm so sorry about Lennon. He went through a bad breakup over the summer. He's always been a little dark, but now he's . . ."

"So dark he can walk into a room and suck the light and bright right out of it," Jules says with a grim laugh. "But he truly would be willing to ride with your girls on the subway."

"No need, I'm sure they'll be fine," Nora tells her.

Dark. She doesn't like the word. Not now, not here . . .

Heather touches her arm. "Oh, Nora, when I said he was dark, I didn't mean dangerous. I don't want you to get the wrong idea. He's a good kid."

"No, I know, I'm sure he is."

Keith speaks up. "It's not that. The girls need to get used to looking out for themselves in the city without a man along for the ride."

Jules clears her throat. "Ah, I wasn't implying they needed Lennon to protect them, just that his stop is way uptown, so he can make sure they get off at the right place."

"By *man*, I was talking about me. Not that your son isn't—"

"I get it, it's all good." Jules shakes a spice jar over the curry. "We like strong women in this house, believe me."

"I'm assuming they'll see Lennon on the train sometimes anyway," Heather says. "He takes the same line, probably around the same time, along with everyone else in the neighborhood. How about some wine? Do you like Austrian white?"

They do. Heather pours four glasses of chilled Grüner Veltliner, and lifts hers in a toast. "Here's to old kitchens and new friends."

They clink.

Uneasy, Nora swallows her wine, gazing at a porcelain chimpanzee above the sink, feeling as though its wide-eyed, garish grin is fixed on her.

The monkey thought it was all in good fun . . .

Pop! goes the weasel . . .

Jacob

"Excuse me?" a female voice calls.

Still sitting on the steps, Jacob turns to see someone framed in the doorway of the adjacent row house.

"Are you waiting for someone, or something?"

"Yeah," he calls back, and plucks the name from his memory. "Blake."

She steps out onto her stoop, an older Latina woman with salt-and-pepper black hair. She's wearing a white terry bathrobe, with red cat-eye glasses perched on the end of her nose.

"You're waiting for Blake?"

"Right. We had plans tonight, but he's not here and I can't get ahold of him, so I figured I'd stick around in case he shows up."

He waits for her to tell him that Blake and his wife have gone away to the beach.

She pushes her glasses up as if to get a better look at him. "You've been here a long time."

He pushes himself to his feet, hands and jaw clenched, head down.

"Guess he forgot." He shrugs and starts toward the boulevard.

"Hey!"

He stops but doesn't turn back, fists shoved deep in his pockets.

"You forgot your newspaper."

He curses and contemplates leaving it there, ignoring her, just disappearing around the corner.

But that wouldn't be wise. Not if he ever wants to return to Anna's house. And he wants to, *needs* to, return.

He swivels slowly, pasting on a smile. "Oh, right. Thanks."

She keeps an eye on him as he gathers up the scattered sections of paper. He keeps an eye on her, too, confirming that she doesn't have a phone in her hand, and isn't calling Blake, or the police.

"You have a good night now, ma'am."

She says nothing, but he can feel her scrutiny as he tucks the paper under his arm and walks away.

He strolls around the corner as if he has all the time, and not a care, in the world. As if she hasn't followed him along Edgemont Boulevard. Several times he whirls around, expecting to see her, but she isn't there, and then—

"Hey, watch where you're going!"

Someone crashes into him from behind.

"Sorry." He scans the street behind him, certain he just saw the woman scuttling into an alleyway. But when he backtracks, heart racing, the alley is empty.

Did he imagine her?

Did he imagine Anna, as well?

Has he spent so many years obsessing over her death—that night, that house—that he's finally teetered right over the edge to insanity?

If you're concerned that you might be going insane, then you probably aren't . . .

People who are developing serious mental illness rarely suspect it . . .

Those words, uttered by a prison therapist he'd seen years ago, had brought tremendous comfort. He'd written them down, repeating them to himself like a mantra over the years, whenever doubts creep in.

Okay, so if you aren't insane . . .

And you don't believe in ghosts . . .

That leaves only one possibility.

Anna has come home to Glover Street at last.

Nora

Dinner is delicious, served at a pair of wrought-iron bistro tables in a pergola scented with trailing white jasmine. It perfumes the humid evening air, along with citronella candles and charcoal wafting from a neighboring yard. The night is sequined with stars and fireflies, strings of fairy lights and lamplight in surrounding windows. Jazz from Jules's portable speaker drowns out the city sounds—and "Pop Goes the Weasel."

They linger long after dessert, generous scoops of Jules's homemade tequila-laced strawberry-lime sorbet for the adults, and mint-carob-chip for the teenagers. Nora keeps an eye on them. The younger girls are like longtime BFFs, juggling conversation with texting on their phones and occasionally showing each other their screens. Stacey, too, seems to be having a good time, deep in conversation with Lennon.

At the adult table, lively conversation flows along with the cold, crisp wine. True to her promise, Jules isn't shy about sharing the details of her "sex, drugs, and rock and roll past," as Heather refers to the time her wife had spent in Seattle as a young adult. Jules got caught up with several grunge-era bands in one capacity or another—musician, backup singer, roadie, groupie. Whip-smart and unapologetic, she shares harrowing close calls fueled by addiction and her doomed affair with a long closeted and now dead household name.

"I could have been so much more than I was, but I blew one opportunity after another. I knew my career and my life were going down in flames and I felt helpless to stop it. I used to ask people—random strangers, you know?—if they'd ever seen a falling star, and then I'd say, 'No? Well, you're looking at one right now.'"

"But you survived," Heather says.

"Hell, yes. I turned my life around and became an entirely different person. I'm one of the lucky ones who's seen it all, done it all, and lived to tell about it—thanks to rehab and meeting Heather. I was so damned lucky."

She clasps her wife's hand, their wedding bands glinting in the flickering light.

At the kids' table, voices are rising.

Nora sees Lennon leaning forward, as if delivering urgent information. His sister gives an emphatic nod. Stacey and Piper are wide-eyed, mouths hanging open.

"Hey, guys? Everything okay?" Keith calls.

"Not really, Dad!" Piper jumps up from the table and hurries to his side. "Why didn't you tell us?"

"Tell you what?"

"About the *murders*!"

The word storms the summer garden like a cold front, obliterating the warm wine and tequila afterglow.

Stacey

orry, dude," Lennon tells Stacey as Piper goes flying over to the adults' table with Courtney on her heels. "I thought you knew."

"How would we *know*?"

He shrugs. "I just figured everyone does. I didn't mean to freak you out."

"Yes, you did. The way you said it . . . like it was some cool thing you just couldn't wait to tell us?"

"It *is* cool, if you ask me. I mean, it's—"

"I didn't ask you, and I don't think it's cool. I think it's disturbing." Stacey gets to her feet and trails after her sister.

She thinks *he's* disturbing, her first impression of him now confirmed. She'd changed her mind earlier, when he was talking about school and books and music—normal things. She decided he was an okay guy after all. Maybe even someone she'd want to hang out with, or even . . .

Yeah, no. No *way*.

"Three people were killed in our house! In their beds!" Piper informs their parents, sounding as if she's on the verge of crying.

"*What?*" Mom and Dad say in unison.

Their faces are masked in shadow, but Stacey sees her mother's hand shake a little as she sets down her wineglass.

Courtney puts a hand on Piper's shoulder. "It's okay, you know? It was a long time ago, before any of us were even born."

"Not before any of *them* were born." Lennon gestures at the adults. "Mom knew the victims. It was a family—father, mother, teenage daughter. She was living here then."

"Actually, I moved to Seattle a few years before they were killed. But my parents were living here at the time, and I used to visit."

Stacey turns to Jules, wide-eyed. "Wait, you *knew* the people?"

"Cool, right?" Lennon's tone is sarcastic, and she shoots him a glare.

"Well, nobody really *knew* them," Jules says. "They lived here for, what, maybe ten years? And when I say they kept to themselves, I mean they kept to themselves. My mother used to say Mr. Toska wouldn't have talked to a neighbor if his house was burning down and the neighbor was out front with a fire hose."

"So . . . like, he was snobby?" Piper asks.

"Nothing like that," Jules says. "He worked some kind of blue-collar job. So did my dad—second shift, my whole life. But Mr. Toska came and went at all hours. The wife never left the house—she was sick or something. Maybe in a wheelchair? Something like that."

"What about the daughter?"

Lennon answers Stacey's question. "She was a gawky weirdo."

Heather scowls at him. "Geez, Lennon. What a thing to say."

"Jules always says it." He shrugs. "Right, Jules?"

"Sure. I don't mean it in a bad way. I mean, *I* was a gawky weirdo, too. Still am. And proud of it. *Anyway*, my brain is a sieve, so don't count on me for details, but this family had some serious ties to organized crime."

"You mean, the mafia?" Stacey asks. "Like in *The Godfather*?"

"You've seen *The Godfather*?"

"I read the book."

"Stacey reads everything," Piper informs them. "And she loves true crime. She has twenty-five thousand books about some girl who killed her parents with an axe like two hundred years ago."

"Shut up, Piper!"

For one thing, it was 1892. And for another . . .

Way to drive home the *gawky weirdo* parallel.

Stacey turns back to Jules. "So, *was* it the mafia?"

"Not the Sicilian mafia, but organized crime."

"Then when they were killed . . . was it because of that?"

"Of course it was," Dad says promptly, as if he knows.

Actually, maybe he does. He'd attended Columbia University.

"Do you remember the murders? Were you living in New York then?" she asks him.

"When was it?"

"January 17, 1994." Lennon rattles off the date as if someone had asked his birthday.

Now who's the gawky weirdo?

"I was here in college then," Dad says, "but I don't remember anything about it."

"How can you not remember, Dad?" Piper asks. "Something like that must have been in the news."

"It was all over the news," Jules confirms. "My parents said you couldn't even get up the street for a few days after it happened, with the press."

"Well, all I cared about was girls and beer and sports," Dad says with a shrug. "And the city was a dangerous place back then. Crime rates were high. The news was full of murder."

"But this was a family," Piper persists. "I can't believe you don't remember it."

"I guess my brain is a sieve, too," Dad says lightly.

Mom has been quiet all this time. Now she asks Jules, "Was it a mob hit, then?"

"That was the general consensus. Whoever did it didn't mess around. They were shot in the middle of the night—one, two, three. No one heard a thing."

"The killer must have used a suppressor," Lennon comments.

"What does that mean?" Piper asks.

"A silencer, on the gun," Stacey explains.

Lennon shakes his head. "Suppressors don't really make the shot silent. Just muffled."

"How do you know that?"

"It's true. If you want to look it up—"

"I know it's true. I'm just wondering how you know."

"I know everything," Lennon says with a shrug.

Stacey rolls her eyes and turns back to Jules, gesturing for her to go on.

"Where was I? The murders . . . no one heard a thing . . . Oh, right! It was stormy that night. There's nothing louder than rain on these flat roofs. You'll see tomorrow. The weather's going to be lousy."

"Terrific," Dad mutters.

"Yeah, you're not in LA anymore, but don't worry, you'll get used to it," Heather says. "I did."

"Oh, *please*." Jules shakes her head. "You're always complaining about the weather, California girl."

"Only when it's crappy. Does anyone need more wine?" Heather pours some for herself, and tops off the other glasses without waiting for a reply.

Stacey needs the rest of the murder story. "So the murder was never solved?"

"Nope. Like I said, the family kept to themselves, so there wasn't a lot to go on. They probably wouldn't have been found for days, but one of the neighbors happened to look out her window in the middle of the night and I guess she saw someone breaking in. She called the police, but by the time they got there, it was too late. The Toskas were dead and the killer was long gone."

"What did he look like?" Piper asks.

"My mom said the neighbor just saw a shadowy figure. Couldn't even tell if it was a man or a woman. Like I said, people on the block assumed it was a contract killing, but—"

"More wine?" Heather cuts in, lifting the bottle again.

"You just poured it."

"I *know*." She and Jules exchange a look, and Stacey realizes Heather's interruption was meant to curtail the story.

"What were you going to say, Jules?" she persists. "People thought it was a contract killing, *but . . .* But, what?"

Jules hesitates. "Just . . . you know, hit men don't typically take out the wives and children."

There's a moment of silence.

Stacey clears her throat. "Then who do you think did it?"

This time, Mom cuts in, and the voice that spills from her throat could belong to an overly cheerful pageant finalist trying to answer a tough question. "It doesn't really matter, does it? Who cares what happened years ago?"

"I do. It happened in our house."

"Every house has a history, Stacey."

"Yeah, not a triple homicide, *Mom.*"

Their eyes meet.

Stacey sees an unfamiliar expression in her mother's, stark and troubling.

Is it . . . fear?

Mom, always so self-assured, looks away, into the shadows beyond the flickering candlelight.

This time, when Heather speaks up to change the subject, no one stops her.

Nora

Back at 104 Glover, the climate-controlled house is cool and dry, lamplit and tidy.

Nora takes a long shower, washing the sticky sweat from her skin and the smell of charcoal and citronella from her hair. It's impossible to scrub away the evening's unpleasant ending. The water is steamy and the shampoo jasmine-scented, miring her in the warm, humid garden, hearing those awful words.

Three people were killed in our house . . .

Someone knocks on the bathroom door.

"Mom? I need to get in there."

Stacey.

"Can't you go downstairs?"

"My stuff is up here."

"Okay. I'll be right out," she calls, turning off the spray with a weary sigh.

Wrapped in a towel, she digs through the countertop disorder for her La Prairie night cream. Besides Keith's collection of vitamins and homeopathic remedies, there are too many toiletries and cosmetics, hairbrushes and hair products, two bottles of contact lens solution and cases, her own and Stacey's.

Four people, one full bathroom, and no storage or counter-top in the tiny half bath tucked under the stairs.

How had she thought that wouldn't be an issue?

Other people do it. Families all over the city, crammed into small spaces. The Howells have a whole house. This house, a murder house.

She slathers night cream over her face and brushes her teeth, the unpleasant aftertaste of garlic and alcohol linger-ing along with traces of conversation.

Three people were killed in our house . . .

In their beds . . .

The killer was never found . . .

She pulls a nightgown over her damp head and emerges from the bathroom. Stacey's door is ajar and she's speaking quietly. Is she reading aloud? Talking to herself?

Poking her head in, Nora is surprised to see both her daughters bent over Stacey's open laptop.

Piper is wearing shorty pajamas and orthodontic retain-ers. "But which room?" she asks her sister in a low voice. "Mine or yours?"

"Probably this one, because it's bigger and she was the only—" Stacey breaks off, spotting Nora.

"What's going on, girls?"

"Stacey found this thing online about the murders."

Of course she did, even though Nora and Keith had ad-vised the girls on the short walk back not to dwell on their new home's macabre history.

She sighs and leans in toward the screen. "Let's see."

It's an article from a newspaper archive. The headline reads HEINOUS TRIPLE HOMICIDE and is accompanied by a photo with the caption *Doomed couple in happier times: their wedding day.*

Stanley Toska is swarthy with a mustache and intense dark eyes beneath bushy brows. His bride, Lena, wears a white skirt suit with oversize shoulder pads, and she's smiling beneath a dark cloud of big hair and spackled-on makeup that was all the rage in the '80s.

Nora scans the article, details jumping out at her.

. . . January 17, 1994 . . .

. . . 104 Glover Street in Brooklyn . . .

. . . daughter, Anna . . .

"Creepy, right?"

She looks up to see Piper waiting for her reaction. Stacey is now focused on her phone, typing something.

"It was a long time ago. Long before you two were born."

"Looks like it was my room." Stacey shows Piper her phone. "See? This article says the victims were found in adjacent bedrooms. Yours isn't adjacent to the master."

"Oh, good. I mean, good for *me*. Not for you, Stace. Sorry."

"What are you talking about?" Nora asks, though she has a good idea.

"We were wondering which bedroom was the girl's," Piper says, "because I can't sleep in a room where someone died."

"Yeah, and I'm pretty sure there's a law that you have to inform people about something like this before they decide to move in," Stacey adds.

"I don't know about that. The rental agent didn't say anything to us."

"But how could you and Dad not think it was weird that this place has been empty for twenty-five years?"

"We didn't know. She said it was a brand-new listing, and I think she mentioned that the owner lives abroad."

"Well, Courtney said no one's ever met the owner, so even *he* has obviously never even lived here."

"And Lennon said no one has since the murders, because it's haunted," Piper puts in.

"Girls. This house is not haunted."

"Lennon and Courtney said it is."

"Lennon and Courtney are wrong. There's no such thing as—"

"The murderer got away, Mom. What if he comes back?"

"Piper . . ." Nora shakes her head and presses her hands into her aching shoulders as weariness descends like a weighted blanket.

"Stacey says a killer always returns to the scene of a crime."

"It happened years ago. The killer's long gone, or dead. So that's not going to happen. I promise."

"You can't promise that. You don't know."

"I *do* know. You're safe here. We're all safe here. Come on, let's call it a night. Things will be brighter in the morning." She turns to Stacey. "And don't waste another minute looking up details and scaring yourself and your sister."

"But—"

"We came to New York because we all needed a change of scenery and a positive experience."

"I thought we came because Dad's company made him transfer here for a year."

"Yes. Of course. But everything happens for a reason." *This move, especially.*

"Come on, Mom, that's such a cliché."

"Clichés are clichés because they're true," she informs Stacey. "And we have to make the most of this opportunity. So let's look forward, and not dwell on some terrible tragedy that happened to strangers. Okay?"

Stacey shrugs. "Sure."

After a moment, Piper agrees.

Not convincing, but Nora will take it.

She tells the girls good night and shuffles down the hall toward the master bedroom.

Keith is probably waiting up to discuss the situation. Maybe he, too, is worried about sleeping in a room where people were murdered.

No. When she opens the door, he appears to be deep in slumber.

She flips off the light, climbs into bed, and turns onto her side, her back to her husband's. Listening to his breathing, she can't tell whether he's really asleep.

They've both grown proficient at faking sleep—and other things.

Stacey

Stacey turns off the bathroom light and steps into the dark hall.

Her parents' bedroom door is closed at one end. She half expects to see her sister's open at the other, and Piper having returned to Stacey's room, still too anxious to sleep. But her door, too, is closed.

Stacey's is still ajar, as she left it. Yes, *exactly* as she left it—she counts the floorboards between the threshold and the bottom corner of the door to make sure it hasn't moved. Then, just to be absolutely certain no one crept in while she was gone, she checks under the bed and in the closet.

Empty. Safe.

For now.

She closes the door behind her. Like the others along the hall, it has an old-fashioned china knob on a metal plate with a skeleton keyhole and no key. You'd think after what happened in this house that whoever remodeled it would have updated the bedroom doors with modern locks.

Then again, no one has lived here since the murders, so it didn't matter until now. Maybe whoever fixed it up thought no one would be stupid enough to live in a place where a family had been slaughtered.

No one but us.

She reminds herself that the Lizzie Borden house in Fall River, Massachusetts, became a popular bed-and-breakfast inn. Plenty of people pay to spend the night in the rooms where the axe murders were committed.

That's different, though. The killer is long dead.

And any reminder of Lizzie Borden is the opposite of soothing.

Heart pounding, Stacey goes to the window and lifts the edge of the shade to peer out.

Tonight, the flat roof of the shed next door is empty.

But Friday, she could have sworn she'd seen a shadowy figure there, watching this house through binoculars. She caught just a quick glimpse, and then he was gone.

That was before she knew about the triple homicide. She figured her eyes must be playing tricks on her. Or that her mind was—an option she found almost as unnerving as Peeping Toms.

This evening, heading out with her family, she'd noticed a man sitting on the steps of a house across the street. At a glance she assumed he was just a neighbor enjoying his newspaper on a beautiful summer evening, but then something felt kind of *off*.

Though she couldn't see his face, she wondered if he was the same person she'd seen on the roof—illogical, since she had nothing more to go on than a silhouette and some weird instinct.

Now that she knows about the murders, though, it makes a terrifying kind of sense.

What if the watcher is the gunman who escaped twenty-five years ago? What if he's plotting to murder a new family?

She's glad she hadn't brought that up to her sister when she barged into Stacey's room.

Back home in California, she and Piper had coexisted without much interaction. There were no confidences, mutual friends, or shared interests. They've never been the kind of sisters who really even notice each other.

But here, they only have each other. And tonight, they bonded over curiosity about the crimes and dread of sleeping in this house.

Stacey tells herself that's the reason she didn't tell Piper about the watcher—to protect her from one more thing to worry about. Not because . . .

Well, not because if she mentions her suspicion, she might see that familiar look in Piper's blue eyes. The same look their parents get whenever they worry that something is wrong with Stacey. With her brain.

What if they're right about that?

One night last winter, she'd overheard them behind closed doors, mid-conversation.

"She's a teenager. Growing pains are normal," Dad was saying.

Stacey assumed he was talking about Piper, a freshman who'd been pestering them for more freedom now that she was dating a junior, Billy Underwood. Ever since sixth grade, Stacey had referred to him as *Bully* Underwood, if only in her own head. He's outgrown the mean-spirited middle school hobby of tormenting girls like Stacey, but she hasn't forgotten, or forgiven him, and is glad his romance with his sister was short-lived.

"Seeing a mental health professional is *normal*, Keith," Mom said. "Pretty much everyone we know is seeing a shrink and is medicated."

"You're not. Piper's not. I'm not."

They were talking about Stacey.

"Yeah, well, *you*," Mom said. "*You* won't even take ibuprofen when you get a headache."

"Because natural healing is—"

"I get it, Keith. But just because you don't take medicine doesn't mean there's something wrong with it."

"And Stacey's mood swings and quirky habits and appearance don't mean there's something wrong with *her*. Maybe she doesn't look like a Barbie doll, but she's got other things going for her."

"This isn't about her looks!" Mom protested. "I think she might be unstable and I want her to see a psychiatrist because I'm concerned for our daughter's physical and emotional well-being. I want to help her."

"And you think her life would be easier if she could feel comfortable at school, find friends, fit in . . ."

"Well, wouldn't it?"

"Yes. And so would yours."

"How dare you?" Mom's voice was low with fury. "How dare you insinuate that I—"

Stacey fled. She didn't need to hear more. It was nothing she hadn't heard before, thanks to Bully Underwood and his friends calling her fat, ugly, and crazy back in the day. Yet it stung even worse, hearing it from her own parents. Not in those same words, but in equally hurtful ones.

That night, she vowed to change the one thing she could control: her appearance. She'll never be a Barbie doll like her mother and sister, but she's a lot healthier than she used to be.

As for the rest—mood swings and quirky habits don't make a person crazy. They make her normal, like Dad said. She doesn't need a psychiatrist.

She drops the shade, turns away from the window, turns off the light, and climbs into bed.

Nora

This time, Keith really is sleeping, and Nora is certain she'll soon follow, courtesy of the busy day and boozy dinner.

But every attempt to lull herself with pleasant thoughts boomerangs her to the triple homicide.

Leave it to Stacey to unearth an article about the case as soon as they got home. She'll want to know everything about it. For someone like her, knowledge provides a measure of control. The more information you have about how terrible things happened to other people, the better equipped you are to ensure they don't happen to you.

Only sometimes, terrible things happen to people through no fault of their own.

"Keith?"

Her whisper doesn't interrupt the steady snoring. Nor does the soft creaking of the mattress when she gets up and grabs her phone from the nightstand, or her quiet footsteps across the room.

She opens a drawer and reaches way into the back. There are several prescription bottles hidden beneath her clothes. She opens her phone screen to cast enough illumination so that she can read the labels. Finding the right bottle, she shakes a pill into her hand, swallows it without water, and returns to bed.

She closes her eyes, waiting for sleep, knowing this time it will come.

But not soon enough.

She thinks of Stanley and Lena Toska, dead on this very spot.

Hit men don't typically take out the wives and children.

She hears Jules's voice, her tone almost glib, as if she were sharing innocuous gossip and not another family's tragedy.

She hears Keith's rhythmic breathing.

She hears the echo of stealthy footsteps on the stairs a long, long time ago. Long before her girls were born. But no, not before she was.

When sleep comes at last, it's laced with nightmares of bullets and bloodstains, and a killer fleeing in the night, and an echo of her daughter's frightened voice . . .

A killer always returns to the scene of a crime . . .

Stacey

Tuesday morning, as Piper takes the world's longest shower heedless of the others waiting to get into the bathroom, Stacey lies in bed dreading the school day ahead and listening to her parents in the next room.

It's not like she's actively eavesdropping. And the walls of this old house aren't as thin as they are back home. But under this roof, the residents are in close proximity even when they're in their own private space. Sometimes you can't help but hear what's going on in the next room.

She thinks of the family shot in their beds. Of the daughter who died in this room, and the parents in the next. Had the girl heard anything? A confrontation? An intruder's footsteps? The fatal shots in the adjacent room?

Lennon's comment echoes back to her. *Suppressors don't really make the shot silent. Just muffled.*

In this moment, Stacey can hear the hangers scraping along the metal pole as Dad rummages through the closet. He's trying to figure out what to wear to the office, wondering whether to dress up or down. Mom is offering advice, as if she knows anything about anything.

Unlike the rest of the family, she gets to lounge around

at home all day with the dog and do whatever she feels like doing. She doesn't have to plunge into an unfamiliar world populated by strangers, hoping to find acceptance.

Maybe things will be different here. It's not like Stacey needs to make a bunch of friends, or any, really. But it would be nice not to spend every weekday in queasy apprehension. Her old school had prided itself on its anti-bullying campaign, abolishing schoolyard picks in PE and hanging *Kindness Counts* posters in the corridors. But that didn't eliminate the endless awkward moments and pervasive reminders of her misfit status.

"I can't believe she didn't tell us," Dad says on the other side of the wall, and Stacey assumes he's talking about her, since she doesn't tell them anything.

"Well, I checked New York's stigmatized property rules, and it turns out listing agents aren't required to disclose things like that."

"Like a triple homicide? Doesn't it seem only fair that she'd tell us?"

"If she had, there's no way we'd have moved in here. But it's not like we're in danger, right? Or do you think—"

"No! Of course we're not in danger." There's a pause, then Dad adds, "But maybe we should install some kind of alarm system, with camera surveillance, just in case—"

"Keith, no! Can you imagine how upset the girls would be if we did that?"

"You don't think it would make them feel safer?"

"I think it would make them feel like we're lying when we tell them there's nothing to worry about. And if you honestly think there is, then why are we even living here? Maybe we should move out. But we'd have to find another place right away, so—"

"No, never mind. That's not necessary. Not unless something happens. And nothing's going to happen."

Someone bangs on Stacey's door, and she cries out, startled.

"It's just me," Piper calls.

"Yeah, no kidding."

Piper opens the door a crack. She's wrapped in a towel and has another one wrapped around her head.

"Hey! You don't just barge into someone's room."

"I'm not *in*, and anyway, I knocked."

The sisterly bond forged Sunday night had been fleeting. Yesterday, she and Piper had alternated moody silences with bickering—about hogging the bathroom, about whose turn it was to unload the dishwasher, about whose fault it was that Kato threw up a sock, about whose sock it was.

"Why aren't you up? It's your turn," Piper says.

"Let Dad go first."

"Don't you think you should? I mean, you want to make sure you have enough time to get ready, right? Fix your hair, put on makeup . . . since it's a new school and everything."

"Don't worry, Pipe. I won't embarrass you."

"I didn't mean—"

"It's fine. Just go."

"I'm going." Piper heads back down the hall.

"I mean to school. Don't wait for me. I'll go when I'm ready."

"We have to wait for Dad anyway."

"Wait, what? We're supposed to go on our own. That's why he showed us how to take the subway the other day."

"I guess he changed his mind."

"He did," Dad informs them, now in the hall. Stacey sees him, shirtless in pajama bottoms, tanned and muscular like some California surfer.

"You're kidding, right? You want to take us to school on our first day? This isn't kindergarten."

"I'm going to the office anyway. We can all go together until you get used to things."

"But that's not what you said!"

Piper speaks up. "Stacey's right, Dad. You told us we'd be fine after we practiced on Saturday."

Saturday—right. It dawns on Stacey: that was before they'd found out about the triple homicide. But a quarter-of-a-century-old crime wouldn't have any impact on their commute unless they really are in danger, right?

Stacey thinks of the person she saw—or thought she saw—watching the house, and watching her.

She thinks of her parents' doubts about her mental well-being; of her own doubts; of her chance, today, to make a fresh start.

That won't happen if she brings up the watcher. If her parents believe her, they'll freak out and move them all right out of this house. And if they don't believe her, they'll probably haul her off to a shrink.

Two lousy alternatives are enough to convince her, for now, to keep the watcher to herself.

Nora

Nora stands on the stoop watching her daughters head toward the subway with backpacks over their shoulders.

In the end, Keith agreed to let them go as planned, as long as they stick together. They are, and yet not—both plugged into earbuds, lost in their own music and thoughts. Their school uniforms are identical and yet not—Stacey's white polo shirt is untucked and her pleated powder blue skirt pulled low so that it grazes her knees; Piper's shirt is tucked in and her waistband is rolled so that her hemline rides halfway up her thighs. She's wearing white knee socks and black flats; Stacey, black knee socks and black sneakers. She has her old black military parka over one arm, likely as a security blanket since there's no rain in the forecast.

As they reach the Edgemont intersection, Nora lifts her hand to wave as she had ten minutes ago when Keith departed for the office. But unlike their father, the girls don't look back before disappearing around the corner.

Well, good. That's a good thing, isn't it? Maybe they're excited about starting their new school. More likely, they're relieved to escape after so much family togetherness. She can't blame them.

Alone in the house at last, she turns the dead bolt and after a moment's consideration, slides the security chain. It's cast iron and original, according to the listing agent who'd shown off historical door hardware and neglected to mention the historical triple homicide.

She turns away from the door and steps over Kato, the world's worst watchdog, asleep underfoot. Her eye falls on the marble console table, where the pineapple sage is starting to wilt. She picks up the vase and goes into the kitchen.

No midcentury kitsch or retro earth tones here. No monkey figurines. Everything is sleek, modern, and monochromatic.

Using kitchen shears, Nora trims the bottom inch from the sage stems and fills the vase with fresh water, then sets it on the counter. Bright September sunbeams emphasize the splashy red blooms against the white marble counters and subway-tile backsplash.

In drought-plagued California, she wouldn't dream of running the dishwasher unless it was filled to capacity. She shouldn't do it here, either, with only a few coffee things and cereal bowls.

Just this once, she promises herself, throwing in a detergent pod. Because she craves order, and there's only so much she can control.

As the dishwasher hums into action, she grabs her phone and steps outside.

The soft morning air smells of damp soil. She crosses to a weathered teak bench, moss-slicked brick pavers cool and slightly uneven beneath her bare feet. She sits and dials Teddy.

The line rings, rings, rings . . . voice mail.

"It's me again. I was hoping I'd get you this time. Everyone's left for work and school and I finally have the place to myself. I wanted to fill you in on everything, but . . . oh, well. Call me back if you can. Just not after midafternoon here, because I'm not sure what time the girls will get home. They take the subway to Manhattan. Can you believe it? They're getting the hang of city life. I hope you're safe, Teddy, wherever you are. Miss you . . . love you . . . Bye."

She pockets her phone and allows the stillness to settle over her.

Birds chirp and foliage rustles in the breeze. A garbage truck grinds and halts its way along the adjacent block, a plane hums low overhead, and neighboring window air conditioners drone and drip. But in this verdant corner of the world, the morning hush holds the urban clamor at bay.

Anyone in earshot could have heard her on the phone. Had she used Teddy's name? She doesn't think so, but even if someone had overheard her talking to "Teddy," it would be meaningless. She's surrounded by strangers here.

Surrounded.

She gazes at the walls of windows above the garden. Some are open. Neighbors could be eavesdropping. Watching.

She stands and walks slowly into the house, resisting the urge to look back over her shoulder. Inside, she locks the door after her and gazes out, heart pounding as though she's just narrowly escaped—

She screams as something grazes her legs from behind.

"Oh, you scared me, you crazy dog!"

It's mutual, based on startled barking that doesn't immediately subside. She watches Kato closely, wondering if he's agitated because there really is someone out there. But then the barks morph into the whiny-whimper that means he needs to go out.

"*Now?*" She contemplates getting the leash and taking him for a walk. Then she looks again at the dappled garden.

There's work to be done there. The rental agent had mentioned that a landscaping company comes every Wednesday morning and if they wanted to keep the contract going they could.

"We do," Keith decided, without consulting Nora. "Just like at home."

"Wait, I tend to the garden at home."

"The garden, yes. But you don't mow the grass or prune the trees. We need someone to do all that on this property."

On this property, there are no real trees to speak of. Nor, for that matter, is there much grass. But there are droopy dinnerplate dahlias that beg for stakes, faded zinnias that need deadheading, peonies that should be divided . . .

Well, *should* isn't the right word. They *can* be divided, if you're itching for a reason to get outside and dig.

Nora has been since she arrived.

"Come on, Kato, let's go out." She holds the door open and he trots over the threshold without hesitation. He wouldn't do that if there were an intruder in their midst, would he?

She shoves her feet into her rubber garden clogs and follows him outside.

She begins by trimming the straggly bramble border, where she can keep an eye out for Peeping Toms. She's put her concerns aside by the time she's moved on to the zinnias and dahlias, and the sun has ridden over adjacent rooftops. Dog days, but Kato long since retreated back into the air-conditioned house. She should do the same, at least to fetch cold water, a hat, and some sunscreen. But she has one final task to accomplish.

Her phone vibrates with a text as she carries a long-handled garden rake and sharp spade to the peony bed. Probably Keith, checking in from the office. It can wait. This can't.

There are three broad, waist-high clumps of glossy foliage, one in front of each basement window. Back in May, their huge pink blooms would have scented the entire garden. Now she breathes in cedar mulch and damp mineral compost, raking layers away from the plant's base.

She begins to dig, grateful this spot along the house's brick foundation is relatively free of thick tree roots, rocks, and perhaps centuries-old war weapons scattered beneath the rest of the yard. She grunts softly with every thud of the shovel. Sweat trickles and tickles along her hairline, and she pauses to blot it against her upper arms.

At last, the large root ball lifts from the ground, the tangled network of threads snapping far below. Almost . . . almost . . .

She angles the shovel beneath the plant and rocks her body weight on the handle. The blade makes contact with some-thing solid. Panting hard, pausing to get a better grip, she wonders if it's a fieldstone, or perhaps another cannonball. . . .

She pries the plant loose, heaves it up, and plunks it down in a hail of dirt. Peering into the hole, heart pounding, she sees a severed worm oozing slime, a crumbling of loam, and beneath, a broad patch of flat, uniform, and thus man-made surface.

In that moment, her phone rings. She straightens, yanks off her glove, and answers the call.

But it's not Teddy's voice that responds to her breathless "Hello?"

"Nora? Everything okay?"

"Who . . . ?"

"It's Jules. I've been texting you, and when you didn't answer I figured I'd call."

"Oh! Sorry, I've been busy in the garden since the girls left for school."

"Great, then you haven't had lunch yet."

"I—no."

"I'll be right over." She sounds so decisive, as if they'd made plans that slipped Nora's mind.

But she's not the one who has problems with memory. That's Jules.

"I figured you might be lonely today, so I made a big salad. And I just baked a double batch of carob chip cookies. First day of school tradition in our house. Yeah, maybe they don't taste *exactly* like chocolate, but our kids love them and yours will, too. See you in two minutes!"

Nora hangs up, returns the phone to her pocket, and looks again at the object in the hole.

Two minutes.

She bends down and with a trembling hand, brushes the dirt from a rectangular metal box.

Jacob

A fter Sunday's encounter with the neighbor across from Anna's house, Jacob had avoided Glover Street.

It wasn't difficult yesterday. His in-laws were hosting their annual Labor Day pool party on Long Island—attendance mandatory. They live so far out east that you have to take two subway transfers and two train transfers to get there. Three and a half hours each way, lugging bags of outdoor gear and the casserole Emina insists on making every year, though it stinks up the trains and no one, not even her parents, eats steaming cabbage pie at a picnic.

Meeting them at the station, his father-in-law predictably mentioned that if they'd driven, they could have made it in half the time, even with traffic.

"I don't understand why you don't just get a car," he said in his Slavic-accented English.

"And I don't understand why you never even taught your daughter to drive," Jacob returned as Emina climbed into the back seat with the kids.

"Because the man drives. He buys the car, and he drives it."

"It doesn't matter anyway," she told her father. "We can't

afford a car, we have nowhere to park it, and we can get anywhere we need to go using public transportation."

She, of course, doesn't know the truth about Jacob's fel-
ony conviction, driver's license revocation, prison time. No,
his wife believes what he tells her. Or if she doesn't, she
knows better than to question him. She was raised in an old-
fashioned household; respects her husband and maybe fears
him a little, even after a decade of marriage.

"You could have gotten here hours ago if you had driven,"
her father went on. "That is all I'm saying."

No, it wasn't all he was saying. Maybe to his daughter, but
the old man's eyes narrowed at his son-in-law.

Jacob ignored the glare and settled back in the passenger's
seat. He had other things to think about.

Anna.

This morning, he'd left home before dawn and walked by
her house once, twice, three times, before the shades opened
downstairs and lights came on. By that time, the rest of the
block was stirring and he retreated to a bus stop bench on
Edgemont Boulevard. From there, he could keep an eye on
the subway entrance on the opposite corner, watching for
Anna, just in case . . .

Having convinced himself that he'd imagined her, Jacob
didn't expect her to appear. When she did, he leapt to his
feet, jostling the woman beside him.

"Hey! What the hell is wrong with you?"

He ignored her and raced across the street against the
light, dodging the rush-hour traffic crawl.

Anna was wearing a school uniform and carrying a backpack, accompanied by one of the blond strangers. He followed them, joining the throng plodding through the turnstiles and down to the Manhattan-bound platform.

When the train came in, he boarded the same car she did, on the opposite end. It was crowded. He stood against the door, forcing disgruntled passengers to push past him at every stop.

He kept an eye on Anna as they rumbled into Lower Manhattan, prepared to disembark wherever she did. She was plugged into earbuds and lost in a private world, eyes half-closed as she clung to the overhead pole.

The blonde nudged her as the train screeched into the Houston Street station. Anna shook her head and held up her index finger. At the next stop, she nodded and they got off.

So did Jacob, along with enough other passengers that Anna wouldn't have realized she was being followed even if she'd looked back over her shoulder. Yet he found it disturbing that she didn't.

You've changed. You've let your guard down. How could you, after what happened to you?

But then, how could she be here at all, after what happened to her?

Out on the street, the girls paused, getting their bearings. They seemed to argue, pointing in opposite directions and then consulting their phones before heading west.

Jacob trailed them at a distance, all the way to a beige brick building with tall windows and a sign: *Notre Dame School.*

Now he remains on the sidewalk staring at the building long after Anna has disappeared inside.

What can she be doing here? The uniform indicates that she's a high school student, but she'd been a college freshman when they met. When she *died*.

So . . .

All these years later, she's not dead, and . . . and younger? Still in high school, living in her house with strangers?

He must have missed something—some detail that will make the pieces fall into place.

"Sir?"

He turns to see a police officer. She's Black, sturdily built, and looks like she means business.

"What are you doing here?"

"What?"

"We had a complaint from the school."

"A *complaint*?" About to go on, he sees the look on her face. "Sorry, I know what it looks like, but I . . . my girlfriend went to this school, a long time ago. She died, and I was just remembering . . ."

Unmoved, the cop shrugs and tells him to move along. He can feel her watching him all the way to the end of the block.

He buys coffee from a cart near Jackson Square Park and settles on a bench inside the wrought-iron fence. The dog walkers, stroller-pushing nannies, and dozing vagrants pay no attention to him.

He stares at the cast-iron fountain, no closer to figuring out the mystery surrounding Anna's reappearance or how he could have forgotten that she hadn't died after all. Unless time travel is possible, or ghosts or zombies are real . . .

His phone nudges with a text.

Emina. She's sent a photo of their two sons posing on the

sidewalk in front of the building. They're holding backpacks and dressed in new shirts, heading off to second grade and fourth—no, wait, it's third and fifth this year.

Pulsing dots appear beneath the photo. She's typing.

A moment later, her message comes in: **They did good in case u were wondering.**

He hadn't been wondering. He'd forgotten all about his sons' first day of school. He hadn't given them, or his wife, a second thought when he got up in the dark this morning and left the house.

They'd likely assumed he'd gone to work early. He does that sometimes. He's an independent electrical contractor, and the hours vary.

He stands, tosses his empty cup into the garbage, and heads back toward the subway, thinking about Anna's miraculous return.

Nora

Jules stands on the doorstep bearing a large glass bowl and covered tray. She's wearing a sunflower-colored headwrap and a purple tank dress that bares her arms and legs, her dark skin shimmering with sweat and wafting patchouli oil.

"You look like you're having a fun day!" She grins, gesturing at Nora's grimy self, then leans in to pluck a small twig from her hair.

"Oh . . . sorry. I was . . . I . . . I'll get cleaned up."

Jules is already heading toward the kitchen as though she's been here many times before. "No worries. Take your time. I know my way around."

Nora closes herself into the half bath under the stairs, exhales through ballooned cheeks, and leans toward the mirror. Her fingernails are embedded with soil and her face is smudged with grime. Her sweat-matted blond hair hasn't seen a brush since yesterday. She uses her fingers as a comb and washes up the best she can, thinking about the metal box she'd hastily concealed beneath a stack of yard cleanup bags in the shed.

As soon as her guest is out of here, she'll get back out there and open it.

Jules has set out plates and cutlery on the breakfast nook table and is unspooling paper towels to use as napkins. "Do you have salad tongs? I didn't want to go snooping around for them."

"Yes—have a seat, and I'll finish setting the table. Can I get you some ice water, or coffee, or . . . I think we have wine."

"Water's fine. With lime, if you have it?"

"We do."

Nora opens the fridge and takes two green glass mineral water bottles and a lime. She slices it quickly, keeping a watchful eye on the shed through the window.

"I hope you like fennel. I'm trying to imitate a salad they make at our favorite Italian restaurant . . . Nora?"

She turns away from the window. "Sorry. Just thinking of all the things I have left to do out there."

One thing. One really important, nerve-racking thing.

She does her best to put it out of her mind as they settle in over lunch. Jules tells her about a crazy morning in her own household, with Heather searching high and low for her MetroCard, Courtney hogging the shower, and Lennon repeatedly hitting the snooze button and late for school.

"On top of all that, one of the dogs had an accident that everyone stepped over and ignored so that I'd be the one to clean it up after they all left the house. I was going to leave it there, but it stunk to high heaven, so . . . sorry, wrong lunch conversation topic," she adds, as Nora pokes at her salad, still contemplating the box. "You don't like fennel, do you?"

"I . . . hate fennel," she admits, and Jules laughs.

"You're a breath of fresh air, girlfriend. Honesty's a lost art."

"But the best policy, right?"

"Unless I'm performing and I ask you how I did. Then you lie your ass off."

"Other than the fennel, this is delicious. And I'm not lying my ass off, I promise."

"Good. Heather and I had something like it at this amazing little place we love on Mulberry Street. I've been trying to re-create it. The owner won't give me the recipe. Old family secret, he says."

Mulberry Street . . .

All around the mulberry bush . . .

Nora had finally gotten the song out of her head, but it's back, tinkling and taunting her, redolent and elusive, attached to a memory she can't seem to retrieve—maybe because it's one she'd deliberately buried.

Jules is asking her how her morning went.

"Pretty well, I think. By the time I got downstairs, the girls were ready to leave."

"And they didn't bother you? How'd you pull that off?"

"They're pretty self-sufficient, and I normally get up early, but . . . jet lag. I'm still not used to the time difference."

In reality, she'd lain awake again last night, thinking of the murders in the master bedroom, and down the hall. Every time she closed her eyes, she saw blood-spattered walls and floors. Yes, the stains have long since been scrubbed away, sanded over, painted over. Yet she's certain they remain, lurking beneath the surface, indelibly soaked into wood and plaster and her mind's eye.

"This is so not fair, Nora."

"What isn't fair?"

"You get to sleep in, your kids are self-sufficient, and your husband is great—even your dog. He's not under the table driving us crazy begging for scraps." Jules jerks a thumb at Kato, out cold on the doormat. "I bet he never craps on the floor or eats MetroCards. And *you*, Nora . . ."

"I don't do that, either."

The quip is met with a hearty laugh. "Yeah, no, what I mean is you're perfect, too."

"*Stop trying so hard, Nora,*" Teddy's voice echoes in her head. "*Perfection doesn't exist.*"

"*Sure it does. I have everything I ever wanted: a husband and children, a beautiful home, good health, financial security . . .*"

"*Any of those things can disappear in an instant. Be careful, my love . . .*"

"*I'm always careful.*"

But is she? Living *here*? Sitting across the table from a virtual stranger? One who managed to work her way into this house uninvited, and says she knew the victims?

"Trust me, I'm not perfect," she tells Jules, keeping her voice light, "and my family isn't, either. I mean, come on . . . *you're* sitting there in a pretty summer outfit, and *I'm* in raggy jeans and covered in dirt."

"Yeah, you look like you're modeling for a laundry detergent ad." When Nora opens her mouth to protest, she adds, "It's a compliment, okay? Just say thank you."

She does, and they resume eating, and chatting.

Nora notices that the pineapple sage blooms and foliage in the vase on the counter have perked up since this morning's stem trim. Too bad she can't do the same. But she's weary, and in her head, the monkey is chasing the weasel round and round the mulberry bush.

Jules asks where she's from, then holds up an index finger. "Wait, I know this! Iowa?"

"No, I—"

"Hang on, my memory isn't completely shot, no matter what my wife says. Um . . . oh, yeah, it was Kansas, right?"

"That's my husband."

"Right! You grew up in Los Angeles, like Heather. Are your parents there? Sisters, brothers . . . ?"

"No siblings, my mom died young, my dad died not long after I graduated from USC, and my stepmom moved away, so . . ." She shrugs. "No family."

"Is that rough?"

"I'm used to it, and I have the girls and Keith, so . . . it's all good." She pushes back her plate, a signal to end the conversation, the meal, the visit. "Thanks so much for bringing lunch. It was delicious."

"Dessert's better, I promise. You're going to love the cookies."

Oh, the cookies.

"And I'll take that coffee now, if it's no trouble. But no wine yet."

Yet? How long is she planning to stay? Nora rises, thinking of the box in the shed and trying to think of a polite way to get Jules out of here. There isn't one.

All around the mulberry bush . . .

Her jaw clenches around a smile. "Caf, or decaf?"

Stacey

tacey takes the subway home alone after school. Piper had stayed in Manhattan to watch soccer practice in some park with a new friend who'd promised to direct her to the right subway line afterward.

The non-rush-hour train isn't crowded. She manages to get a seat and listens to her favorite playlist all the way back to Brooklyn, eyes fixed on the overhead sign that advises her to say something if she sees something.

The slogan is posted all over the city, making her vaguely uneasy.

"What does it even mean?" Piper had asked Dad the first time they rode the subway.

"You know . . . if you see anything unusual, you tell the conductor."

"Like what? Everything's unusual here. How do I know what to tell the conductor? And where's the conductor? And you told us not to look around or make eye contact with anyone so how are we supposed to see anything, anyway?"

Dad answered her sister's questions patiently, trying not to scare her, Stacey could tell.

"You have to keep alert to what's going on around you, but

you don't engage. Just like anywhere else, whenever you're in public, you just put up your personal space perimeter. You make sure you stay in it and everyone else stays out."

Here, that perimeter is smaller than Stacey's accustomed to. With the exception of the wild-eyed mentally ill vagrants and pushy panhandlers, people pretty much ignore each other, even when they're close enough to touch. Yet this morning, she'd felt uncomfortable on the crowded platform and when they were jammed into the car. Visible, somehow, and particularly vulnerable whenever the lights flickered and went out in the tunnel, no matter how she reassured herself that whoever she'd glimpsed watching the house wasn't lurking nearby.

If you can't see anything, you can't say anything, or do anything. In the dark, you're helpless.

She's much more relaxed now, on the return to Brooklyn. Maybe because the First Day jitters are behind her. Or because this trip is faster and smoother. No stalling to wait for congested traffic ahead. The lights stay on. She can see everything. It's better that way.

At her stop, she emerges onto a sunny sidewalk. It's warm out, but she wears her vintage black army coat, tattered with a ripped lining. Back home, she'd more or less worn it out of defiance. Here, it makes her feel edgy and urban. Plus, it hides her Catholic school uniform as she walks half a block to the Edgemont Grind, a café she's visited daily since her arrival in Brooklyn.

Stepping over the threshold, she removes her earbuds and joins the line at the register. The coffee-scented air wafts with classical jazz, quiet conversation, and whirring bean grinders. This place is much smaller than the strip mall coffeehouse next door to the bookstore where she worked back home. The hardwood floors, tin ceilings, and exposed brick walls are vintage, and the stools along the plate glass windows overlook a bustling urban sidewalk instead of a parking lot filled with luxury cars.

When it's her turn, Stacey orders a double shot soy latte from a handsome barista in a Sikh turban.

"For here or to go?"

"To go." She's in no hurry to get home, but all the seats are taken.

"Anything else?"

"No, I'm good." She looks away from the enormous black and white cookies in the glass case beside the register. Lunch was hours ago. She was hungry immediately afterward, and is famished now. She's basically been famished for months.

It's worthwhile, though. She felt more comfortable in her own skin today than she has in school in years. Maybe because everyone has to wear the same frumpy uniform, or because it's an all-girls school with a diverse student body. Her old school wasn't entirely populated by the superficial, homogenous crowd, but most days, it seemed that way.

"Double shot soy latte for Stacey!" a barista calls just as a pair of yoga moms vacate a bistro table.

She grabs her coffee and sits, relieved to delay home a bit longer.

It isn't that her mother asks probing questions. But with her, even an innocuous "How was your day?" bears an undercurrent of concern. It's like Mom's anticipating a negative answer and would prefer not to hear it, but if Stacey gives her a positive one, Mom thinks she's lying.

Glumly sipping her beverage, she wonders why she just can't win with her mother. On the surface, she knows they have very little in common, but sometimes she thinks their personalities are much more similar than anyone else in the family. Mom can be introspective, too. She likes to lose herself in her garden for hours the way Stacey loses herself in books.

A shadow pierces her personal space perimeter, falling over her table.

"Wow, a Catholic schoolgirl out in the wild. Shouldn't you be praying in the chapel or something?"

She looks up to see Lennon.

Sunday night, when he wasn't being a jerk, she'd thought he resembled Julian Casablancas, the lead singer from the Strokes. Almost good-looking, in a moody kind of way.

Today, though, his dark hair is straggly, his brown eyes and thick lashes are masked by sunglasses, and the thin line of dark mustache above his lip is too sparse to qualify as sexy stubble. He's got a backpack over his shoulder as if he, too, has come straight from school, but he's in jeans and a frayed black denim jacket, with a ratty-looking T-shirt underneath. Shouldn't he be wearing a uniform?

"I see you made it back from Greenwich Village in one piece." Exaggerated emphasis on the *Greenwich*. "But uh-oh—where's your sidekick?" He looks around, and bends to check underneath the table. "Lose her along the way?"

"What?"

"Your little sister. Skinny, blond, blue eyes, about yay-high." He gestures with a face-down palm a few feet off the ground. "I thought your dad told you two to stick together."

Her heart jumps. Dad did say it, but how does Lennon

know? Feigning nonchalance, she asks, "Why would you think that?"

He taps his temple. "Psychic."

"Yeah, right."

"What, you don't believe in that? You should."

She rolls her eyes.

"And you know your dad will be upset that you misplaced his favorite perfect golden child on the first day."

Her mouth tightens. Her sister might be perfect—and golden—but Dad's not the parent who plays favorites.

And anyway, Stacey didn't *lose* Piper. She called and checked with Mom first, and Mom said it was fine.

And *anyway*, it's none of his business.

He dumps his backpack on the chair opposite hers. "Watch my stuff. Be right back."

He strides toward the line of people waiting to order and goes right to the front. Flashing a smile at a pimply pair of younger boys who are next, he leans in and says something to them. They exchange a wary glance and step back, allowing Lennon to cut in front.

Stacey rolls her eyes, wishing someone would come along right now and steal his stupid backpack. It's unzipped, his MacBook carelessly sticking out like an invitation to thieves. She also spots a pack of cigarettes, a knotted necktie, the cuff of a balled-up dress shirt, and a well-creased paperback copy of Stephen King's *The Shining*.

If someone tries to grab his bag, she'll let them. She really will. His sister was right. What a jackass.

Stacey grabs a book from her own backpack and opens it to the page she'd marked with a straw wrapper. Staring down at the text, she reads the same paragraph over and over without comprehension, her brain consumed in conjuring clever things she *should* have said to the jackass.

It's just like back in the old days, when the bullies taunted her. She always found herself tongue-tied in the moment, afraid that if she tried to utter a word, she'd cry. The tears came later, when she was alone in bed at night, accompanied by a useless, belated barrage of comebacks as the torment looped back through her head.

Today, she decides, she'll tell Lennon what she thinks of him, and then she'll sail out of here with her head held high.

But when he returns to the table carrying a tray, his folded sunglasses are dangling from the collar of his T-shirt, revealing big brown eyes that aren't just intense, but also seem . . . *kind.*

"Double shot soy latte, right?" He puts a steaming mug in front of her like a waiter delivering an order.

"For me? I . . . um, how did you . . . ?"

"I'm psychic, remember? And fluent in café code." He gestures at her half-empty hot cup, with its Sharpie-scrawled *D/S S L Stacey.* Then he sets down a plate. "Got you this, too, and one for me."

She stares down at the oversize black and white cookie. Café code couldn't have told him she'd been coveting it before he got here. It really is like he read her mind, unless . . .

Has *he* been following her? Was he lurking behind her, catching her longing glance at the glass bakery case? Eavesdropping on her conversation yesterday with her father about sticking with her sister on the way to school? Watching her from the shed behind the house Friday night, or from the steps across the street on Sunday?

All she'd seen that day was a male figure mostly concealed by an open newspaper. He was wearing jeans and smoking a cigarette. Could it have been Lennon? And then . . . what? He'd gone back home, snuck upstairs, and come back down to greet her and her family? Why would he do that?

"I figured we could hang out for a while, but you don't have to eat that if you're not hungry. I just wasn't sure if you'd ever tried one, and you should, if you're going to live here. It's a New York thing."

"Wh . . . *what*?"

"Yellow cookie, more like a flat cake, half vanilla frosting, half chocolate."

Yeah, Stacey knows what a black and white cookie is. Her stammered question was in response to his comment about hanging out. Why would he want to when he doesn't even seem to like her?

"If you want to trade, mine is white chocolate macadamia nut." He's moved his backpack to the floor and now occupies the seat across from her, stirring sugar packets into a mug of black coffee.

"I . . . no, thanks. And thanks."

So much for snappy comebacks.

And for willpower. She breaks off a small piece of the vanilla-frosted side of the cookie and puts it into her mouth. The cookie is dense and moist, the icing pure sticky-sweet sugar.

"Interesting."

She looks up. "What's interesting?"

"You broke off a piece instead of biting it and you didn't go for the chocolate side. That says something about you."

"That I'm boring?"

"The opposite, actually." He shrugs. "I like the vanilla side better, too."

"Really?"

"Yeah. Why? You think *I'm* boring?" He leans in, eyes gleaming.

"No. I'd expect *you* to go for, you know, the dark side. But you're just full of surprises, aren't you?"

His eyebrows shoot up, and a smile plays at his lips. "I'm not the only one."

Stacey's heart jumps. She's not sure what's going on here, exactly. He's acting almost like he's flirting with her; she's almost flirting back.

He bites into his own cookie and says around a mouthful, "So good. Jules always makes these horrible carob cookies on the first day of school and I pretend they're great but they suck."

"Jules?"

"My mom."

"No, I know who Jules is, but . . . you call her by her first name?"

"It's easier. What are you reading?" He gestures at the book still open in front of her.

"Oh . . . it's true crime."

"About . . . ?"

"Uh, Lizzie Borden?"

"Cool."

Unsure whether he's back to sarcastic, she breaks off another little piece of vanilla-frosted cookie and pops it into her mouth.

"So we're both reading about crazy people who go after their own families," he says, and shows her *The Shining*. "Only your axe murderer isn't fictional and she was guilty as hell."

"You think so?"

"You don't?"

"No, I do."

But how do you even know anything about it?

"I mean, who else could it have been?" He ticks off on his fingers. "Not her sister, Emma—she was out of town. Not the uncle John Morris who was visiting them—"

"Morse. But close." *Amazingly* close.

"Yeah, Morse. He had an alibi. Definitely not the maid Bridget. I bet she knew something, though, right?"

"Probably. I . . . I mean, wow. I can't believe you know so much."

"Why? *You* do."

"Yeah, but I'm . . ."

"Smarter? Special?"

"No! I was going to say . . ."

Not *crazy*. Because she isn't crazy. She might not even be all that unusual, though it's the word she chooses to complete her sentence.

"Yeah, well, unusual is a good thing," Lennon says. "Beats the hell out of boring any day."

For the first time in a long time—or maybe ever—Stacey decides it might be true.

Nora

Any other time, Nora might have enjoyed afternoon coffee and chitchat.

Jules is fun, fascinating, and pleasantly opinionated. She's as comfortable discussing politics and pop culture, literature, and even horticulture as she is her sordid past, curtailed career, and being a "burnt-out fallen star," as she calls herself.

"I don't know what would have become of me if I hadn't met Heather. She convinced me to stop hating myself, because it wasn't my fault. Addiction is a chronic illness, just like anything else, you know?"

Nora doesn't, but she nods.

"It's not easy getting past all that. You do whatever you have to do, and if you're lucky, you survive, you know?"

Nora does. She nods again.

Jules looks at her watch. "Guess I should go. The kids will be home soon."

She should probably offer a polite protest, but it's all she can do not to grab her visitor's arm and manhandle her toward the front door. The journey back through the house seems endless, with Jules pausing along the way to pet Kato, now sleeping on a dining room chair, and to admire the décor.

In the front hall, she double-takes at the sepia family portrait on the stair wall.

"Wait, is that . . . ?" She walks to the foot of the steps, peers up at it, then turns to Nora. "It is! Where did you get this?"

"It came with the house, like everything else. Why?"

"Damn, I was just thinking I was pleasantly surprised this place isn't creepy after all, considering—you know. But *that*—" She gestures at the picture. "That is creepy. You know what it is, don't you?"

"The family that used to live here?"

"I don't know if they *lived* here, but one of them is definitely *dead*."

"They're all dead. It's from the 1800s."

"No, I mean, dead in the picture. Look at the daughter. See how her eyes are gaping at nothing? And how the parents are holding her? They're propping her up between them because she's a corpse. Those Victorians were morbid freaks. Post-mortem photography was a *thing* back then."

Nora stares up at the old portrait, heart pounding. "How . . . uh, how do you know this?"

"A few years back, the Met was opening an exhibit on Victorian mourning culture, so Heather dragged me and the kids to a historical museum that had a similar collection. There was a display of pictures just like this—families posing with their dead loved ones. *Memento mori*. Know what it means?"

She shakes her head.

"'Remember you must die.'" Jules shudders and steps toward the door. "Thanks for everything, Nora. I can't wait to tell Ricardo about you."

"Ricardo?"

"At the urban farm. He'll be thrilled to have a volunteer who actually knows something about agriculture. We can get together this week so you can meet him. Sound good?"

"Sounds good." Nora reaches past her, turns the dead bolt, and opens the door. "Thanks for coming, and for lunch. It was delicious."

"Fennel aside, right?"

"No, I mean it."

"It's nowhere near as good as they make it at that place on Mulberry. You and Keith will have to come with us. Maybe next weekend. Sound good?"

All around the mulberry bush . . .

"Sounds good," she tells Jules, again. "I'll wash your salad bowl and get it back to you later."

"Oh, I forgot—you don't have to do that. I can just grab it." She starts to turn back.

"Don't do that!" Nora protests more sharply than she'd intended. "I mean, why walk down the street with a dirty bowl? Unless you need it right away? I can send Piper down with it—I'm sure she'd welcome the chance to see Courtney."

"Or maybe Stacey will want to bring it back so that she can run into Lennon? Is it just me, or did those two click the other night?"

It's just you.

The last thing Stacey needs is a friend who thinks it's "cool" that she lives in a house where three people were murdered in their beds.

She says only, "You never know with kids that age."

"You're right. Oh, well. Thanks again, Nora. See you soon!" This time, Jules steps over the threshold and is gone.

Nora turns the dead bolt, checks her watch, and after a moment's consideration, slides the cast-iron chain. Piper won't be home for a while, but Stacey could show up any minute. She'd texted well over an hour ago to say she was heading for the subway.

This won't take long.

Out back, she finds the garden cast in shadow now, and the morning hush long gone. She hears sirens and honking traffic, a construction site jackhammer, planes buzzing overhead. Children are shouting and laughing beyond the bramble hedge, in the yard behind 106 Glover.

The shed door creaks when she opens it. A shaft of sunlight falls in, and she can see dust floating like glitter. The metal box is precisely where she'd left it. She brushes away the dirt and gives the lid a tug. It sticks.

She looks around for something to use to pry it off as the voices of her unseen neighbors float outside.

"Joshua, don't climb so high!"

"I'm not scared, Mom!"

"Well, I am. Get down from there."

Nora picks up the box, wraps it in a yard waste bag, and peers out of the shed to check for nosy neighbors peeking over the hedgerow, or watching from walls of windows. Clasping the bundle to her chest like a schoolgirl embracing her textbooks, she carries it toward the house, trying not to run.

She locks the back door. No chain here because it only opens to the walled-in yard, but that strikes Nora as a serious security breech. She again scans the area for intruders and sees nothing out of the ordinary.

Opening drawers looking for a pry tool, she settles on a butter knife, then turns toward the table.

No. Too many windows here.

She hurries up the stairs, avoiding the dead girl's fixed stare.

Memento mori.

In the master bedroom, she finds Kato napping on the bed. He stirs, eyeing her sleepily. He's just a dog. It's not as if he'll tell anyone about the mysterious box she dug up. Still . . .

"Sorry." She nudges him. "You've got to go."

He closes his eyes.

Nora sighs. "Fine. Stay. *I'll* go."

The bathroom has no windows, and the door has a lock.

She sets the box on the floor of the shower stall, using the bag as a tarp to catch the dirt. She kneels, panting as though from a strenuous workout, pokes the knife tip under the lid, and pries. It comes loose with some effort.

Nora takes a deep breath, lifts the lid, and peers into the box.

Stacey

O nce the ice is broken, Stacey and Lennon have so much to say to each other at the café, and walking home, that they linger at the foot of her stoop debating their opposing theories about *The Shining*, which she's read and Lennon is rereading.

According to him, the main character is possessed by malevolent ghosts who haunt the hotel. Stacey disputes the supernatural angle, convinced he's descending into stark raving hallucinatory madness.

"Let's agree to disagree," he says. "Have you seen the movie? It's one of the only films I've ever seen that does a great book justice. Gotta love batshit-crazy Jack Nicholson."

"Yeah, it's pretty good. I liked *Carrie*, too."

"Book or film?"

"Both. I actually refer to it in my college essay," she says. "I wrote it over the summer."

"Me, too. Which topic did you choose?"

"The one about overcoming obstacles. How about you?"

"Same." He exhales Marlboro smoke through his nostrils. "I'll read yours if you read mine."

"Sure, maybe sometime."

"What's it about?"

Bullying, and no *way* is she sharing it with him.

"I just told you. Overcoming obstacles."

"What kind of obstacles?"

"You know . . . just . . . dealing with school stuff."

"Like being a blood-soaked prom queen and murdering all the mean kids?" At her glance, he grins. "You said you mentioned *Carrie* in it."

"Oh . . . yeah, no. What's yours about?"

"Trying to find my father."

"Your . . . father?"

"Sperm donor. Whatever you want to call him." He'd put on his sunglasses as they left the restaurant, even though the street is cast in late afternoon shadow. But she doesn't have to see his eyes to know there's a gleam in them as he adds, "You *do* know it takes two people to reproduce? I'd be happy to explain how it works, if—"

"No, I was just . . . curious about . . . you know. Who he was. Like, if your moms knew him."

"Nope. He was literally a sperm donor. This is stupid, but sometimes I tell myself he might have been a musician, and now he's famous, and we get onstage and play together."

"Like . . . Julian Casablancas?"

He lights up. "You like the Strokes?"

"I love the Strokes. And you kind of look like him."

"I get that a lot. But I doubt he's my sperm donor, you know? It was probably just some broke college kid trying to make some cash, and he's probably a total loser now."

"Then . . . I mean, why would you want to find someone like that when you have two parents who love you?"

"*You* wouldn't. You've got a mother *and* a father. But if you were being raised by two fathers, and no mother, then I bet you'd want to find her, even just to see what she was like at your age—what she looked like, how she turned out . . ."

The last thing Stacey wants to do is compare herself to her mother at that age—or now, for that matter.

"You're right. I have no idea what it's like for you. It must be hard."

"Yeah. I don't really feel like talking about it, so . . ." He drops his cigarette stub on the sidewalk and grinds it out with his shoe.

She's always considered smoking a disgusting habit, but somehow, it doesn't seem so bad anymore. She hadn't been tempted when he'd offered the open pack, but maybe she should have at least tried it. Just to see what it's like. And so that he'd think she's cool, or sophisticated, or . . .

You're an idiot. You know better than that. What is wrong *with you?*

Lennon pulls out his phone. "Give me your number."

"Oh . . . sure."

She rattles it off, and he enters it into his contacts.

"Cool. Maybe we can meet up in the park later or something."

"Um . . . you mean . . ."

Does he mean, like a date? She can't tell, without seeing his eyes, whether the smile curving his mouth is genuine or sarcastic.

"You know where it is, Stacey. I saw you there."

"What?"

"That wasn't you? Walking the pug?"

She's taken Kato to that dog run every day since they moved in. "You saw me? Why didn't you say hi?"

"It was before we met. I knew who you were, because I saw you here." He gestures at the house. "And then there. But you were wearing earbuds. And so was I."

She digests that, unsettled—only because she'd thought she'd seen someone watching her the other night. If not for that, she'd probably be glad he'd noticed her, right? She wouldn't be wondering, in a tiny corner of the back of her mind, if he's some kind of psycho stalker.

"I, um, need to get inside. My mom's probably freaked out wondering where I am."

"Yeah? Has she been texting you?"

"I'm sure she has." She checks her phone. There are no texts from her mother, just one from her father asking how her first day was.

"Maybe I can come in for a while," Lennon suggests.

"Sorry, no."

Her answer is too quick and blunt. He flinches.

"Yeah, that's cool. I just wanted to check out the house because—you know. The murders and everything. I always wondered if there's a vibe here. Like, this famous drummer, Buddy Rich, used to live in our house, and that's why Jules became a musician. Me, too."

"Because there's a . . . drummer vibe?"

"Pretty much. A musical vibe, anyway. Jules believes that everyone who lives in a house leaves a little piece of themselves behind. Even after they're dead."

"So . . ." Stacey gestures at the house behind her. "What? You were wondering if there's a *murder* vibe?"

"Is there?"

"No." Again, her answer is too quick.

"Or . . . maybe their spirits are hanging around."

"They're not."

"How do you know?"

"I just do. I don't really believe in ghosts or . . . vibes."

"I do. I've been doing some reading on it. I'll tell you about it sometime. Or not." He shrugs, gives a wave, and turns toward home. "See you later."

"See you later," she echoes, wishing she could think of something better to say, and wondering whether he's still planning to text her about the park.

Maybe not. Maybe he's changed his mind. Maybe he was only being nice to her because he has a ghoulish interest in 104 Glover, like those people who spend the night at the Lizzie Borden Bed and Breakfast.

That's a first—a guy who's only interested in you for your murder house. Way to go, Stace.

Climbing the steps, she assures herself that Lennon wasn't watching her, or the house. But what if he's right about vibes and ghosts?

She's never lived anywhere with a past. She's never lived anywhere but their California house, and it was newly built when Mom and Dad moved in before she was born. Maybe she did leave a little bit of herself behind there, though— her old self, shed like the extra pounds she'd lost along the way.

She unlocks the door and shoves it open. It stops short,

and she cries out as her arm and shoulder collide with un-yielding wood.

"Mom?" she calls through the crack in the door. She rings the doorbell, and then she knocks. "Mom!"

"Locked out?" Lennon asks from the sidewalk.

"I have a key, but the stupid chain's on the door." She knocks again, harder, using the side of her fist.

"You can come to my house if you want."

"Thanks, but she has to be here. I just—"

Struck by a frightening thought, she goes still.

What if something happened, like . . .

What if the Toska family's killer broke into the house while Mom was here alone?

"What's wrong?" He backtracks toward her as she dials her mother's cell phone. It rings once . . .

Twice . . .

It's going to go into voice mail. Dammit. Dammit! She has to call her father, or 9–1–1—but which?

Dad. He'll tell her that Mom is out running errands and—

But no, she can't be out. The door is chained from the inside.

She's about to hang up and dial 9–1–1 when she hears her mother on the phone. "Stacey?"

"Mom! Where are you?"

"Upstairs. Where—oh, no. Don't tell me I left the chain on the door. Sorry. I'll be right there."

Mom hangs up.

"All good?"

She looks down to see Lennon poised at the foot of the steps, hand on the railing as if he's about to come up.

"All good. You can go." She gestures toward his house. "She's here, and she's coming to open the door, so . . . But thanks again. You can, um . . ."

"Go. Yeah, got it. You want me to run, or can I walk?" The smile is back, and so taut she doesn't need to see his eyes to know he's insulted. Maybe a little bit hurt, too.

"What? No, I . . . no."

"Hey, it's not exactly breaking news that mothers don't like me. My own included. So don't worry. I'm outa here."

Maybe he wasn't just interested in getting inside the house. Watching him saunter off down the street, she wishes she could explain that not wanting Mom to see him here has nothing to do with him.

She'd be annoyingly relieved that Stacey's made a new friend, or think she's finally found a boyfriend, like it means there's hope for her loner loser daughter after all. She'll tell Dad, and of course Piper will find out because she always does, about everything. The three of them will ask questions, or just give Stacey these probing looks and exchange glances with each other, and it will be a freaking nightmare.

By the time her mother opens the door, Lennon has already disappeared inside his house.

"Sorry, Stace! I forgot about the chain." Mom is flushed and breathless, like she'd run a great distance instead of just down the stairs. She's wearing the same jeans and T-shirt she'd had on this morning, her blond hair in a straggly ponytail, and there's dirt on her clothes and hands.

"Were you in the garden?"

"Earlier. I was just about to take a shower when you knocked."

"Oh, well . . . I was worried that something happened to you."

"Nope. All good."

She doesn't seem worried that something might have happened to Stacey, though she should have been home nearly an hour ago. Nor does she ask where Stacey's been, or about her first day of school.

That's a good thing. A great thing. She should be relieved. But as her mother turns back toward the stairs, Stacey finds her preoccupied smile unsettling.

"Mom? Should I put the chain back on the door?"

"Hmm? Oh—no, that's okay."

Her mother hurries up the flight, goes into the bathroom, and closes the door. The pipes groan as she turns on the tap.

Stacey's gaze falls on the Victorian portrait above the stairs. Father, mother, teenage daughter, same as the Toska family who'd lived—and died—here a century later. The people in the portrait are unsmiling and stiffly posed, as was typical in the era, with the exception of Lizzie Borden. Poring over historic photos of her as a young woman, Stacey had noticed that she appeared to be biting back amusement, despite living in a miserable household with her father and stepmother. The smile, she decided, was a maniacal gleam of insanity, like Jack Nicholson in *The Shining* when he went on an axe-murdering rage against his family.

Climbing the steps beneath the previous residents' solemn stares, Stacey notes that these parents have their arms around their daughter, and hopes all of their lives played out much more happily than the Toskas'—and the Bordens'—had.

Nora

Back in the bathroom with the shower running into the empty stall, Nora retrieves the metal box from the hamper where she'd stashed it.

Stacey's arrival had interrupted her contents inventory—relics of the lives the Toskas had left behind before they came to New York, and cash. So much cash.

The rubber bands around the inch-thick stacks of big bills have dried and snapped. She riffles through one and calculates ten grand. There are at least a dozen packets the same size, maybe a few more, though she doesn't bother to count them. The money isn't as compelling as the personal items.

There's some jewelry—a man's thick gold watch, a woman's sapphire necklace, a baby ring engraved with the initial *A*. Brass candlesticks and a hand-embroidered sash, antique and from a foreign land. A key attached to a simple hardware store ring.

A photo album.

It's wrapped in layers of tissue, the edges disintegrating beneath her fingers as she peels them away.

This is not a vintage leather-bound heirloom volume, but a cheap, spiral-bound one. The pages have space for writing along the margins, and the mounting area is sticky and over-laid in shiny plastic sheets.

She flips through the first few pages of baby pictures. Glossy black curls frame a chubby face, huge eyes with dark lashes, and a delicate rosebud mouth that's smiling in every shot. She'd been such a happy baby, a sweet and innocent little thing. The snapshots are accompanied by notes: *two weeks; first Christmas; first tooth; first birthday; favorite toy . . .*

Hands trembling, Nora snaps the book closed and reaches for a manila envelope. She pries the rusted metal clasp prongs, lifts the flap, and pulls out a stack of paper.

The first is a muddy black-and-white photocopy of an Arizona driver's license issued to Stanislav Shehu and set to expire on his birthday in 1982.

The man in the photo, clean-shaven with a crew cut, is unmistakably Stanley Toska. His eyes are hard. His mouth quirks in a smirk.

Nora flips the page. Another photocopied Arizona driver's license from the early '80s shows a pretty brunette. Her name, before she became Lena Toska, had been Magdalena Shehu.

Like the baby, her daughter, she has dark, wavy hair, big eyes, and thick lashes, but there's nothing sweet and inno-cent about her. She's wearing heavy makeup, and a sly smile.

Nora's seen enough for now. She shoves the papers back into the envelope.

There's just one more thing in the bottom of the box.

A handgun fitted with a suppressor.

Jacob

"Where are you going?"

Emina has come up behind him in the hall, watching him zip up a jacket that's too warm for September. But it's black, with a hood, and deep pockets for the new binoculars he bought on the way home from work.

"Out."

"Out, where?"

It's a bold question, unlike her. He glares, and she looks away quickly, as she should.

"The boys have been asking again for a pet, Jacob, and I thought—"

"I told them no pets!"

"Not a dog or cat. They know that. But they thought maybe a pair of hermit crabs would be okay. They're small and they live in a terrarium and—"

"Fine."

"Fine? You mean it's okay?"

He nods. He might have said a kangaroo is okay, just to shut her up and get her off his back right now.

"Oh, thank you! Thank you!"

She looks tired tonight, with circles under her blue eyes

and her fair hair caught in a straggly ponytail. And she's getting fat, stomach bulging under her sweat top, thighs thick in stretchy pants that pill on the insides where her legs chafe.

She'd been pretty and petite when they met. Jacob was in his mid-thirties and more than a year into his parole, Emina in her early twenties and itching to settle down. The youngest of four sisters who were all happily wed with families, she was sick of being single, sick of living with her parents and their nagging, sick of her long commute and her administrative job at a midtown corporation.

Marriage was a logical step for both of them. He hasn't regretted it much until now.

Emina doesn't follow when he turns and walks away, past the dark living room and the kitchen where the supper dishes are drying on the drainboard and his sons sit at the table doing homework.

This small apartment is still, but as always, there is noise and movement from the neighbors—footsteps creaking above, water running below, muffled voices and droning televisions all around.

The bedroom is white—walls and woodwork, bedding, doilies on the bureau and nightstands. There's a crucifix on the wall above the bed. Jesus with bloody wounds. Every time Jacob looks at it, he remembers that awful night . . .

Anna. I have to get to Anna.

He retrieves the binoculars he'd stashed in a drawer, tucks them into the jacket, and exits. He expects to find Emina still waiting in the entry hall, but she's come to her senses and is gone, leaving him to make an uncomplicated exit.

He makes his way along a wide corridor wafting with

cooking smells and takes the ancient elevator down eight floors to the street. His building, like the others that line the neighborhood, is vast and populated by working-class families and immigrants. The streets are safe if you're local and know which blocks to avoid, especially after dark. That means the walk to Anna's neighborhood takes nearly half an hour tonight.

Emina texts him. **Stop 4 creamer on way home.**

Can't, he responds, irked, and sees the wobbling dots that mean she's got something to say about that. Of course she does. She's got something to say about everything. He's so damned sick of her, and the kids, the dreary home, his work.

Need it 4 my coffee tmrw, Emina informs him.

He scowls. **Then U get it.**

On Glover Street, a dog is barking. Night construction rattles on a nearby roadway, and there are sirens. Always sirens and jackhammers, here in the city.

He'd heard them that January night, too. The noise had been jarring then, because he'd been gone for a while, living in a quiet college town. He remembers wondering how he'd ever maintained his sanity amid incessant wailing and pounding. Maybe he hadn't. Maybe madness had claimed him and he'd never even realized it, despite what his doctor had told him.

"If you're concerned that you might be going insane, then you probably aren't. In my experience, people who are developing serious mental illness rarely suspect it."

Rarely isn't *never.*

104 Glover is well lit tonight, shades drawn on all the windows. He stays on the opposite side of the street and

walks on past to the intersection. Edgemont Boulevard is busy as always, traffic in the streets, people on the sidewalks, shops and restaurants open.

Lingering on the corner, he lights a cigarette. Nobody gives him a second glance. He could be a diner who stepped out of a nearby café for a smoke.

From here, he has a clear, diagonal view of 104 Glover.

He's not sure how long he stands, steeped in smoke and memories, before the front door opens and Anna emerges.

He blinks. If she disappears, then this is just . . .

But no. She's still there, heading down the steps, wearing jeans and a hooded sweatshirt. She has a dog on a leash. She's holding her phone, looking down at it, the open screen glinting.

She seems like a regular living, breathing human being.

And she's alone. *Finally.*

He starts toward her, mind racing. What should he say first? Should he ask her what's going on, or—

As she reaches the sidewalk, a figure steps out of the shadows.

Jacob stops short.

Anna doesn't appear startled, though. No, she was expecting it. Expecting *him,* a shaggy-haired young man who reaches down to pat her dog, and then walks her toward Edgemont with a proprietary air. Anna looks back over her shoulder at the house, as if to see if anyone's watching from there.

They aren't, but Jacob is, wondering whether she'll spot him here, on the opposite corner. When she does, she'll run toward him. His heart pounds, and he throws his half-smoked cigarette to the pavement, preparing to welcome her into his arms at last.

It doesn't happen, though. The stranger escorts her around the corner like a prison guard. She doesn't look back before they disappear in the opposite direction, but Jacob is almost certain she noticed him.

Part
Two

Nora

The metal box Nora dug up in the garden on Tuesday remains hidden on the shelf in the shed. Her family hasn't even noticed the sturdy padlock she bought for the door. Chances are they won't, but even if they do, they won't think twice about it. She's the only one who spends time out back. The girls are busy with school and Keith is working long hours. He hasn't even asked Nora how she's filled the last couple of days.

Now, Friday morning, standing before the bureau mirror knotting his tie as she makes the bed, he comments that she's up early.

"I'm meeting Jules and her friend for coffee to talk about volunteering for the urban farm."

"That's great. It'll give you something to do."

She stiffens. "I have plenty to do."

"I know, I just meant—I've been worried about you, Nora."

"Why?"

"Because you moved here for me, and—I guess, after everything that happened back home last spring, I don't want you to resent this move if it doesn't work out."

If *what* doesn't work out? The move? Or their marriage?

Their eyes meet in the mirror. She quickly looks away.

She resumes arranging the pillows in a precisely layered row across the top of the bed. "It's already working out, isn't it? It's worked out. We're here. Your job is good, school is good, the house is good, *we're* good."

"But are *you* good? Because you seem . . . different since we got here. Or maybe just for the last few days, since we found out about what happened here."

"Different how? You've barely seen me."

He hesitates. "Right. You're right. Maybe it's me. Maybe I'm the one who's not good. I keep telling myself what I told the girls—that it doesn't matter what happened here in the past, to strangers. But we didn't need this right now, you know? After . . . everything. We just wanted this to be all about positive energy. Healing. Looking forward."

"That's what it is, Keith."

He shrugs.

She shrugs.

He picks up his bag and jacket, walks over, and leans in to kiss her. "I love you. I just want us to be okay again."

"We are. I'll see you tonight."

"Not until late. I have that dinner, remember?"

Right. Dinner with colleagues. "Have a nice time."

"Yeah, it's just work."

Are the words forced? Is his smile forced?

Is it really just work?

A year ago, six months ago, doubt wouldn't have entered her mind.

"Oh, and Nora?" Keith turns back in the doorway. "Thanks for doing this for me. The move. Everything."

For him.

She holds a smile until he goes. Then she sinks onto the edge of the bed, hands clenched, remembering the July afternoon when he'd called to tell her about the job relocation.

"Where's the new office?" she'd asked.

"New York."

"New York!"

"I know. There's no way. We can't move across the country, even if it's just for a year."

But then he admitted Cooper hadn't given him a choice. His only option was to look for a new job on the West Coast, and that could easily have taken a year. He'd suggested going alone—flying back and forth every couple of weekends, with Nora and the girls visiting on school breaks, but she pointed out that would be more disruptive for everyone than a clean break.

"It's a year," she said. "We'll get it over with and then we'll come home. Or . . ."

"Or . . . what?"

"Maybe we'll want to stay. Who knows? Maybe we'll love it."

"Nora, trust me, *you* won't love New York. You've only been there a handful of times, as a tourist, to sightsee, take in a show, eat in nice restaurants, stay in luxury hotels. You've never lived there. Living there is . . . it's not the same thing. Not cushy, like your life in LA."

"Who says I need cushy? And neither do the girls. It'll an adventure. It'll be good for us."

Had she really believed it then? Does she believe it now?

She waits until Keith and the girls have left for school and work to emerge from the bedroom, phone in hand. As she descends the stairs, Kato trots in from the living room and shoots her a reproachful look. At least, that's how it seems; how it's seemed all week. Like he *knows*.

"But you don't," she informs him. "Come on. You want to eat?"

His ears perk up, and he follows her to the kitchen. She dumps food in a bowl for him and sets it on the floor. Then she surveys the scattering of toast crumbs and coffee grounds on the counter, along with a few stray items one of the girls unloaded from the dishwasher and left for her to put away.

If you don't know where something belongs, don't guess, she's told them many times. *I don't like things out of order.*

She learned long ago to control the few things she can in this world.

Ordinarily, she wouldn't bypass the kitchen without tidying it, but late yesterday afternoon, a call had popped up on her phone from an unknown number. Nora answered and heard static, then Teddy's voice in distant snatches before the call dropped.

Frustrating, but typical.

As a naturalist studying climate change, Teddy frequently travels to far-flung places. They'd last connected by phone almost two weeks ago, when they were both busy packing— Nora for New York, Teddy for an expedition deep into a South American rain forest. The conversation had been bittersweet.

"I wish I weren't going to be out of touch now, of all times, Nora. This move is going to be so hard on you. I still don't think it's a good idea."

"I know you don't, but I have to do this."

"Just leave me messages and let me know how you are, my love. I worry."

With good reason.

On the heels of her latest tense discussion with Keith, Nora is uncomfortable calling Teddy from inside the house.

The other day, he'd suggested a surveillance system, then told her to forget he'd said it. But she hasn't forgotten. What if he'd gone ahead and installed cameras without her knowledge? What if he can see and hear everything that happens in this house when she's alone here?

Careful, Nora . . . Careful who you trust . . . You know better than anyone . . .

She steps out the back door with her phone. Autumn is in the air. A cool wind stirs foliage that bears the first hints of tawny undertone.

She dials. It rings just once, and then, "Hello? Nora?"

"Yes. Oh, Teddy . . ." She pauses to regain her composure. "I'm so glad to hear your voice."

"We just got back to base camp last night. I've been thinking about you nonstop, worrying. How's it going so far?"

"It was so good, and then . . . Keith and the girls found out, Teddy. About the murders."

Stacey

tanding on the subway platform as a southbound train approaches the station, Stacey checks her watch, and then her phone. It's too soon for this train to be Lennon's. Only a minute has passed since he'd texted **Pulling into stop before yours. In front car. See you in 5.**

She steps back against the wall as people around her press forward to board. It's only been a few days, but the rhythm of subway ridership resonates with her like a familiar song.

The doors glide open. There are announcements. Those waiting to board are asked to stand aside to let passengers off, to be aware of the gap between the platform and the train, to move all the way into the car.

The doors glide closed. The train roars away and the people who disembarked disappear through the exit turnstiles at the opposite end of the platform, leaving Stacey alone.

She pushes her hands deep into the pockets of her army coat. She can hear distant rumbling along the tracks and a hollow drip of water somewhere in the tunnel.

She checks the time again.

Three minutes.

Already, other passengers are trickling in to align them-

selves along the platform, because you can't be alone in public for very long in this city. That's a good thing, and a bad
thing, depending on the circumstances.

She's developed a sense of who's harmless and who isn't,
giving a wide berth to potential perverts, beggars, and
psychos.

She stares at a now familiar *If you see something, say something* sign. She's come a long way in the week since they
arrived in New York.

Really, in a few short days. So much has happened since she
ran into Lennon at Edgemont Grind on Tuesday afternoon.

That night, he'd texted her, as he'd promised.

> **Ready to walk the dog in the park? I can meet you.**

She'd hesitated.

> **Is it safe at night?**

She hated herself for asking, but she wasn't quite bold
enough—or maybe stupid enough—to just go along with
something like that. Especially when she wasn't entirely convinced he hadn't been stalking her.

She braced herself for a sarcastic answer, or an unsettling
one, and was caught off guard by the sweet, gentlemanly reply.

> **I won't let anything happen to you.**

That clinched it. Lennon isn't someone to fear. If anything, he's someone who will protect her.

Maybe she'll even confide in him about the watcher.

A few times this week, she's had that same uneasy suspicion that whoever killed the Toska family is still hanging around.

She's read enough true crime books to know that isn't completely far-fetched, because the killer always comes back.

Or has she simply read enough true crime books to conjure a sinister scheme where there's nothing to worry about?

She hasn't *seen* anything, so she hasn't *said* anything, to Lennon or anyone else. Not yet.

She checks her phone. Two minutes.

Her thoughts return to Tuesday night. Her mother barely batted an eye when Stacey said she was taking the dog for a walk. Her father, just home after a long first day at work, told her to stay on the brightly lit, heavily populated main drag. Only Kato protested, giving a lazy little whimper as she fastened the leash on his collar and dragged him out the door.

She was relieved to find Lennon waiting for her in front of her house. Earlier, as she was doing her homework in her room, she'd lifted the shade several times to make sure no one was on the shed roof. As she and Lennon headed toward Edgemont, she was as concerned that her parents might be spying on them from the house as she was that someone else was out there, watching the house, watching her.

She supposed it wasn't unusual to feel anxious that night, out with a boy for the first time in the city, or . . . ever.

But it wasn't just that. She felt vulnerable. She kept thinking about the murders as they walked to the park. It wasn't deserted, as she'd anticipated. There were other dog walkers, guys shooting hoops, loitering kids, old men playing chess.

She did notice a smattering of loners who might have scared her if she were on her own. But Lennon held her hand securely, and she finally felt safe. For a while. Until he pulled her off the path into a grove of trees and kissed her.

Then, she felt like she'd stepped off a precipice, whirling and twirling and not caring where, or whether, she landed.

One minute to go, but already there's a rumbling approach and headlights in the tunnel.

She runs a quick hand through her hair and boards the front car. It's crowded.

She looks for Lennon. By the time she realizes he's not here, the doors have closed. Grabbing a pole as the train lurches forward, she awkwardly types a one-handed text.

Where are you?

The reply comes a minute later.

Just outside your station. Stopped. Congestion ahead.

Dammit.

On wrong train, she writes.

The message is met with a sad face emoji.

Three wobbly pinpoints appear, meaning he's typing something, but her phone loses the signal in the tunnel.

She'll have to ride to Brooklyn alone and wait for him. That's fine. He won't be far behind her.

It's just that connecting on the train gives them extra time together, and time with Lennon is amazing, even if they're just riding along on a subway that's too crowded for conversation. Especially then, because it means they're jammed up against each other.

They pull into the next station and her phone signal bounces back, vibrating with Lennon's response.

Get off at Chambers Street and wait for me.

"Sorry, excuse me . . . excuse me, sorry . . ." Stacey shoves her way toward the door, pushing through the sea of passengers pressing forward to get on. She steps off the train as the doors close behind her.

Waiting alone again on a deserted platform, she thinks about Lennon. Ever since Tuesday, her thoughts have been focused on him. And schoolwork, when necessary. But that's about it. She hasn't been online, or watching TV, or reading. Even the triple homicide at her house no longer seems particularly frightening, or as fascinating as it did when she found out.

People shuffle onto the platform. A couple of middle-school-aged boys, an elderly nun, a businessman with a satchel. She moves a little farther away from him, in case he's a creep, and closer to the nun.

Making eye contact, she offers Stacey a beatific smile and steps closer. "Hello, my child."

"Hi."

Her smile widens, and Stacey sees that she's missing several teeth.

A headlight appears in the tunnel. The train is coming.

The woman produces a cup from the folds of her habit and holds it toward Stacey, revealing a masculine, hairy forearm.

"Got a few bucks to help my church?" She—he—shakes the cup, rattling change.

Unnerved, Stacey sidles away as the train pulls in, and Lennon's dark head pokes out of the front car.

"Hey," he calls.

"Hey," she says, hurrying toward him, relieved when the doors close behind her, leaving the "nun" on the platform.

"I missed you." He pulls her into his arms as the doors close behind her, holds her steady against him as the train jerks forward.

"I missed you, too."

He's wearing black and denim, same as always. He changes out of his school uniform before getting on the train, dress shirt and tie wadded up in his backpack. He smells like fabric softener and cigarettes.

He kisses her deeply, just like that first night they went to the park; just like every time since.

Pulling back is torturous, but she manages.

"What's wrong?"

"People," she whispers, close to his ear.

"What people? There's no one around."

No one equals a weary-looking man with a squirmy toddler on his lap and an elderly woman sitting with her head back, eyes closed. Neither is paying any attention to Stacey and Lennon.

"If you want to be alone, we can go to my house," he tells her as they settle into a seat well away from the others.

"What do you mean?"

"Nobody's home right now."

"How do you know?"

"Promise you won't tell?"

"Tell who what?"

He holds up his phone. "How I know where they are."

"What do you mean? How do you know?"

He opens a screen and tilts it to show her a map with three scattered pin drop icons, each pulsating a different color.

He points to the pink one. "Here's my sister. She's still at school. That's Brooklyn Friends."

He zooms in on the screen and Stacey leans in to see that the pin is over a rectangle indicating a building near Borough Hall. Then he zooms out and shows her the other pins. The green one is Heather, in midtown Manhattan. The yellow is Jules.

"Where is she? Is that Boulevard Apothecary?" Stacey asks.

"Nope, next door—the Edgemont Grind. So we're not going there today. Good thing I saw this."

"Do they know you're tracking them? Your family?"

"What do you think?"

"They don't? But . . . how did you do this?"

"Stealth Soldier—an app. It's easy. Want me to show you how?"

"No, thanks. I mean, I don't really care where anyone is, as long as they're not bugging me."

Surprisingly, they haven't. No questions or unsolicited advice, even from her mother. Not that they've seen much of each other this week. But when they cross paths, Mom doesn't ask questions. She's quieter than usual.

Maybe she's bored. She's the only one who doesn't have anywhere to go every day. But then, she didn't in California, either, and she always seemed okay with that.

Maybe she's homesick.

Or maybe she's afraid, being alone in the house every day, knowing another family was murdered there.

"So are you coming over, or what?" Lennon asks.

"When is your mom coming home?"

"Later."

"How much later? How do you know she won't show up while I'm there?"

"She won't. Not that she'd care anyway. She likes you. She thinks you're smart and kick-ass."

"She said that?" Stacey tries to hide her pleased smile. "So you told her about . . ."

She can't bring herself to say *us*, as if that's a thing. As if they're . . . a couple, or something.

"I don't tell her anything. But after you left our house Sunday night, she said you're smart. And she liked that you spoke up when I was giving your mom a hard time. She said she respects a girl who won't take shit from anyone, including me."

"She said *that*?"

"Yep. Not to me, but I heard her talking to Heather."

"So, um . . . when were you giving my mom a hard time?"

"When I thought you guys were from Kansas or something and that your mom was shocked that a lesbian couple got pregnant . . . Remember? She said something lame about how she was just surprised by the retro kitchen."

"It wasn't lame. It was—"

"Hey, you don't have to defend her again. Anyway, Jules said your mom was probably just freaked out by the pregnancy because—"

The brakes screech and the intercom crackles an announcement, drowning him out as the train pulls into a station stop.

"What did you say? I couldn't hear you."

"Nothing."

"About what Jules said about my mom?"

"Forget it." He waves his phone at her. "Let's go to my house. I'll make sure no one comes home while you're there. I can set an alert that'll ping me when they leave the perimeter."

"What perimeter?"

"Whatever I set." He types on the phone app as the train rumbles forward again. "There. I'll get a notification the second she leaves the café."

"Wow. You're like a high-tech spy. Why do you need to keep tabs on your family?"

"Because they bug me. Here, let me see your phone for a second." Lennon holds out his hand.

"Why?"

"I just want to show you something. Wait, it's locked. Why do you have a stupid code on it?"

"Because that makes it secure. Why *don't* you have one?"

"Because it takes for-freaking-ever to do anything."

"It takes one second," she says, thinking it's an interesting contradiction in personality—that someone so tech savvy would be so careless.

"A waste of a second. Seconds add up."

"Maybe you should aim for a little more patience."

"Maybe you should aim for a little more efficiency. Here, unlock it."

He sounds like he's delegating tasks to an underling, but she sighs and enters the four-digit pin. Lennon doesn't even pretend to look away.

She tells herself that's okay. She can change the code when she gets home. Not that she has anything to hide from him, or that he has any reason to spy on her, but still . . .

He takes her phone, presses a couple of buttons on his phone, and then on hers.

"What are you doing?"

He grins, showing her his screen. There's a fourth icon now, red and heart-shaped, pulsating in the East River.

"That's you," he tells her. "We're in the tunnel between Manhattan and Brooklyn right now."

"That's . . . me? The heart?"

"You deserve to be more than a boring circle, since you're my girlfriend." He smiles.

The word catches her off guard. She's his *girlfriend*?

He says it casually, as if it's common knowledge. Is that how these things work? One person says something that transforms the other person into something without their . . .

Permission?

It's not as if he's done something to her; violated her in some way. And even when he first held her hand, put his arm around her, kissed her—he didn't ask if he could do any of those things. He just did them.

She wanted him to.

Does she want to be his girlfriend?

They have a lot in common, like . . . he texts in full sentences, with punctuation. She likes that. She does the same thing.

And he reads. Not just sci-fi novels or comic books, but everything.

They never run out of things to say. He's smart, funny, interesting . . .

But some things about him make her a little uncomfortable. Like, he can be so direct, though that's probably just the New Yorker in him.

"I'll put Stealth Soldier on your phone so you can track me, too," he says, intent on her phone, expertly thumb typing and scrolling. "So you'll always know where I am, and I'll always know where you are. We'll never miss each other on the train again. Cool, huh?"

She hesitates.

Maybe you shouldn't overanalyze or question things. You should just accept, and trust. Just be . . .

His *girlfriend.*

"Cool," she says, and the train rushes on through the tunnel, lights flickering like lightning bolts.

Nora

Stepping into the Edgemont Grind, Nora spots Jules alone at a table for two by the window. She's scrolling through her phone, wearing a hoodie and jeans, sneakered feet propped on the other chair.

Nora hurries over, still breathless as though she just ran a mile instead of walking around the corner. "Hey, Jules. Sorry I'm late. I heard from a friend back home. I haven't talked to her in a while, and I lost track of time."

Most of that is true, though the call had been hours ago. It's a quarter past three now. The day passed in a flurry of cleaning and scrubbing, her usual way of coping with anxiety.

"No problem. I'm not in any rush. Wow, you look fancy," she adds, taking in Nora's blazer and blouse.

"Well, I figured since I'm meeting Ricardo, I should probably—"

"Okay, first, every time I've seen him, he's in grimy jeans and second, he couldn't make it, so it's just us. Hey, when you order, would you get me another pumpkin spice latte?" Jules pulls a twenty from the pocket of her jeans. "Even if I won't sleep a wink tonight."

Yeah, that makes two of us.

Nora waves off the money and joins the line at the register, wishing Jules had told her about Ricardo in advance, so they could reschedule. He's the only reason she pulled herself together and dragged herself here.

She'd have preferred to stay in today. But Teddy had thought it was a good idea for her to get busy with the urban farm.

"It's a great cause. Food insecurity is a serious crisis. Go meet the guy this afternoon and find out what you need to do, Nora. You'll feel good about helping out and it will be healthy for you to get out of that house on a regular basis."

Keith's similar comment had irked her this morning. Coming from Teddy, who knows her so well, it seemed like sound advice.

But then, even Teddy doesn't know everything.

"Hi, what can I get for you?" The female barista has full sleeve tattoos on both arms, face piercings, and a purple mohawk.

"Oh . . . pumpkin spice latte and . . ." Nora hadn't even bothered to look at the colorful chalkboard menu. "You know what? Just . . . make it two."

"Name?" she asks, black Sharpie poised to write it on the cup.

"Nora."

"Short for Eleanor?"

"Um . . . what?"

"That's my name." She points to the plastic tag pinned to her tank top. "But I go by Ellie."

The name hits her like a bullet.

"I'm . . . I'm just . . . Nora."

She steps aside to wait for her order, feeling as though she's perched on top of a rickety ladder and wishing she could dive out the door.

"You're strong, my love. You can do this. You can do anything. You chose this path, and you've come this far . . ."

It's what Teddy had said this morning, when Nora had found herself in tears.

"I should have listened to you. I shouldn't have done this."

"But you said you had no choice, Nora. The move was for Keith's job."

"I know, but . . . I should have let him come alone. Or we could have lived in Manhattan, like he wanted. I shouldn't have—"

"Stop wasting time on *should*, Nora. You know you can't go back and undo anything. You can only go forward, and you have two choices. You can stay where you are and try to make it work, or you can go."

"Going would be complicated. Uprooting the girls, and Keith . . ."

"Then you've made your choice. Stay, and find a way to deal."

Yes. She'll stay in Brooklyn. And she'll stay in this damned café. She'll deal. She's been dealing for years.

Stacey

"Welcome to my room," Lennon says, opening the door. "It's exactly the same as yours, so nothing you haven't already seen, right?"

"How do you know that?"

"How do I know what?"

"That I have the same room? I never mentioned where mine is, and you've never been in my house . . ."

"Isn't it obvious?"

"Not really."

She pushes away the memory of the figure on the shed roof, watching her. It wasn't Lennon. It probably wasn't anyone. Just a weird shadow or something.

"Our houses are identical. The master bedroom is at the front of the house. The older sibling gets the next best room." He shrugs. "I'm not wrong, am I?"

"No."

"Okay, well . . . come on in."

She crosses the threshold and he closes the door behind her.

His room is identical to hers in terms of layout and size, but it feels smaller and darker. Every horizontal inch of space is crammed with books, electronics, and clothing; every inch of vertical covered in blackout curtains, posters, and hooks that hold more clothing, bags, and gear. The trim and patches of wall that are visible are painted the color of blackberries.

She studies the posters, an eclectic mix of politics, modern art, a marijuana leaf, Radiohead, the Beatles . . .

"Are you named after John Lennon?"

"Yeah, and Courtney's named after Courtney Love. Jules knew her, back in the day. She pretty much knew everyone."

Including the dead family at 104 Glover.

"She knew the Beatles?" Stacey asks.

"She knew *everyone*."

"But I mean . . . the *Beatles*?"

"Well, she once saw John Lennon on Central Park West when she was a kid on a class trip to the Museum of Natural History. She waved at him and he blew her a kiss."

"My dad rode in an elevator with Paul McCartney last year."

"Cool. Maybe they'd have named you Paula if it happened before you were born."

"I doubt it. In my family, we're not named after anyone."

"Well, in mine we are, and I'm lucky Jules named me after John Lennon and not Dweezil Zappa, whom she actually knew really well."

Stacey smiles. "I like that you said *whom*."

"I like that you like that. Here, I'll take your coat."

He gestures at her black parka, and she can't think of a reason to keep it on, other than that it makes her feel safer, somehow. She shrugs out of it and he drapes it over a floor lamp.

"Should you do that? I mean, isn't it going to catch fire?"

"Not if I turn off the light."

"Wait, don't, I . . . I'll just hang on to it."

"Okay, well . . . have a seat." He moves a heap of clothing off the bed.

It's the only place to sit, so she does, clutching her backpack and perching awkwardly on the edge of the mattress with her army coat draped like a lap robe.

She notices a pair of binoculars hanging over the back of a chair, and her heart pumps slush through her body.

"Why . . . um, what's with the binoculars? Are you into bird-watching or something?"

"Birds? No, hockey. Ever tried to follow a game from the worst seats in the upper level?"

"No, but you obviously have." She looks around for more evidence of a passion for sports, and finds none. "I didn't know you were a hockey fan."

"My moms like it, so every once in a while, we go." He sits beside her, takes the backpack, and sets it on the floor. "Man, that thing is heavy."

"Yeah, well . . . books. You, uh, have a lot of them." She gestures at the built-in bookcase, identical to her own. His, though, is overflowing. "You really like sci-fi and fantasy."

"Don't you?"

"They're my least favorite genres."

"What's your favorite?"

"True crime."

"Right. Lizzie Borden. Too bad there's no book about what happened at your house. I'm going to write one someday."

"Really?"

"Yeah. I've read a ton of stuff online about it, and Jules knows a lot about it, since she knew them and everything. Hey, she told me about the corpse picture at your house? I want to see it."

"Corpse picture?"

"The spooky family with the dead girl."

"The Toskas? We don't have any pictures of—"

"No, not them. *Memento mori*."

"What are you talking about?"

"Wait—you don't know? Your mom didn't tell you?"

"Tell me what?" Stacey's heart is pounding.

"Jules was over there the other day and she said there's this picture of a family from the 1800s . . ."

Ah, the portrait above the stairs. "The people who used to live in the house."

"I guess. Parents with their dead kid."

"What? It's not . . ."

Or is it? Envisioning the portrait, she sees the somber couple embracing their daughter . . . or are they holding up her corpse?

Lennon tells her that it was common for grieving Victorian families to memorialize their lost loved ones in one final portrait—an art called memento mori.

"It means—"

"I know what it means," Stacey says with a shudder. "I took three years of Latin."

Memento mori. Remember you must die.

"It's pretty bizarre that something like that would be

hanging in a house where a mother, father, and daughter were murdered a hundred years later," Lennon comments. "Don't you think?"

Hell, yes, she *thinks*. But she says nothing, thoughts spinning.

"Sorry to freak you out," he goes on, "but I figured you knew."

"How would I know? That's not our picture. It came with the house. It was there when we moved in."

"But I can't believe your mom didn't mention it to you after Jules told her."

"*I* can. My mom doesn't want Piper and me to be afraid, living there, because of what happened to the Toskas. She already said not to dwell on that because it was a long time ago, but . . . God. No wonder she's been so . . ." She shakes her head, remembering the dead-bolted door the other day, and how quiet and distant her mother has been all week.

"She's been so . . . what?"

"I bet *she's* scared."

"Of what?"

Maybe Mom, too, is worried that the killer will come back. Maybe she, too, has seen someone watching the house.

"Forget it," she tells Lennon. "I mean, it's not like some weird nineteenth-century corpse portrait has anything to do with the Toska murders."

"Unless . . ."

"What?"

"Never mind. You said you don't believe in that stuff."

"*What?*"

"You know . . . ghosts. Or vibes."

THE OTHER FAMILY

145

"I don't."

"But if something bad happened to that family in the 1800s . . ."

"Apparently, something horrible happened to them if their kid died," she points out.

"Exactly. Maybe whatever happened to their family cursed the Toska family."

"This isn't *The Shining*, Lennon, okay?"

"Okay." He inches closer and puts his arms around her. "Why are we even wasting time talking about this?"

He kisses her, and she tries to lose herself in it, in him.

But when she closes her eyes, she sees the dead girl's grim gaze, and the silhouette of a man on the roof with binoculars.

Nora

Jules is pleased when Nora rejoins her with a pair of pumpkin spice lattes. "Oh, good, you like them, too. Heather thinks they're too rich and cloyingly sweet."

Sipping the beverage, Nora decides Heather is right.

"Hey, thanks for sending my salad bowl over with Piper last night," Jules says. "Courtney was glad they got to hang out for a while. I guess they made plans to go shopping on Saturday."

Nora nods as though she knows, though Piper hadn't mentioned it. Or maybe she had, and Nora had been preoccupied. Her younger daughter's been full of chatter the last couple of days about how much she loves her school, her new friends, the city.

Keith's "stick together" rule was shattered by day two. Piper heads to school an hour earlier than Stacey and home an hour later, meeting with teachers and using the Academic Center in an effort to stay on top of the new curriculum. Stacey has adapted far more quickly, as a senior accustomed to the high school workload, and a better all-around student.

Jules leans in across the table. "Not only that, but Stacey

and Lennon are . . . I don't even know what they call it these days, do you?"

"Um . . . that depends on what 'it' is."

"If I said *dating*, my kids would roll their eyes like I did at that age when my mother used that word. *Dating* is dances and movies, you know? This is more like . . . hanging out."

"Like Piper and Courtney."

"Not like that. Something's going on, but . . . I take it Stacey didn't tell you?"

"No." That, Nora would have noticed, preoccupied or not. Stacey's been quiet the last few days, but it isn't unusual.

"Lennon didn't tell me, either. Courtney did."

"He told her?"

"God, no. He doesn't tell anyone anything. She probably read his texts. She's good with stuff like that."

"With . . ."

"You know. Technology. Invasion of privacy." Jules shrugs. "My daughter is the nosiest person in the world. She's always snooping around, spying on the rest of us. Good thing we've got nothing major to hide, right?"

Nora hopes her own "Right" doesn't sound as hollow to Jules's ears as it does to her own.

"Anyway, Lennon and Stacey have been meeting up here after school and in the park the last few nights, in case you were wondering."

"*Here* after school? In this café? So any minute now, they might show up?"

"Right."

Nora looks to the window, surveying the steady stream of pedestrians.

"*Were* you wondering?" Jules asks her.

"No, I mean . . . Stacey walks Kato after dinner, but she's supposed to stay on Edgemont. I can't believe she's going to the park alone after dark."

"Not alone. With Lennon." Jules peers at her. "Ah, that's even worse?"

"I didn't say that!"

"It's written all over your face, girlfriend."

"I'm sorry. It's not about your son—I'm sure he's a great kid, and—"

"Yeah, no, he's not. Definitely not a *great* kid, unless you have a soft spot for surly geniuses. He's a pain in the ass. Not that I don't love him more than life itself, but—anyway, he's not a horrible kid, either, as far as I know. So you don't have to worry about that."

I have to worry about everything. You have no idea.

Nora sips the milky, syrupy coffee and says nothing. She keeps an eye on the window, watching for her daughter, as Jules, capable of carrying both sides of the conversation, tells her about Lennon's bad breakup early in the summer.

"They were only together a few months before she dumped him, but he was crazy in love, and you'd have thought he was widowed after fifty years of marriage. Heather and I didn't think he'd ever smile again. Come to think of it, *has* he?" She tilts her head, like Nora might know. "But at least he's back to eating and sleeping and bathing. Poor kid. You know what it's like at that age when you get your heart broken, unless . . . wait, you were the girl who always had a boyfriend in high school, right?"

"Me? High school boyfriends? No."

"Oh, come on. You never had a first love who wasn't your husband?"

"Well, *that* . . . yes. But it didn't end well."

"Does anything? So what happened? One of you cheated?"

Nora forces a laugh, and a lie. "Exactly. How'd you guess?"

"Oldest story ever. I've been the *cheatee*, and the *cheater*. How about you?"

"Same."

"Wow, really? You mean you're not as perfect as I thought! If it makes you feel any better about Lennon and Stacey, he was the good guy when he and his girlfriend broke up. She was the one who cheated. Not him. He was loyal. Crazy about her. He fought to keep her. It doesn't mean he won't break your daughter's heart, but if that's what you're worried about, he doesn't have that particular strike against him."

Is that what she's worried about? That Stacey will be hurt in a relationship?

Of course that's part of it. Certainly the only part she'd admit to Jules.

"Can I ask you something?" Nora asks. "If they meet here every day after school . . . why are *we* here?"

"For one thing, everyone comes here. It's the best café in the neighborhood."

"And for another thing . . . ?"

"Isn't it obvious?" Jules grins. "I mean, aren't *you* curious about what's going on with them?"

Nora digests that, wondering if Jules had ever even invited Ricardo to join them today.

Careful, Nora . . . Careful who you trust . . .

She doesn't trust Jules.

Injecting her tone with wry nonchalance, she says, "Well, I guess we know where Courtney gets it."

"Hey, at least I don't hack people's phones. Mostly because I have no clue how to do it. Enough about the kids. What have you been up to all week?"

It's an innocuous question, Nora knows, but she breaks eye contact, again shifting her gaze to the plate glass window. "Oh, you know . . . settling in, getting organized, exploring the neigh—"

She breaks off, staring in disbelief at a man who's stepped out of the pedestrian parade to lean toward the window and look inside the café. He's wearing a red flannel work shirt, untucked and unbuttoned like a jacket over a dark thermal Henley, just as he did when she knew him.

"Nora? Are you okay?"

"I . . ."

The man cups his hands alongside his face, as if to block the sun's reflection on the glass. As if he's searching for someone.

Not her. He looks right through her.

She squeezes her eyes shut. When she opens them again, he's gone.

But she didn't imagine that he was there—or someone who looked just like him. Farther down the street, she glimpses a patch of red flannel before he disappears into the crowd.

Jacob

The last couple of afternoons, he'd made it to Anna's subway stop in plenty of time to settle in on a bench and wait for her to appear after school.

She rides the subway to and from Manhattan with the shaggy-haired stranger. He accompanies Anna to the café, too, and walks her to her house afterward. In the evenings, he waits for her in the shadows beneath the stoop and escorts her to the park.

When Anna isn't with him, she's with the blond people who now occupy the house. She's never alone.

To Jacob, it now seems as if they've imprisoned her.

Is it because she's been brought back to life like . . . like something out of a science fiction movie?

Is she even Anna?

Whenever he spots her, he's certain she is. But afterward, he wonders if she was just a random brunette . . . or if there was even a girl at all.

Occasionally since her death, he's glimpsed her out of the corner of his eye and whirled around to find no one there.

Or he's done a double take at a young woman on the bus or walking past on a crowded street. It always turns out to be a stranger who resembles her. Sometimes, not even all that much.

This girl, though . . . she doesn't just look like Anna. She lives in her house. In her damned room.

Is *that* the reason he's been seeing her again since Friday? Had the moving van and open front door triggered power of suggestion so that some wistful, subconscious corner of his brain conjured her?

Maybe.

There's no sign of her today. But he was delayed getting to her neighborhood, courtesy of a rewiring project out in Canarsie that should have taken half the time.

It was a residential job in an old house. The owner, an elderly widow, followed him around like he was going to steal something and kept asking questions. Her husband had been an amateur electrician who'd cobbled things together behind those old walls. Sorting it out had been a frustrating, painstaking process. He barely held his temper in check.

Now he walks along Edgemont, hoping he isn't too late. He has to find Anna. He needs her to be alone this time, just like the old days.

"Sometimes I feel like I've been alone and lonely all my life," she'd told him, so long ago. "I used to cry myself to sleep, wishing I had just one friend."

"Well, now you do. You have me."

She'd smiled, and nodded. "Now I have two friends. You, and Ellie."

Nora

"M om!"

Nora opens her eyes. The room is bathed in Saturday morning sunlight. Piper is standing over the bed.

"Mom, are you okay?"

"I'm fine, just . . ." She pauses, overtaken by a yawn. "What time is it?"

"Almost eleven."

"Eleven!" Nora sits up. "How did I sleep so late?"

"Dad said you're still on California time."

"I guess I am," she murmurs, but that's not it.

Yesterday afternoon, she could have sworn she'd glimpsed someone from her past peering through the café window. She wanted to believe it wasn't him, but the truth is, it *could* have been. For the rest of the day, and well into the night, she wondered about it.

Grateful that Keith was having dinner in the city, she'd gone to bed early. She was still awake when he got home close to midnight, but feigned sleep when he climbed into bed, smelling of whiskey and the hard rain that was falling on the flat roof above their heads.

"Nora?" he whispered, boozy and hopeful. "Hey, I missed my beautiful Barbie doll."

She lay on her side, eyes closed, and heard him sigh and mutter, "Guess Malibu Ken's not getting lucky tonight."

He was asleep within minutes, snoring loudly the way he does when he drinks. It was close to dawn when she got up and took one of the secret prescription sleeping pills she'd brought with her from California.

Now, limp and hazy, she looks at her younger daughter, never much of an early riser herself. Piper's blond hair cascades in waves that probably took her an hour to create with a hot iron. She's fully made-up and accessorized, wearing her favorite jeans, sweater, and boots.

"Going somewhere?" Nora asks, shoving her hair out of her eyes and rubbing them with her palms.

"Shopping! With Courtney! I told you last night. You said you'd leave your credit card on the hall table for me in case I see something I need."

Did she? Maybe.

"My wallet's on the dresser. Take it."

Piper pounces, tossing a sly grin over her shoulder with "Your wallet?"

"Funny. My Amex. And don't use it unless you have to."

"I won't, unless I find those boots I told you about."

"You have boots. You're wearing boots."

"Not snow boots. I need snow boots, remember?"

"It's snowing?"

"Not yet, but when it does, I'll be ready." Piper waves the card at her. "Thanks, Mommy. Bye."

She disappears into the hall and pounds down the stairs,

leaving the bedroom door open. Nora gets out of bed, stretching, and looks out the window in time to see Piper descend the steps and bounce off down the street to meet her friend.

In the hall, she sees that Stacey's door is closed and the bathroom is vacant. No sign of Keith. For once, no one knocks as she takes a long, hot shower, dries her hair, puts in her contacts, and applies light makeup. Back in the bedroom, she dresses in jeans and a zipped navy blue hoodie and makes the bed. It's going on noon by the time she descends the stairs.

Keith is in the kitchen, cooking something on the stove and talking to someone. Not Stacey. Hearing a familiar voice on speaker, Nora realizes one of his sisters is on the phone. He has three, all married with children and living within a mile of each other and their parents.

"I'll check the plane fares and see if we can make it work."

It's Sherri, his older sister. She's the bossiest one, according to Keith, though they all fit that bill in Nora's opinion.

"That would be great, Sher," Keith says. "I just need to make sure . . ." Turning away from the stove to reach for something, he spots Nora. "Hey, Nora's up. Let me talk to her about it and get back to you, okay?"

"Sure. Good morning, sleeping beauty," Sherri calls.

"Good morning," she calls back. "Say hello to everyone for me."

"I will! See you soon! Bye, guys!"

She hangs up. Keith reaches for his phone, propped against the backsplash, and puts it into his pocket.

She catches his eye and raises a brow at him. "'See you soon'?"

"Sherri wants to come for Thanksgiving."

"Come *here*?"

"Right." He turns back to the stove, stirring something in a cast-iron pan.

"They've never wanted to spend Thanksgiving with us."

"That's not true. They invite us every year for Thanksgiving and Christmas."

"To *Kansas*."

Before the girls were born, Keith and Nora had made a few holiday trips, but decided that it would be too difficult with babies and toddlers. They'd established their own traditions—Thanksgiving dinner for four at a Beverly Hills restaurant, and Christmas-week ski trips with friends.

"Your family never came when we invited them to visit us for the holidays—or ever," she tells Keith.

"Because they don't like LA. But they watch the Macy's Parade on TV every year, and they want to see it in person."

"Do they want to see *us*?"

"Of course they do! But if you don't want them to come, I'll call Sherri back before she gets the whole family all excited about it."

"The whole family? Your other sisters, and your parents?"

"I'm hoping. It would be nice, don't you think?"

"It would be really nice," she agrees.

For you, and the girls. But they don't like me.

From the start, the in-laws were cordial to Nora, but nothing more.

"Is it because they're overprotective of you, or because I'm not from Kansas?" Nora asked Keith after their engagement.

"It's because you're a skinny blue-eyed blonde, and my sisters are jealous."

No, that wasn't it. His sisters are also blue-eyed blondes. The entire family has wholesome, sturdy, seemingly effortless good looks.

"They wouldn't like anyone I married," Keith claimed.

She didn't buy that, either. She'd seen his old girlfriends in group family photos on his mother's mantel.

But she wasn't bothered that her in-laws didn't embrace her. She didn't need a trio of Midwestern girlfriends or a new set of parents. She only needed Keith, confident that if he ever had to choose between his family and her, he'd choose her.

That was long before the trouble last spring. Now . . . she's not sure.

"Are you hungry?" he asks, sampling from the spoon.

"What is it?"

"Tofu stir-fry."

"For breakfast?"

"Lunch. Breakfast was ham, egg, and cheese on a roll from that deli around the corner, and that was hours ago."

"Wow. Guess your hangover was pretty awful."

"What makes you think I had a hangover?"

"Classic remedy. Why else would a health nut touch a greasy gluten bomb?"

He smiles. "You know me so well. I've had my fill of cholesterol and carbs for at least a week. Oh, I got you one of those yogurt parfaits you like."

"With the mango and chia seeds?"

"Yep."

"Thanks. You know *me* so well," she says, turning toward the fridge so that he can't see her face.

Because really, even after two decades of marriage, you can only know what you see, and what the other person is willing—or able—to share.

Stacey

Yesterday afternoon, Stacey had been relieved when Lennon's phone pinged a warning that Jules was on her way home.

She couldn't stop thinking about the corpse photo and she wanted to get home and see for herself.

Plus, things were moving a little too fast between them.

That wasn't entirely Lennon's fault. Unaccustomed to physical relationships, she found herself careening like a thrill ride passenger even though she was perfectly capable of taking control and hitting the brakes.

When his mother's imminent interruption loomed, Stacey leapt to her feet, adjusted her clothing, and grabbed her stuff.

Lennon, phone app in hand, told her to relax. "She's still on Edgemont and she's a slow walker."

Stacey is a fast one. She made it all the way up the block without catching sight of Jules rounding the corner.

Mom wasn't home, so she was able to take a closer look at the Victorian portrait above the stairs.

Lennon was right. If you know what you're looking for, it's pretty obvious that the girl is dead.

People had to stand still for a very long time to be photographed back then. The daughter's image is precise, while the parents are slightly blurred. Her eyes are vacant, and there's a mottled look to her skin.

Stacey retreated to her room to search the internet for information about memento mori and early residents of 104 Glover Street. She pretty much stayed there for the rest of the day. Night, too. She'd been planning to go to the park with Lennon, but the weather turned.

Don't you like to walk in the rain? he'd texted as she sat in her room listening to the downpour hammering on the flat roof, punctuated by deafening thunderclaps.

This isn't rain. It's a monsoon.

He'd tried to convince her, saying they could go to the café, or she could go over to his house even though his moms were home, or he could come to hers.

My mom is home.

Sneak me into your room.

No way!!!! she replied, though she's never been a fan of excessive punctuation.

Tomorrow, then. I have a guitar lesson at 2:30.

What time is it over?

Let's hook up before. I'm not waiting that long to see you.

She slept restlessly, and every time she woke up, she thought about the binoculars she'd seen in his room. It makes sense that he'd use them to watch hockey, right?

It does now, in the bright light of day. Last night's fears are forgotten and she's looking forward to seeing him, eager to share what she uncovered last night about the people in the Victorian portrait.

It's going on noon when she leaves her room wearing jeans, sneakers, and a long-sleeved black top. She used to wear a lumpy sweatshirt over it because it was too snug and low-cut. Now she likes the way it fits.

She'd borrowed her mother's makeup, blown her hair dry straight and sleek, and perched a pair of sunglasses on her head the way her mom and Piper do. She's not imitating them. It's just a convenient way to keep the lenses from getting scratched until she needs to wear them.

Lennon wanted to meet her out front, same as usual, but she insisted on connecting in the park. She told him it was because she had to do a couple of neighborhood errands on the way, not wanting to admit it's because her parents might see him.

They're both home today, hanging around the house. She hears their voices in the kitchen as she descends the stairs, trying not to make a sound. She's not sneaking out, exactly, but she doesn't feel like answering any questions.

She resists the urge to pause and take another good look at the Victorian portrait, now that she knows what she knows.

"Stace? Is that you?" her father calls as she reaches the bottom step.

She pauses, offering the ceiling an eye roll and headshake as she calls back, "Yeah, it's me."

He appears in the archway, holding a wooden spatula. "I made stir-fry if you're hungry."

"No, thanks. I'm going out for a while."

"Where are you going?" her mother asks, popping up behind him.

So damned perfect, both of them. Golden, fit, and attractive, with cosmetic dermatologist–enhanced wrinkle-free faces and cosmetic dentist–enhanced smiles.

"I'm going for a walk, same as always."

"Without Kato?"

Right. The dog.

"Where is he?" Stacey asks, as if she'd intended to grab him.

"He's asleep. I took him out earlier. I'd be sleeping, too, if it weren't such a beautiful day," Dad says. "If you wait five minutes, I'll go with you, Stace. Maybe we can go check out that—"

"I kind of just wanted to listen to music." She waves her phone and earbuds.

"Oh, right. Go ahead."

She hates that he looks disappointed, that she feels guilty, that she can't just admit she's meeting someone.

But Lennon didn't make a great first impression on her parents the other night, or even on Stacey herself. She doesn't feel like defending him, or her own choices, to a perfect couple whose lives are ridiculously uncomplicated compared to her own.

All right, maybe that's not entirely the case. There had been a brief time back home, before the school year ended, when she'd been concerned that something might be wrong with one of her parents, or maybe between them. She can't even remember what, specifically, triggered her speculation. Neither ever seemed sick, and it wasn't like they were fighting. Her parents tended to have levelheaded discussions about disagreements, as opposed to full-blown arguments.

Whatever was going on, if anything at all, Stacey hadn't expended much time or energy stressing about it. She had enough to deal with between her schoolwork, college boards prep, and diet and exercise program.

"Okay, well . . . I'll see you guys later," she says.

Mom nods. "You look nice. I like your hair that way."

"Thanks."

"Have a nice walk." Her father drapes an arm over her mother's shoulders. "How about you, Nora? You want to go to the park or something?"

"No, I've got to change the sheets and do the laundry."

"Do it tomorrow."

"You know I do it on Saturdays, Keith."

Mom really needs to get a job or something. Just because they can afford for her not to work doesn't mean she should be a housewife.

Stacey doesn't hang around long enough to hear the rest of her parents' conversation. She doesn't care how they spend their Saturday, as long as they're not going to the park.

Outside, she pauses on the stoop to put on the sunglasses, insert her earbuds, and start the new Beatles playlist she'd made last night. John Lennon drowns out the city sounds, crooning the sweet lyrics of "If I Fell" as she heads out into a sun-drenched, shade-dappled day.

A slight breeze stirs golden leaves from overhead branches and the ground is littered with them, blown down in the overnight storm. The block hums with leisure activity. Stacey passes a young couple with a helmeted child on a bike with training wheels, a couple of kids with ice cream cones, and a male couple wearing cardigans and strolling along holding hands.

She's about to round the corner when someone steps into her path.

The man is middle-aged, a stranger with a dark crew cut, bushy eyebrows, and a razor-stubble-flecked face. His expression is urgent and he's saying something to her.

Wide-eyed, Stacey yanks out an earbud in time to hear, "Anna!"

Nora

Sitting across the table from Keith, Nora toys with her yogurt while he eats his stir-fry and tells her about last night's dinner.

"It was one of those old-school Manhattan steak houses where everything is expensive and all the sides are à la carte. I had the works—a New York strip, scalloped potatoes, creamed spinach, and then cheesecake for dessert."

"*You* ate all that?"

He grins. "When in Rome, right? I probably should go for a run instead of a walk today. And we need to find a fitness club around here. Let's go look for one this afternoon."

"I can't."

His smile fades.

"Keith, I'd love to, but I've got a million things to do around here. I told you, the laundry, and I have errands . . ."

"I'll help. I'll go with you. I haven't seen you all week. I miss you."

"I miss you, too, but you don't have to spend your day off doing chores and errands." Seeing a familiar flicker of mistrust in his blue eyes, she adds, "Let's go out to dinner tonight. Jules suggested a few places we should try."

"Okay. That sounds good. How was your community garden meeting yesterday?"

"Urban farm. And Ricardo couldn't make it. We're rescheduling."

"For when?"

"I'm not sure. Why?"

"If it's on the weekend, I can come, too."

"*You* want to volunteer?"

This time, he doesn't grin or say *when in Rome.* He fixes her with a gaze that makes her want to get up, get away from him.

"Nora, don't you think we should be trying to find things we can do together, after . . . ?"

After.

"Sure, but . . ." She lifts the yogurt cup again, stirring it even though she likes to eat it layer by layer, staring down at the unappetizing goo. "I mean, you don't even like gardening. There are plenty of other things we can do."

"Things that don't involve Ricardo?"

She plunks down the yogurt container. The weight of the spoon topples it over, spilling yogurt onto the table. Ordinarily she'd jump up to clean it, but she stays put, eyes narrowed at her husband.

"I've never even met Ricardo, Keith."

"But you did go to the café yesterday."

"Yes, I went. With Jules. Why does it matter? And how do you know? Do you have me under surveillance or something?"

"Of course I don't have you under surveillance. You used the debit card there. It's a joint account. I had to move some money yesterday, so I noticed the transaction."

"Seriously? And now you're questioning me, like . . . like . . ."

Like you don't trust me.

Heart racing, she can't bring herself to say it.

"Come on, Nora . . . after everything we've been through, you can't blame me if I'm a little . . ."

"What?"

"Nothing. Forget it."

"No, say it, Keith. What are you? A little . . . ?"

Suspicious.

But if he's not going to voice it, she's not going to force him. It's not like she needs to hear it. It's not like she doesn't know.

He pushes back his chair and stands. "I'm going to go for a run."

She stares at the spattered yogurt after he leaves the kitchen and goes upstairs.

Even then she doesn't move, feeling as though he's watching her, thinking again of what he'd said about wiring the house with cameras.

Was it because he's worried that the elusive killer is going to return to this house twenty-five years later? Or because he thinks she's up to something behind his back . . .

Again.

Jacob

Anna!"

It's actually happened. She's alone at last, right here, right in front of him. She's close enough to touch, though he doesn't dare.

She's just standing there, wary and startled. Her eyes are hidden behind large sunglasses but what he can see of her face is familiar.

"Zemra ime," he breathes.

Heart of mine.

She flinches and steps back, then cries out as he reaches for her arm.

"It's me," he tells her. "I'm—"

"Hey!"

He whirls to see two young men in cardigan sweaters.

The larger of the two steps between Jacob and Anna, turning to her. "Are you okay? Is this person bothering you?"

Her head moves. It's barely a nod, but the man takes it as a reply.

"You heard her," he tells Jacob. "Get out of here."

"Who the hell are you to tell *me* what to do? Anna, tell this . . . *person* to get out of here."

People are starting to glance in their direction.

"You need help over there?" a burly looking guy calls.

"Yo, there's a couple of cops down the street. You want me to go get them?" a young woman asks.

Cops? No, no cops.

"Anna," Jacob says. "You have to . . . just tell them who I am . . . tell me who you are . . ."

He needs to hear her voice. Now. Not just in his head.

Do you believe in ghosts, Jacob?

At last, she opens her mouth.

"Leave me alone. Please. I'm not Anna."

Nora

Sitting at the yogurt-spattered kitchen table, Nora thinks back to last April, when Keith caught her in the lie that had threatened—is still threatening—to destroy their marriage.

She'd told him she was going to the Coronado Flower Show, same as she had every spring of their lives together. But when she reached San Diego she kept right on driving, heading south of the border.

Teddy was always in Baja California at that time of year, studying gray whale migration patterns.

As cities go, Ensenada was relatively safe, but just like anywhere else, if you look like a tourist and you let your guard down, things happen. During a stroll along the idyllic but crowded waterfront, Nora's phone went missing.

She presumed it had been stolen.

"At least it wasn't your passport," Teddy said, "or you'd be stuck here for a while."

"That might not be such a bad thing. Don't you wish we could just stay here forever?"

"Your life is back in California, Nora, and mine is wherever my work takes me. The whales have moved on, and I need to do the same."

Of course she knew that. There was never enough time together.

Too soon, she was on her way home, unaware that a good Samaritan had found her phone on the promenade, called her home phone number, and talked to Keith. He knew everything.

Well, not everything.

But enough to shake up the most stable relationship she'd ever had.

Now, she hears his sneakered footsteps descend the stairs. The front door opens and closes as he leaves without a good-bye.

Looking up at last from the spattered yogurt on the table, she spots the vase of pineapple sage she'd moved from the hall table and revitalized earlier in the week. The stems droop, the leaves are dried and curled, and faded red blooms have fallen like wounded soldiers.

Salvia elegans symbolizes healing, Teddy's voice reminds her.

The move to New York was supposed to help heal Nora's marriage. It was supposed to heal a lot of things. So far, though, it's done just the opposite, dredging up unwelcome memories, and . . .

Hallucinations.

Because yesterday, she could have sworn she'd seen a familiar face peering through the café window.

Jacob.

Stacey

At first, Stacey had thought the man was a street person, maybe a panhandler, like the nun on the subway platform.

Then she heard "Anna" and she knew.

He's the one who's been watching the house. Watching her. He thinks she's the girl who was murdered there with her parents.

"I'm not Anna." Her voice warbles, but she stands tall, buoyed by the strangers who'd rushed to help her, the knowledge that the police are nearby, and an unexpected surge of inner strength. She stares him down as if he's a schoolyard bully.

His eyes are dark, and his expression is intense. Not insane, like Jack Nicholson in *The Shining*. Not that that means anything.

He shrugs, turns, and walks away without another word. She exhales.

"You okay, honey?" asks one of her cardigan-clad heroes.

"Yeah, I'm just . . . Thanks for helping me."

"No problem." They continue on their way.

The onlookers have already dispersed, but someone is hurrying toward her from Edgemont.

Lennon.

"Stacey? What the hell was that?"

"You saw him?"

"I saw a commotion. I was over there, waiting for you." He points up the boulevard.

"You were supposed to meet me in the park."

"*You* were supposed to be running errands. But you were home all morning." He holds up his phone like a lawyer presenting evidence.

Right. The tracker. Heart-shaped. She's his girlfriend.

She needs to tell him she doesn't like the app, and to get rid of it. But not in this moment. Her newfound steely core has gone liquid, and she feels tears welling.

"What happened, Stacey?"

"This guy just . . . he thought I was someone else." She scans the busy street, making sure he's not still there, watching her.

"Yeah, they do that."

"What?"

"Pickpockets, scammers. They stop you and get you talking. Did he take your wallet?"

"I don't have a wallet. And he wasn't a pickpocket, Lennon. He was . . ." She takes a deep breath, then shakes her head. "Let's just go to the park. I need to get out of here."

"Okay, come on." He puts his arm around her as they walk.

The gesture strikes her as more possessive than protective.

She tells herself that's only because she's still disturbed by that damned tracker. She wishes she found it romantic that he wants to know exactly where she is, but it's creepy.

She shudders, and Lennon pulls her closer.

"Are you cold? Want my jacket?"

"No, I . . . maybe I should go home. I'm kind of freaked out right now."

"No, we should go to the park, like we said."

"But—"

"Come on, Stacey. This is New York City, not Kansas."

"I'm not from Kansas."

"I didn't say you were. All I mean is, stuff happens here. You just need to get used to it."

Yeah. Maybe he's right.

The park is busier than ever, populated by the usual dog walkers, runners, cyclists, and skaters. Today there are picnicking families, kids' birthday parties, and weekend sports leagues with spectators on the courts and fields.

Stacey scans the crowds and landscape for the man, afraid he's going to step into her path again, or that he's lurking nearby.

Every bench they pass is taken, but there's space on the low stone ledge surrounding the fountain. Lennon lights a cigarette as they sit, and his tobacco smoke mingles with the sweet scent of pot wafting from a group of kids nearby.

"Wait." Stacey holds out her hand as he starts to return the pack and lighter to his jacket pocket. "I'll take one."

"You don't smoke."

"Does it calm your nerves?"

"Yeah." Looking pleased, he holds out the pack.

"I won't get addicted, will I?"

"Nah."

"So you're not?"

"Me? That's different."

"Why?"

"Jules," he says, like that means something.

"What are you talking about?"

"I'm an addictive personality, like her. She was a crack addict."

"Crack?"

"Back in the '90s, a lot of people were. And addiction is hereditary. So as long as your parents are as squeaky clean as they look . . ."

"Definitely." She plucks a cigarette from the foil and looks at it, checking to see which end goes into her mouth.

"Let me." He takes it from her, puts it into his own mouth, and lights it, shielding the flame from the breeze. "Here you go."

"Wait. Show me how." She's seen enough movies and TV shows where someone chokes, sputters, and gasps on their first attempt at smoking.

He demonstrates how to hold it between her forefinger and middle finger, how to take in some smoke without inhaling it deeply into her lungs, how to exhale, how to tap the ash.

He hands it to her. "Go ahead."

The first cautious drag isn't particularly pleasant. By the third or fourth, she gets the hang of it.

Lennon gives pointers like a coach teaching her how to pitch a ball. "Right. Great. See? You're a pro."

She raises an eyebrow. "A professional smoker? Yeah, that's not a thing, Lennon."

"Professional wiseass is a *thing*." He grins. "Nerves calmed down yet?"

She shrugs, watching a couple stroll by, arm in arm. They look dreamy and content, lost in conversation and a private world free of Peeping Toms and unsolved murders.

"He called me Anna," she says after a few moments, without looking at Lennon.

"Did he see you come out of the house?"

"I guess so. He must have been watching. Not just now, but I think I've seen him hanging around. On the street, and . . ."

What will happen if she tells him the whole story?

He'll either take her seriously, or he won't. If he does, he might want to do something about it. Like tell the police, or his moms, who will in turn tell her parents. And her parents will either take her seriously, or conclude she's mentally unstable, just as they suspected.

"Stacey?"

"You can't tell anyone about this, Lennon. Promise me you won't."

"I promise." His eyes are kind. He's her protector, just like she thought.

"I think I saw him on the roof of the shed behind our house the other night, watching me through binoculars."

She lifts the cigarette to her lips.

Maybe people like smoking so much because when you're having a conversation you'd rather not be having, you get to do something other than say things you'd rather not be saying and then wait for the other person to say something you'd rather not hear.

"Wow. So do you think he's just some psycho who's into true crime? Or the one who did it?"

"You mean the one who killed the Toskas? You think that guy could have been the murderer?"

"Don't you? He called you Anna."

"I know, but . . ."

Dammit. He isn't supposed to support that theory. He's supposed to argue it.

"Who else could he be?" he asks.

"I don't know. He said something in a foreign language."

"French? Spanish?"

"I have no idea. Nothing I've ever heard before. Do you think he was just some random vagrant? A pickpocket? A ghost?"

"Not a ghost."

"You're the one who believes in the paranormal."

"Right, and spirit doesn't just pop up on a busy street in broad daylight."

"'Spirit'? Why can't you just say ghost? Or at least, 'a spirit'? *Spirit* is so . . . it's . . ."

"It's the proper term, if you want to get scientific and specific."

She does not. She only said *ghost* to show him—and herself—that the man could have been anyone.

Anyone other than the escaped killer returning to the scene of the crime.

"I really don't think there's anything scientific about paranormal stuff, Lennon."

"You'd be surprised. I read that—"

"And I really don't think there's much that can surprise me right now. Did you see him?"

"Was he wearing a cardigan sweater?"

"No."

"Was he Black?"

"No."

"Then I didn't see him. Maybe you imagined—"

"I didn't. Everyone else there saw him, too, and interacted with him. Would that happen with a ghost?"

"I doubt it. And anyway, whose spirit would he even be?"

"Um, the *murderer's*?"

"We don't know that the murderer has crossed over to the Other Side. Now if you were talking about being home alone and Anna popping up, or one of her dead parents . . . *that* might be spirit."

Stacey inadvertently takes a deep drag on the cigarette. The smoke enters her lungs. She manages to expel it without choking as Lennon talks on about unsettling supernatural scenarios involving the late Toska family haunting 104 Glover.

As soon as Stacey regains her ability to speak, she changes the subject. Sort of.

"Hey, I did some research online yesterday about the dead girl in the Victorian portrait."

"Oh, yeah? That's cool. What'd you find out?"

"A lot, actually."

She tells him about John and Margaret Williams, who'd lived at 104 Glover in the nineteenth century. It was John who'd discovered the Revolutionary War cannonball when the house was being built. She'd found an 1876 newspaper article about Brooklyn's role in the Revolutionary War a hundred years earlier. There was a photo of John standing on the steps, proudly holding his historic find. The house is easily recognizable, as is the relic that now sits beneath glass in the hallway where—according to other newspaper articles from the 1880s—a teenage Gertrude Williams had died in a tragic accident.

Or was it? John Williams had never recovered from the economic downturn following the Panic of 1873, and made plenty of enemies through unscrupulous business dealings. Margaret had reportedly mentioned seeing a strange man scrutinizing the house in the days before Gertrude's fatal fall down the steep stairway.

"And that's where her parents hung her picture? Pretty morbid, if you ask me."

"It's *all* morbid, Lennon. Within a few years of her death, they were facing financial ruin and they lost the house. Margaret wound up in an asylum. Years later, she supposedly made a deathbed confession to murdering her daughter."

"Sick. Like a reverse Lizzie Borden without the axe." He tosses his cigarette stub to the ground and crushes it under his black Doc Marten, then takes hers from her hand and does the same. "How'd you find all this information?"

"I went through real estate records for the house, and then genealogy records. I had to join one of those ancestry research sites."

His eyes widen, and he looks away.

"What?" Stacey asks. "Why did you look at me like that?"

"Like what?"

"Like . . ." She touches his arm. "Tell me."

"Tell you what?"

"Whatever is making you act strange all of a sudden."

He appears to be weighing something, then shrugs and gives a little nod. "I kind of thought you'd mention it the other day when I brought up looking for my birth father, and you didn't. Not then, and not ever. So obviously, you don't like to talk about it. And listen, that's cool. You don't have to. Not even with me, even though I get it, better than anyone. Maybe that's why we're so alike, you know?"

"I don't know. I have no idea what . . . *what* don't I like to talk about?"

"That one of *your* parents isn't your birth parent, or maybe both aren't, and you're adopted."

Jacob

Shaken by his encounter with Anna, by her denial, Jacob walks.

He smokes, and he recalls that sleet-pelted January night.

Even after twenty-five years, the details remain vivid.

The house had been dark when he arrived, but not deserted. No, they were home at 104 Glover on that last night of their lives, upstairs in bed, all of them: Stanley, Lena, Anna.

He knew where to find the hidden key to the front door. Anna had told him about it. Not because she thought he'd ever use it, but because sometimes when they were together, secrets came tumbling out. Not all of his secrets. Not even close. And not all of hers.

But she'd told him that Stanley had once locked her out overnight, furious that she'd left the house without her keys and thus failed to dead-bolt the door behind her. After that, Anna duplicated her key and hid it in a crevice behind a loose brick on the foundation beneath the steps.

That January night, he realized she must have shared that secret with someone other than him. With Ellie. Because when he looked for the key, it wasn't there.

He walked around the block to Edgemont Boulevard. Back then, the corner brownstone was a private residence, dark and slumbering. He crept over the stoop railing onto the adjacent flat roof of the shed behind 102 Glover. From there, it was a short drop into 104's walled-in property.

There was no hidden key among the ground level windows in the back brick foundation. Nor were there security bars. But the middle window had a broken interior latch. He jiggled the wooden frame, and it slid up.

He made his way through the dark basement and up the stairs, positioning his feet along the railing edge of the treads so that the steep wooden steps to the main floor wouldn't creak. There was no way to avoid a telltale squeak when he opened the door to the kitchen, and he braced for confrontation.

All was still on the other side. The scent of overripe bananas and Comet hung in the air along with Stanley's lime aftershave, barely perceptible, like a footprint oozing in mud.

He made his way in pitch blackness through the dining room, living room, hallway, up the stairs. The master bedroom door was ajar, flickering blue light from the television. It was tuned to a local newscast, yet another story about ice skater Tonya Harding, whose bodyguard had just been charged in the previous week's attack on her rival Nancy Kerrigan.

Through the wedge of the doorway, he could see the bottom half of the queen-size bed. The bedspread covered a human form on the far side. The near side appeared empty, covers pulled back. A heap of clothing was just visible on the floor beside the bed.

He walked on down the shadowy hall. Anna's bedroom was dark and still. He hesitated before reaching for the wall switch, heart pounding with bruising might.

Lamplight dribbled over bookshelves lined with paperback novels, clothes draped over doorknobs and filling a wicker hamper, stuffed animals arranged on a chair. There was a Nirvana poster her friend Ellie had given her, because Ellie loved grunge music and wanted Anna to appreciate it, too.

In a matter of months, Kurt Cobain would be dead.

And Anna . . .

Oh, Anna.

Anna was in the bed, huddled beneath the pink-and-white-polka-dot quilt . . .

Jacob has spent years trying to forget what she looked like when he left her that night. Yet his last glimpse of her remains indelible: dark, bullet-shattered head on a darker pillowcase that should have been pastel pink.

Above the headboard, Kurt Cobain hung like Jesus, staring through a straggly blond fringe of golden hair, and more polka dots, red ones, spattered over the poster and the white wall.

Blood. So much blood.

Anna's blood.

The next day, Jacob returned to 104 Glover to find police cars, a medical examiner's van, satellite news trucks, a throng of onlookers held back by yellow tape and barricades. He was there when all three bodies were carried from the house, shrouded on gurneys.

He was in Green-Wood Cemetery a few days later when they were buried. There were no mourners in attendance, only cops, reporters, and gawkers. He watched from a distance as the earth swallowed three coffins.

He'd witnessed it all firsthand. But even if he harbored a shred of doubt about anything he'd done or seen that January, there's no denying concrete evidence. The internet is full of press coverage, details about the police investigation, autopsy reports, death certificates, unequivocal identification of the bodies at the morgue by next of kin . . .

Yeah, no. Anna's death hadn't been a figment of his imagination.

How about her return?

Maybe, when you spend two and a half decades thinking about someone, obsessing over her, really—maybe your brain conjures what it longs to see.

But if that's the case . . .

If she'd sprung from his own mind, then she wouldn't have said the words that had filled him with confusion. With rage.

Leave me alone . . . I'm not Anna . . .

Yes, she is.

She's Anna, and he's *not* going to leave her alone. Never, never again.

Nora

The Edgemont Grind is busy on this sunny Saturday afternoon.

Alone at a window table for two, Nora sips black coffee. Her laptop is open to a garden design website, but she's watching the street. Watching for Jacob. Just in case he was actually here yesterday. Just in case he comes back today.

If Teddy weren't out of reach again, Nora might call to ask, "Do you think I'm going crazy? Or, in this city with nine million people, could I possibly have seen someone I used to know?"

And not just anyone . . .

Teddy would want to know who she'd seen, opening the door to other questions with answers Nora isn't willing to give.

A text alert pops up on her laptop.

She opens it. Heather.

Happy Saturday. Jules said we're having dinner with you guys!

That's news to Nora.

Uncertain how to respond, she sees three quivering dots

as Heather types something else, probably that she meant to send the text to someone else.

But the next message is **I'll grab a reservation. Is 8 p.m. good?**

Is she being manipulated?

Or could she have made plans and forgotten? There are so many blank, fuzzy spots in her days lately. But she doubts this is one of them, and she's hardly in the mood to socialize.

Then again, she and Keith are already planning to go out. Does she really want to be alone with him after that conflict in the kitchen?

She types, **Sure! Sounds fun!**

Even as she hits Send, she knows she should have at least asked Keith about it. She'd better tell Heather she just has to double-check with him.

Too late. Before she can backpedal on her acceptance, a new text pops up. This one is from a restaurant app, informing her that Heather Tamura has made a reservation for four people at eight o'clock at an Italian restaurant on Mulberry Street.

Jules had mentioned something about it the other day, when she came over for lunch with the fennel salad. Nora had forgotten all about it, but clearly Jules, with her self-proclaimed lousy memory, had not.

All around the mulberry bush . . .

Nora's memory, too, is lacking. The tune spins an intangible recollection of something sweet and delicate as cotton candy, and—

"Mom?"

The past dissolves as she whirls to see Stacey.

Her daughter is holding a steaming latte and a plastic shopping bag from the drugstore. Nora looks around for Lennon, remembering what Jules had said about the two of them, and how Stacey had styled her hair and makeup before leaving the house. Now she looks windblown, and her makeup is smudged. Her contacts were probably bothering her and she'd rubbed her eyes. She couldn't have been crying . . . could she?

"What are you doing here, Mom?"

"I'm . . . drinking coffee." Realizing her cup is empty, Nora adds, "Well, I *was*. I mean, why else do you come to a coffee shop?"

Her tone is too bright. Defensive.

"You told Dad you had a ton of stuff to do."

She's not accusatory, exactly, but Nora bristles.

"I *did*. And this is my reward for getting it all done. How was your walk?"

"It was . . . you know. Fine."

"Did you go shopping?" She gestures at the bag.

"What? Oh . . . yeah. I needed some stuff for school."

"Do you want to sit down?"

It's clear that she doesn't, and Nora doesn't want her to. But here they are, and Stacey sits.

"Just for a few minutes. I really need to get home to . . . study."

"It's Saturday. You're a senior."

"It's a new school. I have . . ."

"A ton of stuff to do?"

"Exactly." Her smile is faint.

Nora closes her laptop, reminding herself to erase her internet history later. When she first got here, she'd entered the name *Jacob Grant* into the search engine, something she hadn't wanted to do on the home Wi-Fi in case Keith would somehow be able to see it.

She hadn't gotten a single hit. Not even when she added the few details she'd known about him back in the '90s. But then, would he have given her his real name?

"Stacey, have you been crying?" Nora asks, getting a better look at her eyes.

"No!"

"Yes, you have. What happened? Did Lennon do something that upset you?"

Stacey hesitates. "What do you mean?"

"You don't have to— Look, I know you guys have been . . . I'm not sure what you're calling it, but Jules said you're . . ."

"His girlfriend?"

The word is bigger and far more specific than whatever Nora had been reaching for, but her daughter gives a decisive nod. "Yeah. I mean, that's what he says."

"Wow. That happened pretty quickly. You haven't even known him a week."

"So? Dad always says you guys fell in love at first sight. You eloped right after you met."

"Not *right* after. And we were much older."

And I never would have done that if my father were still alive. I was so alone, and then Keith came along . . .

"You weren't 'much older,'" Stacey says.

"Well, there's a huge difference between seventeen and twenty-five, Stacey, in case you're thinking of—"

"I'm not! God, Mom. I'm not getting married. Don't worry."

She sips her latte. Nora lifts her own cup, remembers that

it's empty, and sets it down again. She can't tell Stacey that she's not worried she might elope with someone like Keith, but because Lennon reminds her of someone else. Someone dangerous, who preyed on a lonely misfit.

But Lennon isn't Jacob.

Stacey glances at her phone, lit with a text.

"Is that from him?"

"No."

Nora knows it's a lie. She can tell by the way Stacey quickly closes the screen; by the flash of guilt on her face; by the way she refuses to make eye contact.

I was once your age, Nora should say. *I get it. I understand more than you think.*

She can be that mother, right? She can offer empathy and comfort, words of maternal wisdom, anecdotes from her own past.

Made-up anecdotes. But close enough to the truth.

I understand. I know what it's like to fall for a guy like that.

"I should go," Stacey says.

"Wait—why were you crying?"

"We had a fight."

"About what? You don't have to tell me," she adds because she's not that mother. Not to Stacey. And Stacey's not Piper. She doesn't share confidences.

She takes a deep breath. "He said I was adopted."

Nora's heart jumps. "*What?* Why would he say that?"

"Genetics. You and Dad and Piper all have blue eyes, and mine are brown, so he said that either one or both of you can't be my birth parent. So I told him that you wear colored contact lenses, and then he said . . . you know what? It doesn't matter."

"Stacey? What did he say?"

She sighs. "That he wasn't surprised to hear that, because you strike him as someone who's fake."

Nora clenches her fists on her lap beneath the table. That little . . .

How dare he? How dare he say that about her? To her daughter? To anyone?

"But not just you, Mom. He said our whole family seems superficial and plastic, except for me."

What is there to say to that? Any of it? That it isn't true? That he has no business making assumptions about their family, and based on what?

"So . . . is it because of how we look? Is that what he means?"

"What else would he mean? It's not like he *knows* any of you. Except . . ." She toys with her cup, rolling it back and forth between her palms.

"Except *what*?"

"Nothing. Forget it. It's over."

"You broke up? Good. I'm glad. You don't need—"

"I mean the *argument* is over, Mom. He said he was sorry, and I forgave him."

"Okay, well that's . . ." Again, Nora picks up her empty cup and sets it down. "That's just terrific."

"What?"

"You *know* it's offensive to judge people based on what they look like, whether you're talking about the color of someone's eyes or hair or skin or—"

"Yeah, I know that. I'm not stupid and insensitive!"

"And you *know* you're not adopted."

Her daughter says nothing, toying with her phone.

"Stacey, you can't possibly—"

"I've never seen any pictures of you pregnant with me. Or, like, holding me as a newborn."

"No pictures? You think that means I wasn't pregnant with you and I'm not your biological parent?"

"No, but . . . I mean, you have pictures from when you were pregnant with Piper. You have pictures holding her in the hospital, right after she was born."

"I'm sure I have the same pictures with you, somewhere."

"Really?"

No. Not really.

Be that mother, Nora. You need to fix this. You don't need to tell her the whole truth, but a small truth is the only way to fix this.

"All right, so . . . maybe Lennon was right about me being . . . what did he say, shallow?"

"Superficial. And plastic, and fake."

"The thing is . . . I hated having my picture taken. It was because of my nose, okay?"

"What?"

"I *hated* my nose."

Stacey looks at her. *Really* looks at her, examining her as though she isn't just taking in her features, but as though she's seeing who Nora used to be.

The scrutiny is unnerving. She forces herself not to squirm in her seat, forces herself to maintain eye contact, to be the mother, *that* mother, the one her daughter needs right now.

"Your nose is perfect, Mom."

"This isn't the nose I'm talking about. I mean the one I had—the one I was born with . . ."

"I broke it when I was a kid, and . . . it didn't heal properly."

"How did you break it?"

"Skiing." Nora shrugs. "And every time I looked in the mirror, I remembered . . ."

"The accident? Did you fall? Or ski into something?"

"Right. Yes."

"Which?"

Is Stacey asking because she's trying to catch her in a lie, or because she's curious?

"Both. I skied into a tree, face-first, and fell."

"That must have been really painful."

"It was. Finally, when you were about a year old, Dad said that if I hated it that much, I should have cosmetic surgery and get it fixed. So I did."

"And that's why there aren't any photos of you with me, or pregnant?"

"What can I say? I was vain. I'm not proud of it, but it's the truth. You can ask Dad. He'll tell you. And he'll also tell you that you're not adopted and that we are both your parents. Okay?"

She's quiet, digesting this. Nora reminds herself that she can't possibly know the rest of the story. The real story. Even Keith doesn't know that.

Stacey's phone, face up on the table, lights up again.

"Lennon?"

Her daughter quickly darkens the screen.

"It was just a guess. Don't worry. I couldn't see it. And I'm not trying to pry."

Stacey puts her phone into her pocket and shakes her head, mouth pursed, eyes on the ceiling.

After a moment, she asks, "Why don't you like him?"

"I only met him once. I never said I don't like him."

"No, but he felt that. Right away."

"Well, that's a shame, because I can't think of anything I did to make him think—"

"Really, Mom? Seriously? You just said you were glad when you thought we broke up."

Nora looks down and closes her eyes, seeing Lennon, a sharp-eyed stranger. She hears him telling her daughters about the murders at 104 Glover, saying, *I know everything.*

She hears Jules saying, *He won't break your daughter's heart, but if that's what you're worried about . . .*

It isn't. Not entirely.

"I'm your mother, Stacey. I don't want you to lose yourself—your *self*, who you are—in a relationship. I want you to pursue the things you love to do, find new interests, make other friends. And I don't want you getting hurt by some little creep who's not good enough for you."

"Based on what? That he's not *perfect* like you? He's . . . he's *imperfect*, and he's *real*. Like me." She shoves back her chair. "And I know why he had the feeling that you don't like him, because I have the same feeling every day of my life. Every time you look at me, I see it all over your face."

"Stacey . . ."

"Whatever." She stands. "I have to go."

Nora watches her walk away, and she doesn't stop her.

Stacey

H ello?" Stacey calls, letting herself into the house. "Anyone home? Dad? Piper?"

Silence. Kato isn't the kind of dog who races to greet anyone.

She takes one last look outside before closing the door, making sure there's no sign of the man who'd confronted her earlier. And no sign of Lennon. There wouldn't be, because he's in Manhattan at his guitar lesson . . .

Unless he'd lied.

She can't think of a good reason why he would, but she's not sure she trusts him. Or anyone, at this point. Not even her mother.

If she is my mother.

Does Stacey really doubt that, based on some stupid theory of Lennon's?

Of course not. Of course Mom is her mother, based on . . .

What, though? That story about having her nose fixed?

It's not like Mom hasn't had her share of cosmetic procedures over the years. Dad, too. Back home, they were always making the rounds of doctors and dentists, salons and spas, getting nips and tucks, treatments, veneers, injections. Everyone else's parents did the same thing, and so did half the kids at school.

Stacey had never paid much attention.

Now Lennon has made her second-guess everything she ever thought she knew about her family, and herself.

Back in the park, Stacey couldn't wait to get away from him after he said that. But he draped that possessive arm over her shoulders, saying he was going to get her home before he went to his guitar lesson.

"You don't have to 'get me home,'" she protested, "like I'm . . . I don't know, a little kid or a little old lady or something."

"I'm just keeping you safe."

"Well, I appreciate it, but I have a few things I need to do on Edgemont, so . . ."

"Do you think that's a good idea? With that lunatic killer running around thinking you're a dead girl?"

No, she did not. But she didn't appreciate his proprietary attitude toward her.

They parted ways at the Boulevard Apothecary. She told him she had to pick up a few things.

"You're not sick, are you?"

"No, I just need some stuff for school."

He frowned a little, like he thought she was lying, and she was. He didn't need to know she'd decided to get some cigarettes of her own, along with cosmetics and hair product so that she wouldn't have to keep borrowing her mother's and sister's. Her mother didn't need to know that, either. Or anything else.

But when Stacey walked next door to the Edgemont Grind, there she was.

She was stunned to see her mother, and mostly dismayed, but also maybe a tiny bit relieved. If the strange man popped up again now, Mom wouldn't let anything happen to her. Maybe she'd admit to Stacey that she's been spooked, too, about living in the house. Maybe she'd tell Dad they have to get out of here, move back to California.

Is that what you want?

Right now, Stacey isn't sure. She only knows that telling her mother about the conflict with Lennon had been a bad idea. Telling her about the stranger who'd called her Anna would have been a worse one.

Good thing the conversation blew up before she could mention it.

Mom already wants her to see a psychiatrist. At least she had, back in California. She probably still does.

Maybe you should. Maybe you imagined that man.

Lennon hadn't seen him, and he was right across the street.

The others had, though—the guys in the cardigan sweaters, and a few people who'd come running to her rescue . . .

Unless they weren't real, either.

She peers out the window alongside the door. If they're out there on Glover Street now, watching the house, then they're only in her head, like the eerie crowd Jack saw in the hotel bar in *The Shining.*

They're not there.

"At least you're not crazy," she murmurs to herself, turning away to see a human shadow looming in the hall. She screams, loud and high. Somewhere in the back of the house, Kato starts barking.

"Stacey!"

It's just her father. She presses a hand to her racing heart.

"Sorry, Dad, I . . . I didn't think . . . I asked if anyone was home when I came in."

"I just got here. I was out back looking for Mom, but she's not there. I wanted to show her—I joined a fitness center." He's wearing sweats and sneakers, and holding a membership folder.

As he tells her about the facility's state-of-the-art equipment, she nods as if she's interested, wishing she could escape to her room.

"I got the family membership, so you and Piper and Mom can go, too."

"I'm really not much of a gym person, Dad." Like, not at all.

"That's okay. Piper and Mom will go. I wonder where she is?"

"Mom? She's at the Edgemont Grind. I just saw her there when I stopped for coffee."

A strange look crosses his face. "Who is she with?"

"She's by herself."

"Is she meeting someone?"

"I don't think so. She has her laptop."

"Huh."

Stacey turns toward the stairs. Her gaze falls on the Victorian portrait.

"By the way, Dad . . . did Mom tell you about . . ." She points at the photo. "Memento mori?"

"What?"

Stacey explains, his eyes widen, and he ascends the stairs to examine the portrait.

He turns back to her with a grim nod. "It does look that way. But I doubt Mom knows about it, because she would have mentioned it."

"To *you*. Not to Piper and me, because she doesn't want us to be scared to live here."

She hesitates, longing to tell him about the watcher, and Anna . . .

Then she sees the troubled, distracted expression in his blue eyes. Now isn't the time.

"You're right," he says. "Mom doesn't want to say anything that might upset any of us. Do me a favor, and don't mention it to Piper, okay?"

Stacey promises that she won't, tells him she's got some studying to do, and escapes to her room.

She dumps the contents of the shopping bag on her bed. She examines the toiletries and then stashes them in the back of a drawer.

She opens the pack of cigarettes, takes one out, and holds it the way Lennon had shown her. She's tempted to light it and practice, but her father might smell it. So she stands in front of a mirror and goes through the motions to see how she looks.

Wow. Much older and much cooler.

Back home, she wouldn't have dreamed of smoking. None of the smart kids did.

Right. Because they know it's stupid and addictive and toxic.

Why, if Stacey knows that, too, does it seem like a good idea now?

Because Lennon smokes, and she wants to impress him?

Yeah, maybe that's part of it. But it's the stress, too. The sudden doubt about who she is, and whether her parents are her parents. And living here, with the growing certainty that someone's watching the house, watching *her*. Maybe he's just some random creeper. Or maybe he's the escaped murderer.

Everything she's read about the Toska family theorizes that the father's suspected involvement in organized crime had led to contract killing.

Hit men don't typically take out the wives and children.

And a hit man wouldn't return to the scene of the crime. And if he'd killed Anna Toska, he wouldn't be looking for her, or confusing a stranger with her, twenty-five years later.

So who would?

She hides the cigarettes in the back of a drawer and grabs her laptop.

Opening a search window on her laptop, she types in *Toska Family Homicide Brooklyn January 1994*, and hits Enter.

Nora

Nora picks up a small flat of potted herbs on the way home from Edgemont Grind. It's late in the season for tender annuals, but she needs a reason not to spend the rest of the afternoon in the house, where Keith will be impossible to avoid.

He's dozing in his leather recliner in front of a televised college football game when she walks in, and barely turns his head at her greeting.

"Where were you?"

"Doing errands on the Boulevard. And I had coffee with Stacey."

"I heard." He's focused on the television.

Maybe because an intense play is unfolding on the field. Or maybe because he's still stewing in the earlier tension between them.

"Jules and Heather invited us to have dinner with them tonight in Little Italy. What do you think?" she asks, as if it's an option and not an accepted invitation with a reservation for four.

"Sounds great."

"Great."

She spends the rest of the afternoon in the garden, planting, weeding, watering, and trying to not think about the past. Jacob.

Nora's dressing for dinner when Piper pops into the master bedroom to return the credit card, weighed down with shopping bags and brimming with anecdotes about her day with Courtney.

"Did you get your snow boots?"

"Boots? Yes."

"Let's see."

"I'll model them for you later. Courtney said you and Dad are going out with her parents, so we're getting takeout and having a sleepover at her house. She's going to kick out her brother. Oh—I almost forgot! Did you know he and Stacey are together?"

"What? He's in her *room*?" Nora hasn't seen Stacey since she got home, but had called to her through her closed bedroom door to say she and Piper will be on their own for dinner.

"Mom! Not right this second. Not in her room! I meant in general. She's—"

"His girlfriend. Yes, she told me."

Piper, who delights in delivering breaking household news, is shocked to hear that. Ordinarily, Nora might experience a prickle of smug satisfaction. But she has other things to worry about, like the long cab ride to Lower Manhattan with Keith, who still seems quiet and distanced.

Then Jules texts to say they'll go together, with instructions on when and where to meet the taxi van out front.

Ordinarily, Nora might take exception to the fact that it isn't a suggestion, but under the circumstances, welcomes the directive.

The conversation in the cab flows, and by the time they get to Mulberry Street, Keith seems like his usual self again. He grabs her hand to help her out of the back seat, and casually holds on to it as they enter Nonna Della's Osteria, a sleek, modern restaurant tucked in to the bottom floor of an old brick tenement.

"When I heard Little Italy," he says, "I was picturing a red sauce tourist trap with checkered tablecloths."

Here they're white, as are the flickering votive candles on the tables, tin ceiling, and fairy lights strung along its perimeter.

"No tourist traps if you stick with us, my friend," Jules assures him.

Tony Bennett sings about leaving his heart in San Francisco as they settle in at a round table for four. A waiter arrives with menus, a pitcher of water, and a basket of hot bread. He's an older gentleman, heavyset and balding, and greets both Heather and Jules with a bow and hand kisses.

"Fernando, these are our new friends, Keith and Nora," Jules tells him. "They just moved here from California."

"California! If the fires don't get you, the earthquakes will," he says in accented English, and turns to Nora. "Beautiful lady. I've seen you on TV, no?"

"Me? No."

Keith puts his arm around her. "My wife may look like a movie star, but she's not an actress."

"A model, then? You look so familiar."

"No." Nora's smile stretches thin.

"You never said that to me when we met, Fernando," Jules says with a fake pout.

"Because you, you're a rock star."

"You knew that just by looking at her?" Keith asks.

"Ah, no, she told me. She tells *everybody*. Everybody who comes through that door."

Even Nora has to laugh at his comical expression.

It turns out Fernando has known Jules since she was a little girl. He used to work at an Italian restaurant in Brooklyn. When it closed, he came here.

"And this one, she followed me," he says with an exaggerated gesture at Jules. "She tells me she'd follow me anywhere, and I say that's fine, as long as you stay out of the men's room."

Fernando presents a wine menu, but Heather tells him they don't need it. "I think we'll have a bottle of the Vermentino, Fernando."

"What? No Barolo tonight?"

"No, we'll stick with white, right, Jules?"

"White," she agrees. "We're having seafood. I've been telling our friends about the tagliatelle with grilled calamari and clams."

She probably has, but Nora missed it. She's never been crazy about calamari, and Keith had sworn off carbs for the rest of the week. She waits for him to say that, and that he and Nora prefer red wine to white, but he doesn't, leaving his menu untouched on the table.

"You don't want to hear about the specials?" Fernando asks. "Because the veal Milanese is—"

"No, thank you," Heather says. "We'll do the tagliatelle, family style."

"And we'll start with the arugula and shaved fennel salad. Thanks, Fernando."

If they'd agreed that Heather would be ordering everything for the table, Nora missed that, too.

Fernando lingers, asking how the school year's going for the kids.

"Courtney loves it, Lennon hates it," Heather says.

"Ah, then everything is normal. And his heart, it's still broken?"

"Not anymore, thanks to their daughter." Jules points at Nora and Keith.

Fernando claps his hands in delight at this news. Keith is obviously taken aback, but says nothing until the waiter has ambled away.

"*Our* daughter? You mean Piper and Lennon are—"

"Not Piper, Keith."

He gapes at Nora. "Stacey? So you knew about this? Jesus, do you tell me *anything*?"

"I do, when I *see* you. You're the one who was out late last night, and—"

"Are you going to get on me for that?"

"No, I'm not going to *get on* you." She clenches her mouth, biting back her fury, and then turns to Jules. "Can you please tell him that you and I had coffee together yesterday, and Ricardo canceled at the last minute?"

"Yep. That's what happened."

"Well, wait. He didn't cancel at the last minute," Heather

amends. "You *asked* him at the last minute, and he couldn't make it."

"That's true. I'm really sorry, Nora. I completely forgot about it until that morning."

"It's fine," she murmurs, focused on Keith.

"You went back there this afternoon, Nora. You said you had too much to do, yet you were hanging around in a café."

"With Stacey."

"She just happened to run into you there. You didn't tell her you were going. Or me."

"You didn't ask me! If you had, I would have told you. Is that what this is about?"

"It's not just . . ." Keith pauses, lowering his voice, leaning toward her. "Lately it just seems like I'm the last to know anything. Even that crazy picture of the dead girl on the stairway . . . Stacey told me about it. You didn't."

Her heart pounds. "I didn't tell Stacey, either. I didn't want to scare her, or Piper. I have no idea how she knew. It's not like I'm confiding in everyone but you, Keith."

Jules speaks up. "I don't want to get into the middle of this—"

"Then don't," Heather cuts in. "Let them work it out."

"All I wanted to say is that I'm the one who told Nora about it, when I was over at the house on Tuesday afternoon. I saw it and I said, oh, memento mori, and she was like, what's that. So I told her. No big deal."

Nora nods, tight-lipped.

Keith clears his throat. "Look, it's fine. It's not about that. I didn't mean to . . . it's just been a long week. New house, new city, new job . . . I'm stressed out, and I guess I just . . ."

"Happens to the best of us," Heather says brightly, and looks around. "Where's that wine? And I'll get a second bottle. I think we all can use it."

Nora sees Jules gazing at her and Keith from across the table, wearing a thoughtful expression.

Stacey

tacey is in the kitchen, famished and rummaging through the cabinets for something healthy to eat for dinner, when Piper appears in the doorway. She's wearing tall boots with high heels, a short skirt, black leather jacket, and oversize hoop earrings. Her face is overly made-up, even for her.

"I'm going."

"Where?"

Piper gestures at the floral quilted overnight bag over her shoulder. "To Courtney's."

"You're looking pretty bougie for a sleepover."

"I like to look bougie for everything."

Stacey can't argue with that, but something tells her that a sleepover isn't all that's on her sister's agenda for tonight. "Are those new boots?"

"Yep."

"Jacket, too?"

Piper nods. "Do you like it? It's nice, right? Oh, don't tell Mom and Dad."

"Why? Did you steal it?"

Piper is indignant. "No, I didn't *steal* it."

"Then how'd you afford it? It must have cost a fortune."

"It was on sale. I got it with Mom's credit card. She gave it to me."

"Wow. That was nice of her."

"You don't have to be jealous. She'd give it to you, too, if you asked."

"I'm not jealous, Piper." She closes one cabinet and opens another. "I don't need Mom's credit card. I have my own money from working at the bookstore all summer back home."

"Well, maybe you should spend it on something other than books. But just so you know, Mom would love to take you shopping for clothes. She's thrilled that you lost weight and you have a boyfriend."

Stacey's appetite disappears. She closes the cabinet. "Mom said that?"

"Pretty much. And by the way, I can't believe you told her about it before you even told me. I had to hear it from Courtney."

"Seriously? I never tell you anything! Or Mom, either. Jules told her, okay? And I really don't want to talk about it."

Piper shrugs. "Your secret's safe with me as long as—"

"It's not a secret."

"—as long as you don't say anything about my jacket, or anything else, in case you hear . . . anything else."

"What would I hear? And from whom?"

"You know, from Lennon. Oh, and you should probably, you know . . . fix yourself up a little before he gets here. Brush your hair, maybe put on your contacts, and some lip gloss and mascara, and some . . . regular clothes."

She's wearing her glasses, and the leggings and hoodie

she's planning to sleep in, and has a plastic banana clip in her hair to keep it out of her eyes. Earlier, she'd scrubbed off every trace of makeup.

"Lennon's not coming over, Piper."

"Courtney said he was."

"Well, he's not."

"How come?"

"He's just not, okay?"

"Aren't you scared to be here alone?"

"No," she lies.

"I would be. Did you guys break up or something?"

"No! Why are you asking me all these questions? I thought you were leaving."

Stacey yanks open the refrigerator door, blocking her sister from view. She studies the contents of the shelves without seeing anything.

"Geez. Bye." Piper's boot heels carry her out the front door.

Lennon had texted Stacey earlier about coming over tonight while their parents were gone.

Caught her off guard; she hadn't even known her mom and dad were going out. Anyway, she'd already spent time with him today, and it hadn't exactly been idyllic.

Can't tonight. Maybe tomorrow, she wrote back.

Tomorrow you won't have an empty house.

Won't have one tonight, either. My sister's around.

Nope. She's coming here.

She found herself resenting that he knew more about her family's plans than she did. And she was uncomfortable with the idea of being alone with him again after yesterday, in his room.

It isn't just that she's worried about how far he'll want to go . . . or how far she'll want to let him go.

He comes on strong even when they're apart. He's been texting her all day. She hadn't answered the one he'd sent from his guitar lesson because she was sitting in the café with her mother. He wanted to make sure she'd made it home, then when she didn't answer, he asked, twice, if she was okay.

He called her as soon as his lesson was over. By then, she was back in her room looking up the Toska murder case.

"Why didn't you text me back?"

"Because I'm busy."

"I thought something happened to you!"

"I'm fine. Calm down—"

"Hey, you're the one who said you were attacked by a crazed murderer this afternoon, and now you're telling *me* to calm down?"

"I never said he attacked me or that he was a crazed murderer!"

Or had she? She no longer recalls exactly what she'd said or even what had happened earlier on the street.

Standing in the kitchen, all alone in the house where three people had been killed, she kind of wishes she'd caved to Lennon's persistence about coming over tonight.

I need some space.

She'd actually typed that when he kept bugging her about why not, though she'd hesitated before hitting Send.

You want space, you got it, he'd responded, and she hasn't heard from him since.

Any other girl would have been excited to spend a romantic evening with her new boyfriend, but Stacey is new to this. She's used to being alone on Saturday nights.

Anyway, she really is busy, immersed in archived information about the murders at 104 Glover.

So, yeah. Maybe there's nothing wrong with Lennon. Maybe there's something wrong with her.

She closes the refrigerator.

Beyond its electronic hum and Kato's soft snoring from the doormat, she can hear the usual street noise, sirens, low-flying air traffic.

The dog doesn't stir when she goes over to double-check the lock, or when she leans past him to lower the shade on the window beside the door.

"You're a lousy watchdog, you know that?"

She pulls down the shades in the kitchen and dining room, too, then does the same at the front windows. Piper hadn't even bothered to lock the door. Stacey turns the bolt and fastens the old cast-iron chain for good measure. When her parents get home, they can knock.

Climbing the stairs, she pauses to look at the Williams family portrait. Gertrude's dead eyes bore into her. She'd died on this very spot. Maybe her own mother had killed her. Maybe she really is haunting this house. Maybe they all are—the Toska family included.

Stacey covers the last few steps two at a time and pauses

to look at her parents' closed bedroom door. They'd probably drawn the shades while they were getting dressed to go out, but she peeks in to make sure.

The shades are pulled down. Everything is in perfect order. She hastily closes the door again. If the Toskas are still hanging around, they're probably haunting this room where they died.

Does that mean Anna's spirit lingers in Stacey's room?

You don't believe in ghosts, remember?

She goes down the hall to Piper's room. The shade covers the lone window that overlooks the backyard. The bed is unmade, a tangle of clothes she'd tried on and discarded, a few with price tags on them.

Stacey spies a large shopping bag on the floor with a receipt sticking out of it. She picks it up and sees that Piper had used their mother's credit card to pay full price for a leather jacket that had cost twice as much as Stacey earned in a month at the bookstore back home.

Mom probably wouldn't care, though. The two of them are so much alike, her mother and sister. So effortlessly attractive. Even Dad. So different, all of them, from Stacey.

But she doesn't really believe she's adopted, does she?

She closes the door to her own room, where she's kept the shades down ever since that first night. She settles on her bed with her laptop to resume scouring online reports for clues about the Toska murders.

She's hardly the first true crime buff to attempt solving an old case. But in this situation, there's very little to go on. The family members hadn't left much of an online footprint leading up to their high-profile murders. That's not unusual, considering they'd died long before pervasive internet and social media.

Still, a lot of old records have become digitalized and she'd uncovered plenty of information about the Williams family, including photographs. In life, posing with fellow schoolchildren, Gertrude's eyes had twinkled with mischief even when her mouth was dutifully solemn.

The Williamses had lived a full century before the Toskas, yet so far, Stacey hasn't uncovered evidence of their existence prior to 1994. The wedding photo of Lena and Stanley had been the only one published in the press.

The more she reads about the murders, the more apprehensive she is about being alone in the house tonight. She might feel better if Kato were with her, even if he's just a lump of sleeping canine. And she's definitely hungry again. But venturing back downstairs holds about as much appeal as calling her parents and telling them to come home because she's scared.

Remembering the cigarettes she'd hidden, she retrieves them and a book of matches from her drawer. This is one way to calm her nerves.

It takes her a few tries to light a match, and when she does, she fumbles and burns herself trying to get a cigarette out of the pack and into her mouth with one hand. Finally, she gets it lit.

How can one cigarette give off way more smoke than two had when she was with Lennon?

She retrieves a damp towel from her laundry basket, rolls it, and wedges it along the door crack. At least the smell won't seep out into the hall, but the small room is hazy and her eyes are stinging. And she doesn't have anything she can use as an ashtray.

She goes to the window, cautiously lifts the shade a few inches, and lifts the sash just that far. Cold night air rushes into the room, diluting the smoke.

Much better.

She sticks the cigarette out and taps the ash, letting it fall into the plant border below, glad the house is made of stone and brick. In California, she'd worry about igniting a deadly, rapidly spreading wildfire, but that can't happen here . . . can it?

She crouches on the floor, takes another drag, and blows it out the window, wondering what her parents would do if they caught her. It's not like they've ever punished her for anything, or even had to yell at her, really.

Because she's never done anything risky or stupid. Until now.

Lennon . . . the cigarettes . . .

Plus, she's breached her own security measures by opening a window—which is precisely how investigators theorized the Toska family killer entered the house that night. Not this one, but down on the basement level. Back then, there hadn't been bars on those windows. There are now. At least in the front. She hasn't spent any time out back, or in the basement.

What if someone—the killer—got into the house earlier and hid down there all day, waiting until tonight?

Stacey's chest constricts. She can hardly breathe regular air right now, let alone inhale smoke.

So much for alleviating her anxiety. The stupid cigarette is only making it worse.

She kneels and opens the window wider so that she can reach out far enough to stub the butt on the exterior concrete sill.

That's when she sees it.

Him.

Cloaked in shadow, a hooded man is on the roof of the shed next door, binoculars trained on the house.

Nora

Heather and Jules deftly ease the friction between Nora and Keith, sharing their own tales of marital discord. Their storytelling skills are well honed, and they hand off lines and cues like a comedic duo.

Nora laughs along, but she's relieved when wine arrives, closely followed by the first course.

"What should we drink to? Or should I decide? Okay, I'll decide," Heather says, as if they'd urged her to.

"Of course you will." Jules rolls her eyes. "Guys, Heather loves to decide things, in case you hadn't noticed."

"Oh, like you don't?" her wife retorts.

"Sure I do. That's why we get along. We're both control freaks."

Keith laughs. "That makes no sense."

"What? Why?"

"Because two strong-willed people . . . don't you clash?"

"Nah, we get each other. How about you two?" Jules asks Keith.

"Do we get each other? You don't stay married almost twenty years if you don't, right?"

Nora's neck muscles clench as she returns his smile, and

she hopes it doesn't show. She imagines what Jules is thinking about Nora's supposedly perfect life now that it's obvious her marriage is anything but.

Heather lifts her glass. "Okay, so anyway . . . here's to New York! Welcome, Keith and Nora. We hope you love our city as much as we do."

They clink and sip.

"I did live here once before, you know."

Nora half listens to Keith as he talks on about his college days. In the background, Sinatra sings about strangers in the night, and she nibbles her salad with a mouth so dry she probably wouldn't be able to tell fennel from chocolate cake.

". . . right, Nora?" Keith asks.

She fumbles her way back to the conversation. "Sorry, I zoned out for a second there. What was that?"

"I was just saying that you could probably fit the entire population of my hometown into this place."

"Just about," she agrees.

"So yeah, to answer your question, Heather, for me, moving to New York at eighteen was pretty overwhelming. But I loved every minute of the two years I got to spend here."

"Why only two years?"

"It's kind of a long story . . ."

It really isn't, but he makes it one, telling Heather and Jules about the back-to-back concussions that had curtailed his days as a Division One wrestler and Ivy League student. Plagued by blinding headaches, confusion, and fatigue, he couldn't focus on his schoolwork and his grades suffered.

"So that was the end of Columbia for me."

"That's terrible. And the same thing happened to me,"

Jules says. "I mean, I wasn't an Ivy League student athlete, but I did have an awful concussion years ago, when I got shoved off the stage during a concert."

"Did someone attack you? A crazy fan?"

She laughs. "Oh, I wasn't performing yet. It was right after I'd moved out to Seattle and I *was* the crazy fan. I stormed the stage, and security threw me off. I hit my head, and thanks to that—and a whole lot of drugs I took before, during, and after—my brain has been mush ever since, right, Heather?"

"Yes, and I love you anyway. But, Keith, your brain doesn't seem as mushy as Jules's. What did you do after you left Columbia?"

"Went home and finished my degree at Kansas State. Then I moved to LA because someone told me I should be an actor, and stupidly, I listened to her. Maybe my brain *was* mush."

"Nah, Hollywood makes sense when you look like Brad Pitt. Trust me, Nora, I'm not flirting with your man," Jules adds. "Just stating the obvious."

"And feeding his ego. Thanks a lot." Nora forces a laugh.

Trust me, Nora . . .

Jules had said she'd moved to Seattle before the murders and occasionally returned to visit her parents. Had she specifically mentioned whether she was there, on Glover Street, on that January night?

"So have we seen you in the movies, Keith?" Heather asks, and he laughs.

"Nope. I moved to Hollywood, and became the world's worst waiter for about a month. One of the regular customers offered me an entry-level corporate job, probably to keep me away from the restaurant. Best move I ever made. I've been in marketing ever since, and that's where I met my soul mate."

"You were in marketing, too, Nora?" Heather asks.

"No, the landscaping company where I worked was doing a job at the office park where Keith worked."

"Yeah, I was sitting outside eating my lunch one day, and I saw this amazing woman in a hard hat and work boots. It was pretty much love at first sight." He smiles at Nora, as if there hasn't been tension between them all day.

Or for months, since Mexico, and Teddy.

Fernando removes the salad plates and refills their glasses from a second bottle of wine. The conversation flows on as if they're all old friends.

But they're not. These people are strangers.

Careful, Nora. Careful who you trust . . .

The crooner playlist plays on and Perry Como's "Catch a Falling Star" transports Nora back to last Sunday night, to the conversation with Jules about her past, and about the murders.

She'd said no one had known the Toska family, that they'd kept to themselves, that the mother was an invalid, the daughter a gawky weirdo.

She says a lot of things.

But don't count on me for details . . .

My brain is a sieve . . .

Jules, with her head injury and checkered past.

"Anyway, when I met Heather at that gallery opening," she's saying now, "I was back in New York and fresh out of rehab, and she was living with someone. So it was vague interest at first sight, but kind of . . . messy."

"Yeah, like politics and wars and hostage negotiations are 'messy.'" Heather lifts her glass. "But, hey, we made it. Here's to happily ever after—for us, and for you guys, too, Keith and Nora."

They all clink and Nora takes a fortifying sip of wine as Heather asks about their wedding.

Keith says, "We eloped to Vegas, and Nora was the world's most stunning bride."

"Hey, so did we! Well, not Vegas, Vermont," Jules amends. "And I was the world's most enormous bride—eight months pregnant with Lennon. My father had just died, I'd moved my mother into an assisted living condo, and we'd just bought the house. It was kind of a disaster because the plumbing in the upstairs bathroom was—"

A cell phone buzzes loudly.

"Sorry." Keith pulls his from his pocket. "Uh-oh. I need to take this."

"One of the girls?" Nora asks, but he's already heading for the door.

Jules looks at her own phone. "Nothing from our two."

Heather does the same. "Nope. And they're together, right? Piper's at our house with Courtney, and Lennon's at yours with Stacey?"

"I'm not sure," Nora admits.

Stacey hadn't mentioned it, but they'd spoken only briefly and it had been with her daughter's closed bedroom door between them. When Nora knocked and told her they were leaving for the restaurant, Stacey said to have a good time and that she was studying.

"If your kids are anything like ours, they only call when

they need money to order food," Jules says. "Or they can't find something."

Heather nods. "Usually because it's exactly where it belongs, and that's the last place they'd ever put it, or look for it. One time . . ."

She launches into another anecdote.

Nora watches the window. Out on the street, Keith is having what appears to be an agitated exchange with whoever's on the phone.

She sees him disconnect that call and place another one that evidently goes unanswered. He hangs up, sends a text, and strides back into the restaurant.

"It was Stacey. She thinks we have a Peeping Tom."

Nora's stomach turns over.

"It's probably Elvira Hernandez across the street," Heather says. "She's super nosy."

"No, it was a man. She said a vagrant was bothering her on the street today, and now she thinks he's watching her from the backyard."

No. Oh, no. The room seems to be closing in, and it's all Nora can do not to flee. She opens her mouth, trying to form a question, but Heather beats her to it.

"Is she sure about that? I mean, how can someone be in the yard? Isn't it completely closed in?"

"Yes, but she said he was on a roof out back with binoculars."

Nora thinks of Jacob, in the neighborhood, yesterday afternoon, and she tries to dismiss a possibility so preposterous and paranoid that she simply cannot let her mind go *there*.

"Oh, some of the new apartment buildings on the block

behind us have roof terraces," Jules says. "The neighbors are always hanging out overhead. No more nude sunbathing for me, unfortunately."

"Except for that one time . . ." Heather grins.

"Right. And that didn't end well. Anyway, it's just city life, you guys. There are people everywhere."

Everywhere. Jules—she seems to be everywhere. Heather, too. Too close, too familiar, too quickly.

"Yeah, it's hard to get used to at first," Heather says. "I used to freak out over every little thing when I first moved here from LA. Just tell Stacey it was probably someone hanging out on his rooftop looking at the sky. There are a million stars tonight. I bet he's just—"

"Then wouldn't he have a telescope?" Nora cuts in. "Not binoculars. He had binoculars."

"I think she said binoculars, but . . ." Keith shrugs and picks up his wineglass. "She was talking really fast."

"I'm sure it's fine," Heather says with the maddening conviction of one who has no clue about the nuances of a situation. "Anyway, isn't Lennon with her?"

"She said no, she's home alone."

"Where's Lennon?" Jules pulls out her phone again and starts typing.

"Tell her to pull down the shades and ignore the guy, even if he is a Peeping Tom," Heather advises.

Nora wants to tell the two of them to shut up. Just shut up, so she can think.

Jules's phone whooshes with a sent text. "Okay, I just told Lennon what's going on."

Nora thinks of her daughter's tearstained face this afternoon. No. They shouldn't be telling him anything. They shouldn't be—

"Look, here comes our entrée!" Spotting Fernando approaching with a large tray, Heather moves the flickering candle and salt and pepper shakers to make room on the table. "You two are going to die when you taste this!"

"Here we are . . . *tagliatelle con calamari e vongole.*" He sets a fragrant platter in the center of the table, and plates all around. "I'll be right back with fresh pepper. You want a little grated Parmesan, too? More wine?"

"All of the above," Heather says with a laugh and drains her glass.

Nora looks at Keith. "We need to go."

"I don't know . . . I mean, the doors are locked, and she's got the dog," he adds, as if Kato is a ferocious Rottweiler.

"Lennon just got back to me." Jules waves her phone. "He's at a party. Sorry. I really thought they were supposed to be together at your place tonight. Stacey should go hang out with Piper and Courtney."

"It's okay. I'm sure everything is fine at home," Keith says. "She just gets a little . . . She's always been an anxious kid."

"That's why we should get home."

"You sound like a new mom dealing with a frantic babysitter and colicky infant," Heather tells Nora, while sending a rapid-fire text on her own phone. "Stacey's a big girl. She can handle it. I just told Courtney she's coming over and to keep an eye out for her."

"What? No! She won't want to do that."

"Why not?"

"Because she'd be embarrassed!" Nora's voice is sharper

and louder than she'd intended. The cozy young couple at the next table falls silent and looks over.

Keith touches her arm. "Nora . . ."

She shakes him off and shoves back her chair. "I'm going to talk to her."

She flees into the night air. The street is crowded and bright, strung with light strings and festive red and green bunting. Chatter, laughter, and jaunty old-fashioned organ-grinder music spill from a rollicking bistro across the way. The air wafts with pungent garlic and cigarette smoke.

Thinking of Jacob, Nora dials Stacey's phone.

She answers on the first ring with a breathless "Mom?"

"What's going on? Dad said you thought you saw someone watching the house? Did you see what he looked like?"

A pause. "No. Why?"

"I don't know, I just . . . I mean, if you think you saw a man, that's the logical question, right?"

"It was dark out there. It was just, you know . . . the silhouette of someone with binoculars."

"And Dad said you think someone approached you on the street this after—"

"I don't *think* things happen, like some delusional crazy person! It happened, and so did this! I didn't make it up!"

"I'm sorry, I didn't mean—"

"Mom, I'm fine now, okay? I'm sorry I said anything. Go back to your dinner."

"Stace—"

She's hung up.

Nora exhales a shaky breath and leans her head back, eyes

closed. When she opens them, she's looking at the sky, stars lost in the ambient glare of neon and light strings.

What now? She can't bring herself to go back into the restaurant.

At the curb, a cab pulls up to dispatch a family of three. Father, mother, teenage daughter. The parents are bickering as they head toward the crowded bistro, the girl trailing behind, sullen and fixated on her phone.

The man has Stanley Toska's swarthy complexion, the woman Lena's worry lines. But the girl . . .

Her gaze briefly meets Nora's as she passes.

The girl has Gertrude Williams's lifeless eyes.

Memento mori . . .

Remember, you must die.

Remember, you are dead.

The roof light on their vacated cab flicks to Available.

Nora considers jumping in.

Where would you even go?

Anywhere, in this moment, would be better than home and better than back to the table to eat food with strangers, her husband included. She doesn't trust them. Any of them.

"Taxi!" A pair of tourists with flailing maps and fanny packs rushes past her and snaps up the cab.

Nora watches it pull away, leaving her stranded on a frenetic street where the lights are garish and the air reeks and the organ-grinder music swamps her like an encroaching tide.

She doesn't recognize the melody, but it triggers a familiar one in her head.

No.

She can't stand here listening to it, wondering about what might have happened in her distant past that has something to do with that song, or with a mulberry bush, a monkey . . .

She pivots back to the restaurant. Through the wide window, she can see Keith, Jules, and Heather, candlelit and animated and twirling pasta on their forks.

She thinks about that first day at the dog run. How she'd just happened to meet Heather.

Brooklyn is the biggest small world in the world, she'd said when Nora marveled that they lived on the same block, just a few doors apart. And Jules . . .

Jules had lived there around the time the triple homicide occurred. She claims she knew the victims. Her son wants to write a book about it. Her son is making Stacey cry, saying that she's adopted, that Nora is a fake.

If not for that chance meeting at the dog run, this new life might have been the healing fresh start Nora had intended. Her family might never have found out about the murders.

None of them, not even Keith, suspects that it hadn't been news to Nora.

Or that the rainy Sunday last month hadn't been her first visit to 104 Glover Street.

Stacey

ammit. Stacey should have known better than to call Dad and tell him about the man on the roof.

She *does* know better.

Stacey's mood swings and quirky habits and appearance don't mean there's something wrong with her . . .

Those words echo back as she paces her small bedroom holding her phone, ignoring the incoming text vibration. It's either from her parents or from Piper.

There's no way Stacey's going to run scared down the street to her little sister, at Lennon's house, no less. No way in hell.

"I can't do that," she'd told her father when he'd suggested it, saying it would only be for an hour, hour and a half at the most, until they get home.

"But why not? If you're scared to stay home alone, then—"

"I'm not scared to stay home alone!" she shouted into the phone.

Yes, she is. But not like *that*. Not like a little girl frightened that the boogeyman might be hiding under the bed.

The boogeyman is right there in the open, watching her, calling her Anna . . .

If you see something, say something.

When she did, her father seemed to assume she only *thought* she'd seen something. And when she insisted that she had, he said that if she thought she was in danger, she needed to call 9–1–1.

She would have, if not for that conversation she'd over-heard months ago.

I think she might be unstable and I want her to see a psychia-trist . . .

"I don't *think* I'm in danger! I am not crazy!" she screamed at her father into the phone.

He told her to calm down. She hung up on him.

A minute later, he'd texted her that he'd told Piper she was on her way.

Dammit, dammit, dammit.

He's the one who'd defended her months ago, when her mother wanted to send her to a shrink. That's why she'd chosen to call him instead of Mom. But tonight, his attitude made it clear that he, too, questions her sanity.

Stacey herself is no longer even certain about what she'd seen.

She pauses again to lift the shade a crack, peering out to check the shed roof for the silhouette of a hooded man. He's gone, just as he was the last time she'd checked, right before her mother called.

Maybe that should make her feel safer, but it doesn't. It makes her wonder if he was ever there. If he wasn't, she might be losing her grip on reality. If he was, he might be edging closer to the house. He might already be inside. He might be—

She cries out, hearing a shrill blast and loud banging noise downstairs.

He's trying to get in through the front door, and she's trapped here, and—

The blast comes again and she realizes it's the doorbell. The watcher wouldn't ring the doorbell and knock like a Girl Scout selling cookies, for God's sake. But her sister would, just as Stacey herself had the other day when she'd tried to let herself in and found that Mom had fastened the chain on the other side.

Checking her phone, she expects to find a text from Piper saying she's here to collect her lame loser of a big sister.

Instead, she sees one from Lennon.

I'm here. Are you okay?

She exhales, relieved. It doesn't matter that he'd upset her today or that she didn't want to see him tonight. She no longer wants space.

She flies out of her bedroom and down the stairs. She unfastens the chain, turns the lock, and opens the door . . .

To a hooded man in black.

She cries out.

He reaches for her.

Grabs her.

"Stacey, what happened? Are you all right?"

Lennon, wearing a sweatshirt, hood up. Lennon, so concerned.

"Why are you here? How did you know?"

"Jules texted me from the restaurant. I had to lie to her—I

told her I was at a party in Williamsburg, because that's where Courtney and your sister went."

"They went to *Williamsburg*?"

"Not Virginia. It's a neighborhood in Brooklyn."

"No, I know, but . . ."

It's not like she hadn't suspected Piper was up to something.

"I'm supposed to be covering for them, and I couldn't let on that I was home, because they aren't."

He wasn't the man on the shed roof. Of course he wasn't.

He always wears black. His hood is up because of the night chill.

"Can I come in?" he asks, and she sees his eyes flick to the hall behind her.

Recalling his fascination with the murders, and how he'd mentioned that he wants to check out the house, she shakes her head. She doesn't want him inside. But she doesn't want to be left alone here, either.

"I'm starving, and I was about to go out and get something to eat."

"I thought you were freaking out about a Peeping Tom, and that the guy from this afternoon is stalking you."

"Oh, my parents blow everything up into a big deal." She reaches behind her, glad her keys and jacket are right there by the door so that she doesn't have to let him in even for a minute.

"I'm thinking pizza," she says, stepping onto the stoop. "Maybe that brick oven place you like on Edgemont?"

The boulevard will be hopping at this hour on a Saturday night. Plenty of people around, just in case . . .

"Sure. That's cool. As long as I get to see you. I missed you."

"Oh, come on. You just saw me a few hours ago."

"I know, but, Stacey . . ." He pulls her against him and murmurs against her ear, "Are you sure you don't want to go back inside? Or come down to my house? Nobody's home . . ."

Yeah, no. That's the last thing she wants.

"If I don't get something to eat, I'm going to pass out." She closes the door behind her and turns her key to lock the dead bolt.

As they head toward Edgemont, she scans the street for the hooded man.

I'm not crazy. I'm not. I know what I saw.

Someone really is watching this house. Watching *her*.

She only hopes he isn't much closer than she thinks, walking beside her with his arm around her like a straitjacket.

Part Three

Nora

Five days after the tumultuous evening at Nonna Della's, Nora's life has settled into a rhythm.

With the girls and Keith coming and going on a predictable schedule, she's available to them when they're here, and when they're not, she focuses on the things that make her most comfortable. Garden chores when the weather cooperates; indoor chores when it does not.

It's been an active hurricane season, with a tropical storm parked offshore for a few solid days of warm, humid rain. Nora reorganized closets and drawers, scrubbed the oven and fridge, scoured all the tile grout in the house, and rented a steamer to deep clean the rugs, drapes, and upholstery.

Yes, it was largely unnecessary, all of it. But anything to keep busy. Anything to avoid dwelling on the past, the murders, Jacob, and the box that remains locked in the shed.

Jules reaches out daily, and not just once. Nora tells herself she's just trying to be friendly, or maybe she's lonely during the days with everyone gone at work and school. She wants to get together for lunch or coffee, even to talk about the community garden, though she admits Ricardo is away this week.

Nora puts her off, blaming the weather, a nonexistent headache, pressing household chores. The more she resists, the more Jules persists, like an ardent suitor.

It's morning now, the first since Saturday with sunlight streaming in. She goes through the house lifting the shades above windows that have been open all week. Kato follows her, energized by air flowing through the screens that's gone from muggy to crisp overnight. In the kitchen, he sits at the back door and fixes Nora with an expectant look.

She opens the door and watches him from the doorstep as he trots into the yard.

Keith usually takes him out for a quick walk. This is the first day Nora arrived downstairs before him, because last night was the first she hadn't allowed herself to take a sleeping pill. She only has a few left, and she'd better hoard them.

Their plastic surgeon back home prescribes them whenever she or Keith has a procedure. Keith never fills his prescription, and is unaware Nora fills hers. She's never used the medication to keep postoperative discomfort from waking her, but she needs it on nights when the past intrudes. Now that she's here, in this house, that's every night.

She gazes at the surrounding rooftops, wondering where, exactly, Stacey had seen the man on Saturday night. Or thought she'd seen him.

She'd texted Nora and Keith at the restaurant to say that she was going out with Lennon. They got home before she did and waited up in front of the living room television, the day's discord hanging in the air between them.

When Stacey came in, she wasn't interested in discussing what had happened.

"It's no big deal," she said, heading for the stairs. "I just want to go to bed. I'm sorry I said anything."

When her door closed overhead, Keith looked at Nora. "I think you might be right about having her see someone."

"See someone?"

"A psychiatrist, Nora." He sighed. "The way she sounded on the phone earlier . . . agitated, barely making sense . . . it wasn't like her at all."

"She's always been anxious."

"Low-key, quiet, *normal* anxious. Not frantic, like some . . ."

"Delusional crazy person?" Nora suggested.

"That's a little harsh, don't you think?"

"Those were Stacey's own words when I was on the phone with her earlier."

"She said she's delusional and crazy?"

"No, she said she's *not*, and that she hadn't imagined the man on the roof."

"Maybe she didn't."

"Maybe not. This was a stressful day for her, Keith. She was upset about an argument she had with Lennon."

"How do you know?"

"She told me."

She braced herself for him to accuse her, again, of keeping secrets from him.

But he seemed to digest and accept it. "What was the fight about?"

"It doesn't really matter, does it? I just think it's possible that the stress might have triggered a panic attack. If she can put it behind her for tonight, so should we, and we'll see how things look in the morning."

Things were brighter on Sunday despite dreary weather. Marital tensions eased by a decent night's sleep, Nora and Keith spent a couple of quiet, companionable hours reading the *New York Times*. Piper didn't return from her sleepover until midafternoon, too weary to be her usual effusive self, and went up to her room to nap.

Stacey, too, spent most of the day in her room. When she emerged she seemed to be her usual self. Keith attempted to bring up the night before, but she shut him down. "It's all good, Dad. You guys were right. It was probably just a shadow from a tree or something."

"Did you say that?" Nora asked him after she'd left the room.

"No. Did you?"

She hadn't, but if that was what Stacey had decided, they weren't going to argue the point.

Now that she finally has Keith's blessing to find a psychiatrist for her, Nora has been weighing whether to look into it. But it had seemed so much more urgent in California. Here, Stacey seems happier, boyfriend troubles and all.

Is it just that here, you have other things to worry about? Or are you afraid that you're the one who needs to see someone? Are you the one who's delusional?

The last few evenings, she's caught the occasional familiar whiff of cigarette smoke in the air and expected to find Jacob lurking in the house, or around it. She looked for him behind draperies and in closets, and in the rainy garden. Jacob, or his ghost.

Of course she didn't find him, just as she hadn't found him online. He might be long dead. Or the name he'd given her back then had been an alias. Either way, it's unlikely that he's stalking the house or haunting it decades later.

Yet even now she scans the rooftops and bramble border, where Kato has done his business and is nosing around. No sign of Jacob. No Peeping Tom.

"Come on, boy," she calls. "Time to go in!"

The dog doesn't come, intent on pawing at something— probably trying to get at a chipmunk. Or, God forbid, a rat.

"Kato!" Nora whistles. "You want a treat? Let's go get a treat!"

His ears perk up and he trots toward her.

Back in the kitchen, she delivers on her promise, and he settles in to crunch on a bone-shaped biscuit as Keith appears.

"Wow, treats at this hour? What'd he do to deserve that?"

"He came when I called him."

"So would I. You're looking pretty hot in that skimpy T-shirt."

"It's your shirt," she reminds him. "Not that skimpy, and I slept in it, and I haven't combed my hair or brushed my teeth."

"So? Still hot. Do I get a treat, too?"

She raises an eyebrow and shakes the box she was about to return to the cabinet. "If you want a liver-flavored cookie, who am I to deny you?"

Keith laughs and steps up behind her, wrapping his arms around her waist. "I'm glad you didn't deny me last night. Every night could be like that, if you didn't fall asleep as soon as your head hits the pillow."

"Yeah, well, what can I say? Cross-country moves are exhausting for everyone." She slips from his grasp and puts the dog treats away.

Keith pours coffee into a go-cup. "By the way, I've got to get back to Andrew this morning. Should I tell him Saturday night's good for us?"

"What?"

"Dinner with Andrew and Marla."

"Right. Great." Nora smiles as if she's looking forward to meeting Keith's old college roommate and his wife.

Much as she appreciates Marla's help in landing the girls at a fantastic school, she hates the thought of socializing with strangers when she's got so much on her mind.

Keith kisses her on the cheek. "Love you."

"You, too."

He leaves the kitchen. Hearing the front door close a moment later, she heaves a weary sigh.

Cross-country moves are exhausting . . .

Keith, you have no idea.

"Moving to New York is a sign," Nora told Teddy on the phone in July, when she first found out. "Please try to understand why I have to do this."

"I don't know that it's a sign, but you don't have to live in that house."

"I do. It's what I'm supposed to do. You're the one who said—"

"Nora, no. Stop right there. I never said you should go back there!"

Of course Teddy knew about the young woman who'd died in this house, in her bed, on that awful night.

"But you said I need to heal, and that I can't heal if I keep running away from the past instead of facing it."

"What you're doing is punishment, not healing. This is a self-imposed penance. Facing the past is one thing, but revisiting it is just—you're tempting fate, Nora."

"Maybe. But I have to do this. Because she was my friend, Teddy. And I owe it to her."

Stacey

Riding the crowded subway to Manhattan, Stacey stands with Lennon in their usual spot beside the door to the next car.

He has one hand braced on the wall behind her, his long arm stretched like a barricade between her and the other passengers. Both their backpacks are slung over his shoulder, though she'd prefer to carry her own. Not just because his insistence often strikes her more as aggression than chivalry, but because he's occasionally inattentive to his own belongings.

Books and clothing, cash, and even his phone sometimes poke up from his bag or pockets, precariously close to falling out. Once, when his dangling school tie trailed from his backpack like a limp tail, she gave it a tug and asked him how a native New Yorker could be so reckless.

"It only looks reckless to you because you're not a New Yorker. I'm always in tune with my surroundings," he claimed. "I know exactly who's around me. Nothing's going to happen to my stuff. Or to your stuff, or you, when you're with me."

She supposes it *is* nice to know that someone has her back

in this huge, unfamiliar, dangerous city. Especially now that Saturday night has faded to an unpleasant memory, a mere blip in their relationship.

He'd been so sweet at the pizzeria, treating her as though she was a precious princess and not an awkward teenage girl who hadn't bothered to comb her hair or change out of sweats before leaving the house. He made her laugh and forget the drama—most of it self-inflicted, she'd concluded by the time they were heading home. She couldn't believe she'd even considered for one second that he might have been the watcher.

She's still unnerved by the figure she'd seen, and by the man who'd approached her on the street. But after five uneventful, ordinary days, she's almost managed to put it out of her head.

School is going well, thanks to interesting coursework, engaging instructors, and a nice girl from her social studies class who'd invited Stacey to join her lunch table. She's getting used to living in the city. The commute, though long, allows her to spend extra time with Lennon.

"Make sure your parents don't rope you into any family stuff this weekend," he tells her, as the train barrels between stops. "This amazing guitarist I know is doing an open mic night and I was thinking we could go."

The car lurches as they round a curve, and he holds her steady. The brakes screech and the lights flicker. *Off, on, off, on . . .*

She spies a familiar face on the far end of the car.

. . . off.

Plunged into darkness, she leans into Lennon and hisses, "He's here."

"What? Who?"

"The guy from the street. The one who called me Anna."

"Are you serious?"

"Yes."

The lights flick on again, and the train jerks forward, pulling into the station.

"Where is he?"

Stacey turns her head to look, but he's no longer visible. Passengers press toward the exit, blocking her view as the doors open. When they close again, he's nowhere in sight.

"I swear he was here, Lennon. He must have gotten off."

"You think he's following you?"

"I mean . . . why else would I keep seeing him?"

"You're right. I have an idea. We're getting off at the next stop."

"The next stop? Why? What about school?"

"You can be late."

"How late?"

"Like . . . six hours?" He laughs.

She doesn't.

"Okay, so you can miss a day. Haven't you ever called yourself in sick? Don't even bother answering that question." He rolls his eyes. "Look, we have to go now. If he's following you, we need to figure out who or what he is."

"*What* he is?"

"Is he a human being, or is he a supernatural being?"

Or is he a figment in my mind, which I'm losing?

Lennon touches her hand. "Hey, it's going to be okay, Stacey. I promise. I've got you."

Jacob

All this week, the rain shrouded Jacob from recognition as he kept Anna under surveillance. She wore a baggy black parka. He saw her dart the occasional wary glance from beneath her hood, but he was invisible in a sea of urbanites similarly concealed beneath hoods and umbrellas.

Not today, though. Today on the train he was exposed, vulnerable as the hermit crab his idiot kid had pried from its shell, played with, and misplaced.

I told you no pets, Jacob shouted at Emina over their son's screams when they found the exposed crustacean shriveled on the floor.

She wept. Stupid, stupid woman.

Jacob is far more fortunate than the doomed hermit crab.

The lights went out just as he saw Anna recognize him on the train. Impulse took over. He ducked and made his way toward the exit as disgruntled passengers shifted and shoved all around him. When the doors opened, he escaped onto the platform and the train sped Anna away from him.

Now he's trapped in a slow-moving pedestrian procession along a mine shaft of a sidewalk. The entire block outside the subway station is tunneled in plywood, with heavy construction equipment rumbling and clanking behind it.

It brings him back to childhood visits to job sites with his old man, who had a hand in it. He had a hand in a lot of things.

Don't tell your mother, Baba would tell Jacob. *She doesn't need to know about every errand we go on.*

There were a lot of errands, a lot of things Jacob didn't tell her, though it was no secret around the house that his father was part of a dark and violent transnational crime syndicate. His mother, whose own father, brothers, and nephews were also involved, did her best to keep Jacob out of it while he was living at home.

At eighteen, he moved to New Jersey, working in an electronics store by day and attending trade school at night.

Two years later, in the summer of 1993, the store closed. He had to ask his father for a loan to pay the rent.

"You need money, I'll hire you."

"To do what?"

"There's a girl . . . I want you to keep an eye on her."

"And then what?" Jacob had asked uneasily.

"Don't worry. All we need you to do for now is watch her."

We . . .

For now . . .

He was given no choice. Anyway, it wasn't illegal to just . . . watch someone.

He drove to Glover Street early on a July weekday morning and parked across from the address his father gave him. He soon saw an older man trudging away from the house in workman's coveralls and carrying a lunch pail.

A couple of hours later, the girl appeared. She was headed on foot toward Edgemont. He got out of the car and followed her to a small supermarket. She emerged fifteen minutes later with a few small bags of groceries, and carried them home.

That was it for the day.

That was it most days—household errands on the boulevard, as if she were a middle-aged housewife. She dressed like one, in long shorts and frumpy flowered T-shirts or blouses buttoned to her chin.

Occasionally she visited the library with stacked books clasped against her chest. Once in a while, she went to the park to meet her only friend.

Ellie's grunge-inspired wardrobe was as trendy as Anna's was plain. Her dark hair fell long and straggly beneath the beanies she wore with combat boots and flannel shirts on even the warmest summer days. She smoked cigarettes and drank beer, and Jacob eventually found out those were far from her worst vices.

"How did you even meet?" he asked Anna, months later.

"In the park."

"I didn't ask *where* you met. I asked how."

"Same way I met you. I was reading a book on a bench and she struck up a conversation."

From a distance, Anna's conversations with Ellie didn't appear to be lighthearted, but he didn't attempt to eavesdrop. He was certain there wouldn't be anything more interesting to hear than there was to see.

He'd been told to watch her and watch her he did, though his attention often drifted to other, prettier girls.

Anna wasn't unattractive, but she didn't adorn and embellish herself like the girls he was dating that summer, the family-sanctioned neighborhood girls who so actively solicited his attention. Anna didn't want to be noticed, with good reason.

Baba believed Stanley Toska was Stanislav Shehu, once a key player in the family's racketeering business. In 1983, they were infiltrated by the newly formed Organized Crime Drug Enforcement task force. Shehu turned informant, violating *besë*, the family's sacred oath of allegiance, and leading to a flurry of arrests. After testifying for the prosecution, he disappeared with his family into the government's Witness Security Program.

Lost in the past, Jacob walks blindly until he reaches the intersection and looks around to get his bearings. Concrete barricades and orange cones funnel bottlenecked vehicular traffic down to one lane as hard-hatted workers jackhammer a gaping hole into the roadway. Cops are shouting directions and stalled drivers honk or curse out their open windows. Stinking garbage spills from bags heaped at the curb, rotting in the sun that glares over it all.

He spies a street sign. Lower Broadway.

Baba used to take him to an old-world restaurant in this neighborhood, where they could get *kajmak* and *qofte* and strong boiled coffee. *Authentic, just like at home.*

His father wasn't talking about Pelham Parkway, but the distant land across the ocean where he'd been born. He'd longed to see it again one day before he died, but that wasn't meant to be.

Wondering if the restaurant is open for breakfast, Jacob

heads toward it, and back into the past. He thinks again of his dead father. Of Anna, back from the grave.

Of Anna, in August of '93, telling Ellie about her impending departure for college as Jacob eavesdropped behind a tree.

"So that's it. She's going away," he told Baba that night. "And it's time for me to go back, so—"

"What do you think this is, summer camp? You're not going anywhere except wherever she goes."

"But, Baba . . . what about trade school?"

"You're no good at that. How long do you think it's going to take you to get through, and then be able to support yourself? It doesn't make sense. You needed money, I gave you a job. Finish what you started."

The "job" was far more appealing than returning to struggle in trade school. The money was good, and his father, uncles, and cousins were finally treating him as something more than a pesky little boy.

For Jacob, it was a new beginning.

For Anna, it was the beginning of the end.

Nora

Dressed in tattered jeans and gardening clogs, Nora finds Kato waiting beside the back door.

"Really? I thought you'd be in a deep sleep by now." She opens the door, and he trots out into the sunshine. "Maybe you should have morning treats every day."

At the word *treats*, he stops and turns, ears twitching.

"Yeah, *no*," she tells him. "Go ahead and do your thing, and I'll do mine."

After a string of monochromatic days, the world is bedazzled, sky and foliage tinted in autumn's burnished gold. The west wind, crisp and layered in a sweet earthiness, has finally chased the sodden tropical air out to sea. The garden is carpeted in petals and leaves.

Nora finds a rake in the shed, trying not to notice the shelf where she'd hidden the metal box.

Cash . . . A gun . . . Remnants of lost lives . . .

Last night, those things pursued her in the restless purgatory between consciousness and sleep, with a dead girl joining the chase.

Don't forget me, the girl whispered. *Forget-me-not . . .*

At first she was Gertrude Williams, but then her face

morphed into the one that's haunted Nora for twenty-five years.

At last Nora dozed off and found herself a teenager again, wandering in a distant, dreamy garden, gathering beautiful blue blooms in memory of her murdered friend. She heard a rustling in the trees and looked up to see Jacob there, watching her. She dropped the flowers and started running, running, running for her life . . .

Just a dream.

She begins raking leaves, dwelling on things she could have done differently all those years ago . . .

Things she could have done differently on that fateful day last April, when Keith greeted her at the door when she returned from her clandestine meeting with Teddy.

He asked her about the flower show as if nothing were amiss.

"It was great," she said, setting her overnight bag on a chair and opening the closet to hang her coat.

"That's all? Just great?"

Her hand froze on the hanger.

"It was . . . you know, a flower show."

"Really, I don't. I don't know."

"There were booths, vendors, presentations . . ." She resumed draping her coat over the hanger, placing it just so on the rod, shoulder seams meticulously aligned.

Then there was nothing to do but close the closet door and face him. When she did, she spotted a dangerous flare in his eyes. He knew . . . something. How much?

"Is that all?" he asked.

She shrugged. "There were some amazing exhibits."

"And . . . ?"

"I don't know what else I can tell you, Keith."

"You can tell me that you didn't go to a flower show. You can tell me that you went to Mexico. And you can tell me why you lied to me. Who is he?"

She opened her mouth, realized that if she tried to speak she might vomit, and clenched her lips in her teeth so hard she tasted blood.

"Is it Greg Whittle?"

Greg Whittle—the newly divorced father of Piper's closest friend. She shook her head, disgusted. How could he even think that?

"No? One of the soccer dads?"

"No!"

"Then who? Your tennis coach? Our financial adviser? Daryl? I've seen the way he looks at—"

"Stop! It's not . . ." Thoughts churning along with her stomach, she thought better of what she was going to say. "He's not . . . he's not anyone you know."

Wildfire engulfed his summer sky eyes. "How long has it been going on?"

"Not long. It was just . . . it was a stupid mistake, a huge mistake. And it's over. I ended it. Because I love you."

He flinched when she put her arms around his neck.

"Keith, please . . . I'm sorry. It's just . . . I miss you so much with all the long hours you're putting in. It's no excuse, I know," she added quickly, "but it's been hard lately."

That part was the truth. A round of January layoffs had

left his firm understaffed and overextended. He'd been working later and on weekends, no longer a part of many things they used to do together, from watching Piper's soccer games to eating dinner.

"It's not like *I* haven't had opportunities, Nora. It's not like *I* haven't been tempted to—but I haven't. Not yet. Maybe I should have, though. Maybe I will."

"Maybe you will . . . what?"

"Have an affair. Or maybe we should both just . . ." He shrugged. "The Whittles aren't the only ones who are splitting up. Every time I turn around, another couple we know is getting divorced."

"You want to get *divorced*?"

"Do you?"

"No." That, too, was the truth. It still is.

"I love you. I'm so sorry, Keith. Please forgive me."

He promised to try, and said he was finished discussing it.

Afterward, looking back, she found that tidy resolution telling. She knew he couldn't just breeze on past her lie and confession to an extramarital affair. Nor could she overlook what he'd said about opportunities and temptation.

Throughout the spring and early summer, she wondered if she was imagining the scent of perfume on his clothes after late nights at the office, or flirtatious undertones when she overheard him on the phone with female colleagues.

Maybe she should have handled things differently.

Maybe, when he'd caught her in the lie, she shouldn't have responded with more lies.

Maybe enough time had passed and it was safe to share

her real story. Not every detail, but enough so that he'd understand who Teddy is, and who Nora really is.

Was.

"I'm not having an affair, Keith," she could have said. "I'm—"

No.

Her hands clench the rake, and she stares down at the pile of fallen foliage.

That first September after she'd fled New York for California, she'd told Teddy she missed the Northeast's gorgeous autumn tapestry.

"Maybe you won't miss it so much if you remember that it's just Mother Nature orchestrating an exquisite death scene. One last glorious burst of vibrant life, and then all those dying leaves turn brown and wither away into dust."

Remember, you must die . . .

She leans her head back and closes her eyes, so damned tired. Tired of everything. Tired of this day, this life, the lies . . .

She sees herself picking flowers in Teddy's long-ago garden, hears Teddy warning her about that provocative swath of forget-me-not blue.

"They're insidious. They creep in and take over. I don't know how they got here, but they don't belong, and I can't get rid of them."

Nora opens her eyes.

A golden leaf dances from the blue sky. So lovely. So deceptive.

Gold . . . Blue . . .

Nora . . .

"I'm not Nora," she hears herself telling her husband. "I'm . . . I *was* . . ."

No.

She blinks away tears as a whispering wind drifts dying leaves all around her.

Stacey

Calling herself in sick to school isn't the worst thing Stacey has ever done, but it's pretty damned close. Lennon, not even bothering to report his absence to his own school, points out that she's a new student, and the woman who answered the office phone couldn't know her voice from her mother's.

Evidently it's true, but it doesn't sit well with Stacey anyway. "If I get caught—"

"You won't get caught."

"You don't know that for sure, Lennon. They might call my mom to double-check that I'm home. Then what?"

"Then detention, like me. You'll survive. And it'll be worth it."

"What will be?"

"What we're doing. You'll see."

"I don't even know where we are."

"Just follow me."

He's still carrying both of their backpacks. The sidewalks in this neighborhood are narrow and crowded, making it mostly necessary for them to walk single file.

This is in an old part of the city, its narrow streets lined with low buildings, mostly storefronts. Plenty of bodegas, sprinkled with the ubiquitous Duane Reade drugstores, Starbucks, plus specialty shops and small trades—shoemakers and seamstresses, florists and butchers and . . .

"Here." Lennon stops in front of a door tucked between a barbershop and a tattoo parlor.

Stacey leans in to read the placard. *"Psychic Medium?* Wait, what is this?"

"She's really good."

"We're here to see a fortune-teller? But I don't—"

"This isn't a carnival, Stacey. She's the real deal. I know her really well."

"You know a psychic really well?"

"I've had readings with her. Jules comes to her sometimes, too."

"Wait, did you tell her we were coming here?"

"Lisa?"

"What? Who's Lisa?"

"The medium."

"Her name is *Lisa?* Wow, that's so . . ." *Normal.* "What I meant was, you didn't tell Jules we were coming here, right?"

"No. And don't worry, even if she knew, she wouldn't tell your parents. She's cool."

"She is cool, but you don't know that she wouldn't tell my parents. They hang out."

"So? Stop stressing. This is going to be good for you. Lisa can tell you what's going on in that house, and with your Peeping Tom."

Stacey doubts that. But they're here. What does she have to lose?

Lennon reaches for the buzzer, but the door opens before he can press it.

The slender, attractive brunette is in her late thirties at most. Her hair is piled on top of her head and held with a banana clip. She's wearing sherpa-cuffed boots, jeans, a New York Yankees T-shirt, and glasses with purple plastic frames.

"Hey, Lisa."

"Hey." She points at Lennon. "You're—"

"Lennon." He shoots a smug glance at Stacey: *See? I told you I know her really well.*

"I was going to say, 'you're not my bagel and coffee.' I ordered it from the deli down the street, and it's taking for-freaking-ever. I was just about to go down there and pick it up myself, but . . . Whatever."

Lisa's New York accent is thick. *Coffee* is *cawffee* and *whatever* is *whateveh.*

"Are you here for a reading . . . Lenny, did you say?"

"Lennon. This is my girlfriend, Stacey. She wants a reading."

"Hey, girlfriend Stacey. I'm Lisa." She holds the door wide open. "Come on up, guys. Let me just check the app and find out what's going on with my breakfast, and we'll go from there."

They step into a dimly lit vestibule tiled in cracked black-and-white-hexagon mosaic. She leads them past a closed door marked 1A, and Stacey can hear a television game show blasting on the other side. At the top of a steep, creaky staircase, there's another small hall and a door, presumably 2A. It's ajar.

As they cross the threshold, a buzzer reverberates. "Oh,

yay, bagel time. Make yourselves at home. Be right back."
Lisa pivots and sprints down the stairs.

Stacey follows Lennon into an apartment crammed with a
mishmash of furniture. Some looks like it belongs in a me-
dieval castle, some like it came from IKEA. Stacey takes in
the stacks of books, collections of knickknacks, gym equipment, a huge TV, and an artist's easel that holds a half-
finished landscape.

"Cool, right?" Lennon asks.

She shakes her head. "I'm uncomfortable."

"Why? I'm here. It's fine. Don't you want answers? Aren't
you wondering whether—"

Lisa's footsteps pound back up the stairs and she's back,
holding a paper bag and a go-cup. "New delivery guy. He got
lost. I'll put this away for after the reading."

"Oh, we didn't mean to interrupt your breakfast," Stacey
says. "We can come back another time, or something."

"Nah. Business before breakfast! Come on. My study is
in the back. So, Lenn . . . did you say Lennon? Like John?"

"Exactly like John. We've actually met a few times."

"You and John Lennon?" She peers at him through her
glasses. "How old *are* you?"

"I meant you and me."

"Oh—sorry. I have a lousy name recall. Faces, too. What I
remember is energy. Anyway, you can wait in here, Lennon,
and—"

"My girlfriend wants me to come in with her. She's a little
freaked out."

"I am not freaked out," Stacey counters. "I'm just . . ."

"First reading?"

"I guess you *are* psychic."

Lisa returns her smile. "So do you want our friend Lennon to come in?"

Emphasis on the *you*.

"Sure. It's fine."

It isn't that she doesn't want him there. It's more that she doesn't want to be *here*.

He puts his arm around her as they cross into a tiny, cluttered kitchen that smells like cat food. Lisa shoves the bag into the fridge and leaves the cup on the counter, then opens a door, steps back, and waves them inside.

The room is so different from the rest of the apartment that it might as well be in another building, inhabited by someone else.

Parquet floors, white walls and ceiling. A chair faces a couch, across a low table. Not castle furniture, not IKEA, all of it beige and rectangular. The table holds a pad and pen, a candle, and a box of tissues. No crystal ball.

Sunlight streams through the lone window, overlooking a brick wall. Lisa draws the shades and the room is dim. She lights the candle and asks them to sit on the couch.

"I'm going to tell you a little bit about how I work," she says, sinking into the chair and looking at Stacey. "And then we'll get started. Okay?"

She hesitates, then nods. "Okay."

Nora

Back in the shed, Nora picks up a large bag of flower bulbs—daffodils, tulips, hyacinths, and crocuses.

Teddy had suggested that she plant a spring garden.

Just like you did when you came home that first year after . . .

Teddy hadn't needed to finish the sentence.

The murders.

Came home—such an innocuous way to describe her escape from the nightmare in New York.

Her father, Victor Montgomery, was the only person in the world she'd ever trusted. But for her, there was no going home. By then he'd sold the modest bungalow where she'd lived with both her parents in what seemed like another lifetime. By January 1994 Dad was remarried and living in his new wife's Spanish Colonial Hollywood mansion. The first time he escorted her over the threshold, he mentioned that the place was nearly a hundred years old and had once belonged to a silent film star.

"I hate old houses," she snapped, thinking of the one on Glover Street.

She hated her new stepmother, too, long before they met.

Despised the very idea of her father embarking on a new journey that had nothing to do with her.

Even though you did the same thing to him?

But she'd had no choice.

Her father had made a conscious decision to marry the utterly inappropriate Theodora Maria Gonzales, twenty years younger and an independently wealthy free spirit.

She was barefoot the first time Nora met her, wearing cutoffs and a tank top that revealed tanned skin, ample cleavage, and a small pink hibiscus tattoo on her shoulder. Her long dark hair was untamed, her pretty face free of makeup and worry lines.

"Call me Teddy," she said with a welcoming smile. "Do you want me to call you—"

"Call her Nora," Dad told her. "That's what she's chosen."

Yes. A derivative of Eleanor, so that she'd never forget . . .

As if she could ever, ever forget.

Teddy nodded. "Nora it is, then. That's beautiful."

No, *Ellie* was beautiful. *Nora* was a part of the lie she'll live with for the rest of her life.

She stared down at her shoes, still covered in Brooklyn mud.

"I lost my mom young, too, so I'm here for you if you need me," Teddy said. "But if you want me to leave, don't be afraid to say it."

"You mean you'll go away if I tell you to?"

Teddy threw back her dark head and laughed. "I mean if you need some space or some time alone with your dad, just say the word. I'm always happy to head outside and play in the dirt for a while."

"Play in the dirt?"

"She's a gardener," Dad explained.

"Gardener by hobby, horticulturalist by profession. I was drawn to it when I was a little younger than you," Teddy told Nora. "I'd lost my parents and a couple of good friends. Making things live and grow was cathartic. If you want, you can come play in the dirt with me sometime."

"No, thanks. But if you want to go do that . . . I'm saying the word."

It wasn't long before Teddy won her over—not just with her garden, but with acceptance, affection, advice, and assistance in building a new life. She helped Nora with admission and tuition at USC, her own alma mater. She helped her move into an off-campus apartment, furnished it, and paid the rent. She inspired Nora to follow in her own footsteps, majoring in horticulture. She listened when Nora needed to talk.

Most importantly, because of Teddy, they were a family again. For a few years, anyway.

Daddy's diagnosis came shortly after Nora's 1999 graduation from USC. He vowed he'd survive into the new millennium, and he did, just barely.

In a cruel twist of fate, Victor Montgomery died in January and was buried on the sixth anniversary of the murders.

The Southern California weather that day was warm and sunny. As Nora stood in the cemetery watching his casket lowered into a yawning grave, she was back in New York on a sleety winter night.

And now . . .

Now she really is back. It's not winter, but it will be. And she's supposed to be planting a spring garden to keep busy and give herself something to look forward to.

"Put it where you'll be able to see it from the kitchen window," Teddy advised. "When those green shoots sprout up in March, you'll feel like a new person."

"Again?" Nora asked, and they laughed.

She grabs a shovel and scouts for a place to dig. She rules out a shady spot where the spreading roots of a neighboring tree will interfere, and settles on a sunny patch around the butterfly bush. Graceful tiger swallowtails and monarchs flit among the fragrant purple cone-shaped blossoms.

She pokes the tip of the shovel into the soil.

Here we go round . . . the butterfly bush . . .

Once again, the damned monkey is chasing the weasel through her head and back, back in time. Not far enough, though, to release the nebulous memory that prods at her every time the tune pops up.

Every shovelful of dirt plummets her deeper into the sorrowful year that followed her father's death.

Bonded in grief, she and her stepmother had done their best to stay busy. Nora landed a job with a sustainable landscaping company and moved into a garden apartment in West Hollywood. Teddy threw herself into volunteerism for Al Gore's presidential campaign, with environmental protection an issue that was close to her heart.

When he lost, following an epic and drawn-out postelection battle, Teddy did some serious soul-searching. One day, she broke some news that Nora probably should have seen coming, but it blindsided her.

"You're *leaving*?"

"It's a once-in-a-lifetime opportunity, Nora, to join an international coalition of naturalists researching the impact of global warming. They need me. I need to do this. I can't keep sitting by, watching what's happening to this world and not doing a damned thing to understand it and to stop it. This is what I should have been doing all along, and I would have been, if I hadn't put my career on hold to marry your dad."

"On hold? So you expected it to be temporary?"

"No, my love. When I made the decision to settle down, it was for life. I didn't want to travel around the world anymore. I wanted to be with Victor. I just never expected to wind up alone in this big old house."

"You aren't alone! You still have me."

"And I will always love you more than anyone on this planet."

"But the planet comes first," Nora said flatly.

"Not first. Never first. Listen, I know I'm not the mother who brought you into this world, and that I couldn't replace her, but in my heart, you'll always be my daughter."

"Then why are you leaving?"

"Because I have to accept this responsibility, just as you have yours that take you away from me."

Nora didn't really. Not then. Not yet. Her job had yet to blossom into a career, and her apartment didn't feel like a home. With Teddy's departure, she felt utterly alone in the world her stepmother had abandoned her to save.

Three weeks later, she met Keith. Six months after that, they were married.

He'd come from a large family and was eager to start one.

He had old-fashioned values. The man should be the bread-winner, the woman should stay at home, just as his own mother had.

Nora was okay with that. She was okay with anything that promised the security, stability, predictability she craved. Okay, too, with preserving her initial instinct to keep her past a secret even from Keith. Sharing even a partial truth—telling him about Teddy, for instance—would open the door to questions, expectations, even an introduction when Teddy came to town.

It was much easier to let him think she'd been utterly alone in the world before he came along. In some ways, it was true.

Most of the time, she's grateful for the traditional life they've built together. Yet just as Teddy could never replace the mother she'd lost, Keith and the girls can never replace the family she'd lost.

Nor the friend.

She looks up at the house, at the room that now belongs to Stacey. She imagines her troubled daughter peering out the window, believing a man was watching the house.

She turns away to gaze at the surrounding rooftops.

No one is there, and no one was there on Saturday night. Stacey imagined it, just as Nora had imagined Jacob's face in the café window the day before.

She returns her attention to the task at hand, forcing her thoughts to the day ahead, burying the past along with the bulbs. Giving the fresh layer of soil a final pat with the back of the shovel, she sighs contentedly, envisioning the tender

green shoots that will pop up in March, all around the butterfly bush . . .

All around the mulberry bush . . .

Spent, she returns the shovel to the shed, locks it, and
looks around for Kato. There he is, snoozing beside the
bramble border where he'd been nosing around earlier this
morning, front paws outstretched.

"Come on, boy! Let's go inside now."

He barely stirs.

"Laziest dog ever," she mutters. "Come on! Treat!"

The magic word does the trick once again. As he stands,
she sees that he'd been holding something beneath his paws.
He trots toward her, carrying his prize in his mouth.

"No!" she calls, anticipating a mutilated squirrel or bunny.

Then she realizes what it is, and the crisp breeze stirring
dying leaves goes glacial as the dog drops a pair of binoculars
at her feet.

Stacey

S tacey sits across from Lisa, hands outstretched, palms up, like the medium's.

"That opens you up to energy and allows it to pass between us," she'd said before they began.

"What kind of energy?"

"Whatever I get. I'll share whatever pops into my mind. Some things might not make sense until later."

So far, everything has, though Lisa seems to be offering insight and advice as opposed to the predictions and warnings Stacey had anticipated, and most of it is generalized.

"You can be introspective, but you'll open up if the right person draws you out . . ."

"Sometimes you feel as if you've shared too much. It's important not to second-guess yourself . . ."

"I see you in a classroom. School is important to you, and you do very well academically as long as you don't let other issues distract you . . ."

Stacey listens to the rhythmic patter with her eyes closed and head bowed, half wishing the woman would say something to convince her of psychic powers, half hoping she won't.

"There are days when you prefer books to people, but remember, you can learn from both . . ."

"You're facing a fork in the path and you'll have to make a big decision. Take your time. Weigh all your options. Don't rush into anything . . ."

Stacey's hands are starting to feel stiff, held in this unnatural position. Wondering how much Lisa is going to charge Lennon for this barrage of platitudes, she steals a glance at him, sitting next to her on the couch, thigh to thigh, shoulder to shoulder. His eyes are closed, and he seems into the reading.

She bows her head again, trying to open herself to energy and absorb the medium's hypnotic monologue.

"You aren't comfortable with uncertainty . . ."

Yeah, well . . . who is?

"It takes a long time for someone to win your trust, but when they do, you're fiercely loyal. Tread carefully. Not everyone close to you is as truthful as you believe . . ."

At that, Stacey's eyes open.

"Someone in your life is hiding something . . ."

Stacey feels Lennon flinch.

Lisa's head is tilted, as if she's listening to a voice only she can hear. "You need to be careful. It could be dangerous."

"*What* could be dangerous?" Stacey blurts, and the woman's eyes fly open. "Sorry to interrupt, but . . . can you be more specific?"

"I'm giving you everything I'm getting."

"But . . . I don't think I *get* what you're getting."

"You need to be careful."

"Don't we all need to be careful? Shouldn't you be more

specific? This is so vague." Her hands close into clenched fists. "I mean, I'm sitting here and you're telling me that someone close to me is lying, and dangerous, and I think I deserve to know who he is and what you think he might do to me!"

Lisa just looks at her, wide-eyed. Stacey can't tell if she's dazed by the outburst, or listening for the silent voices to provide a response.

Lennon puts his arm around Stacey. "Lisa, sorry, but she's been through some stuff, and I'm not surprised you're picking up on it. That's why we're here."

"I figured. I'm getting some dark energy around her. I'll help however I can."

Stacey reminds herself that she doesn't believe in this stuff. That everything Lisa said could apply to anyone who walked in off the street. But she can't unsee the figure watching her in the night, or the wild-eyed man who called her Anna.

"So, dark energy . . . is it spirit energy, or human energy?" she asks.

"Both."

"Stacey lives in a house where people were murdered," Lennon says, "and the killer got away."

"Ah, restless spirit—that explains the oppressive aura I'm getting."

Stacey finds her voice and clears her throat. "Who's the person I trust who's hiding something from me? It's not a ghost, right?"

"*Spirit*," Lennon corrects her. "Not *ghost*."

"I was asking *her*." She inches away from him on the couch, wishing he'd remove his arm from her shoulders. It's so . . .

the opposite of comforting. Everything about this situation is the opposite of comforting.

"What if I believe there really is . . . *spirit* . . . haunting my house?" she asks Lisa. "I'm not saying that's what's—but let's just say there was, and I believed it . . . what can I do about it?"

"You can tell it to leave the premises."

"That's it? Just say get out of here?"

"Not in those words. Be firm, but polite."

"My little sister doesn't leave my room when I ask her to, but an evil spirit will?" Stacey shakes her head.

"You need to *tell*, not *ask*, and I didn't say *evil* spirit. Is that what you—"

"No, I don't think there's an evil spirit in my house. Or any spirit. Forget I even asked. Forget this whole—"

She starts to get up, but Lennon's hand clamps her shoulder.

"It's okay," he says, like he's soothing a frightened toddler. "Let's just listen and see what our options are."

Our options . . .

As if they're in this together. As if he's not a part of the problem.

"I can come and cleanse the house," Lisa tells Stacey.

"*Cleanse* it?"

"I do it all the time. Open the windows, ring a bell, burn sage, convince spirit to move on."

And probably charge a small fortune to remove a curse or some such nonsense.

"Yeah, thanks, but I don't think that would go over very well with my parents, so . . ." Again, Stacey tries to rise. Again, Lennon presses her down.

I've got you, he'd said earlier, on the subway.

"Let *go!*" She pushes his hand off, jumps to her feet, and heads for the door. "I need to get out of here. *Now.*"

She rushes through the apartment, down the stairs, out the door. She can hear Lennon calling her name, and she's certain he's going to chase after her, but he doesn't. She scurries through the crowded neighborhood, blindly turning right, left, left, right.

The warren of narrow streets gives way to one wide avenue, and then another. She slows her pace. There are chain stores and schools and churches, traffic and police cars, just in case . . .

Again, she checks over her shoulder. No Lennon. No watcher.

You don't need the police. You just need to get home.

Needing a cigarette to calm her nerves, she sinks onto a low brick wall in front of an apartment building, and then . . .

No. Oh, no. How could she?

She'd left her backpack behind. No cigarettes. No *wallet*.

But she has her phone and a MetroCard in her pocket. She can use the map app to navigate to a subway, or a ride app to summon a car. She just needs to catch her breath. Her heart is racing and her chest aches.

She leans back. It's not as though Lisa told her anything she didn't already know, consciously or subconsciously. Nor does she believe the "messages" were delivered via supernatural forces . . . does she?

She'd dismiss the entire experience if it weren't for the last few ominous statements.

Not everyone close to you is as truthful as you believe . . .

Someone in your life is hiding something . . .

Everyone has secrets. Everyone is hiding something.

If there's anything to this stuff, anything at all, Lisa could have been talking about Piper, right? She'd spent a fortune on a leather jacket without telling Mom, and she'd snuck out to a party when she was supposed to be at a sleepover.

And what about Mom, with her surgically enhanced face and nose job and dyed hair and dental veneers? Dad, too, for that matter.

Stacey herself has her share of secrets, from her newly acquired smoking habit to her relationship with Lennon. It's not like she tells him everything, either, so, yeah. People keep things to themselves. That's not a psychic revelation, it's just common sense, along with everything else Lisa—

"Stacey."

Lennon is standing in front of her.

He has both their backpacks over his shoulders and is wearing sunglasses and a smile. It might be relieved, or it might be sarcastic. She can't tell without seeing his eyes.

"How did you . . ."

He waves his phone at her.

Oh.

The damned tracking app. She should have known he didn't need to chase her through the streets.

"I'm sorry I brought you there," he says. "I thought Lisa would be able to reassure you."

About what? That her house isn't haunted? That it is, but the spirits aren't evil? That whoever is watching her, and calling her by a dead girl's name, is just some random lunatic?

Stacey shakes her head, tight-lipped.

"Are you okay?" Lennon sets their backpacks at his feet and opens his arms. "Come here."

"Our bags—someone could steal—"

"No one's going to steal them." He pins the straps under his black Doc Martens and repeats, "Come here."

She doesn't feel like being close to him right now, yet she doesn't want to be alone. She stands, and allows herself to be embraced.

"I was really worried about you," he whispers against her hair.

"Because you think I'm in danger? And that somebody close to me is—"

"No! Because I think Lisa's full of shit."

"*What?* I thought you said she was—"

"I was wrong. She doesn't know what she's talking about. Forget it. I'm just glad I found you."

"Yeah, *you* must be psychic," she says, and her voice is as weak as her smile.

Jacob

The restaurant is so close Jacob can taste the *kajmak* and *qofte*. Just one more block.

Steeped in nostalgia, he reflects on the good old days as he walks.

Baba had been a good man in so many ways. A patient father, an affectionate husband, a good provider. Jacob loved him.

For Baba, he'd upended his own life and curtailed his studies to follow Anna to a college town fifty-odd miles north of the city. Posing as a student, he rented a room in a house full of perpetually drunken guys. They assumed he was one of them.

Every day, he left the house with a backpack full of random books he'd picked up at the Salvation Army. He walked around on campus as if he belonged there, and he kept an eye on Anna.

She seemed different. She wore jeans, and her blouses were tucked in, sleeves rolled up, buttons unbuttoned. She no longer pulled her dark hair straight back in a tight headband. Now it waved around her face and cascaded down her back. She still had glasses, but the frames were more modern. She carried herself differently—shoulders less slumped, head held high.

One day, he was sitting with a Styrofoam cup of coffee on a bench in an academic building as though waiting for class to start. Anna really was waiting for a class to start, sitting on another bench. She seemed bored with the open textbook on her lap, twirling a curl around her fingertip as she read. When she checked the clock above his head, their eyes met. He smiled and gave a little wave.

She looked over both shoulders as if expecting to see someone behind her, then gave a tenuous wave in return. He saw her flinch when he got up and walked toward her.

"You're in my Tuesday-Thursday chemistry class, right? Section four in McGovern?" he added, naming one of the largest lecture halls on campus.

"Me? Oh, um . . . no. I'm not taking chem."

"Really? I guess I mixed you up with someone else. Sorry. I'm Jacob."

"Anna."

"Nice to meet you. What are you reading?"

"This? It's for a class." Keeping her place, she closed the book so that he could see the psychedelic cover.

"*The Electric Kool-Aid Acid Test* . . . what's it about?"

"Basically . . . drugs."

"Drugs? Like, what, Tylenol?"

She flashed a smile that was both shy and sly. "Like acid. It's for my Counterculture Lit class."

"That might be the coolest class I've ever heard of."

"It is. There are seats left. You should pick it up before drop/add cutoff."

"Maybe next semester. I've got a full course load."

They talked for a few minutes longer, until an adjacent classroom emptied into the corridor and it was time for her to go to class. Somehow he'd forgotten, until he was watching her walk away, why he was there.

That was the problem with Anna. With *him*.

His father had given him a chance to prove himself and work his way into the family business so that he, too, could earn easy money and respect. But at what cost?

He delved deeper into her life, digging around for the syllabus to every class she was taking. The next time he engineered running into her, it was after her Counterculture Lit class and not before. He knew it was her last one of the day. He struck up a conversation, asking what she was currently reading.

"*One Flew Over the Cuckoo's Nest.*"

"Loved that book," he said.

"You read it?"

He had not. He'd never been much of a reader. But he'd rented the video from Blockbuster and watched it in preparation for this conversation.

"A few times," he told her. "Great, right?"

A shadow crossed her face. "Disturbing. If I didn't have to read it for class, I wouldn't finish it."

"Oh, well . . . I'm a psych major, so it's right up my alley. What's your major?"

"I'm undeclared. Still trying to figure out what I like, and what I want to do."

"That should be pretty easy. What do you like?"

"What do you mean?"

"Got any hobbies?"

"No."

"Pets?"

She seemed to wince. "No, I . . . no."

"Special skills?"

She raised a dark eyebrow. "Like what?"

"Like . . . juggling plates?"

She smiled. But it faded when she asked him why he'd chosen to major in psych and he said, "Because I'm fascinated by the human brain. What makes people do what they do. Why they become who they are."

She didn't tell him that day about her mother, and the reason she never left the house. It would be a while before Anna opened up about that.

That day, he walked her back to her dorm and asked her out for coffee. She got so flustered he almost expected her to look over both shoulders again as if he might be talking to someone behind her. But she said yes.

As they parted, she stopped him with a question. "Where are you from?"

It caught him off guard. He'd prepared a cover story that had nothing to do with his real life. He was planning to say he came from somewhere upstate—Albany, maybe, or Utica.

But he heard himself say, "New York."

"Really? Me, too. I guess that's why your accent is familiar. I was thinking you were from somewhere else, like . . . I don't know, Europe, maybe."

"People say that all the time, but I'm as American as you are. You *are* American?"

"Of course."

That was the truth, he knew.

He also knew by then that her name, the one she'd been born with, wasn't Anna Toska any more than his was Jacob Grant. It was the alias Baba had told him to use, an American derivation and reversal of his real one, Granit Jakupi.

Caught up in his memories, he doesn't realize he's by-passed his destination until he reaches the corner. Back-tracking, he finds a modern CVS pharmacy where he'd thought the restaurant should be, and momentarily wonders if he's on the wrong block. But no, he recognizes the liquor store across the street where Baba often stopped to pick up a bottle of raki.

He shouldn't be surprised that the restaurant has disap-peared, like so many things he remembers from his youth. People, too.

Everyone he'd ever known and loved is dead, imprisoned, estranged, or in some cases, simply vanished. Back when Jacob was serving his own time, he'd heard the rumor that a cousin had testified against his own brother and father in exchange for immunity and a new identity.

Like Anna, who hadn't been Anna until she'd entered the government's WITSEC protection program with her family. She'd been young then—not too young to have forgotten her old name, her old life, the loved ones and home she'd been forced to leave behind forever.

She never told Jacob any of that, though. Five months, all those secrets, and she never told him the truth about who she really was.

Fair enough.

He never told her the truth about who he was, either.

She'd never known, even in the end, about his own underworld connection that would test his loyalty to his family—and annihilate hers.

Part Four

Nora

Nearly a week has passed since Nora found the binoculars and hid them in the shed with the metal box.

Jacob has yet to reappear. She's been watching for him. Waiting for him.

She sits in the garden, chilly now in her sleeveless T-shirt and shorts as dusk pushes a fiery September sky toward the rooftops.

The girls are home, lamplight illuminating their bedrooms overhead. Piper's shades are open and she's clearly visible in the window. She's sitting at her desk, ostensibly doing homework, but her head is bopping to music and she's texting on her phone.

Stacey keeps her shades closed. Not just at night. Always.

Most mornings after the girls and Keith depart, Nora slips into Stacey's shuttered room, raises the shade, and sits in the window, willing him to appear.

She doesn't know what she'll do when he does, or what he'll do.

Why would a contract killer return to the scene of a triple homicide twenty-five years later? Has he been following her all along? Or has someone in the organization been watching the house and tipped him off that there are new residents?

It makes no sense. Even if that were the case, no one could know who they are. Who *she* is. Only two people in the world were privy to the new identity she adopted after leaving Brooklyn twenty-five years ago. Her father is dead. Teddy would never betray her confidence.

She's kept the truth from everyone else in her life, telling herself that it was as much for their protection as for her own. She fully intended to live a quiet life in relative solitude before Keith came along.

She's been thinking about that a lot lately. About how their relationship began, and evolved—not so much a whirlwind romance as an opportunistic tornado that swept her away from the aching loneliness, grief, regret. If he hadn't popped up when and where he had, she'd likely still be alone.

Yet she does love him, and the girls. For a long time, she'd thought they would be enough; that being a wife and mother could fill all the dark, empty places inside her.

"Only you can do that. And you can't expect to heal if you deal with pain by running away," Teddy had told her, early on.

"What else could I have done? Three people were dead. If I hadn't run away, I would have died, too."

"I'm speaking figuratively. Physically, yes, sure, you saved yourself. You escaped your friend's fate. But you *were* wounded."

"I wasn't—"

"*Figuratively*, Nora. If you broke a bone, would you ignore it?"

She shuddered, thinking of her nose. "That's a horrible analogy, Teddy."

"I'm sorry, I didn't mean to—"

"No, I know."

"Let's just say . . . say you stepped on a rusty nail. If you fail to treat it properly, it's going to hurt more in the long run and leave you with ugly scars. You dread the sting of peroxide in an open cut, but without it, the wound can fester and get infected. Do you see what I'm saying?"

She just stared down at the dirt. They were working in Teddy's garden; always in the garden in those days.

"You have to face your injury and tend to it, Nora—seek professional help, get it stitched up, get medication . . . that's how you will heal and move on."

"That's easy for you to say. You don't know—"

"About survivor's guilt? Believe me, I've been there. I told you about—"

"This is different. I didn't *survive* a volcanic explosion that killed a colleague."

"*Two* colleagues," Teddy corrected her. "And what you survived was equally terrifying and tragic, my love. You need help processing this ordeal and putting it behind you."

"It's already behind me."

"Maybe that's how it seems, but you can't just close the door on it like it's an unwanted visitor. It's going to barge back in whenever you least expect it. You need therapy. That's the only thing that saved me from myself."

"I can't go to therapy. I can't tell anyone what happened."

"Haven't you ever heard of doctor-patient confidentiality? Whatever you share will be safe."

"*I'm* safe now. But whoever killed them is still out there," Nora managed to say, heart machine-gunning her ribs. "Please . . . if I tell anyone, even a doctor, I'm going to be looking over my shoulder again. I'm going to feel like I need to run again."

"Don't run again. Don't go anywhere. You're home."

For a long time, it felt that way. California. With Teddy. And with Keith. Then New York came along, yet another opportunistic tornado that whisked her right back here.

All these years, the house had been waiting for her.

But so, it seems, had Jacob.

Her phone lights up in her hand with a text from Keith.

Leaving the office in five minutes, barring last-minute disaster.

She writes back, **Good luck. See you soon. Dinner will be waiting, barring same.**

He sends a thumbs-up emoji. She responds with a red heart, then pockets her phone.

Weeknights are just a matter of getting through a family meal before everyone scatters—the girls to their rooms, Keith to the recliner in front of the television. Typically, by the time she changes her clothes and returns to the living room, he's dozed off, allowing her to escape back upstairs alone.

On weekends, though, he's rested and expects to spend time with her. He'd talked her into joining his health club so that they could work out together and do couples yoga on Saturday. That evening, they'd had dinner on the Upper East Side with his college roommate and his wife.

They were a nice enough couple, but it was one of those meals where the men talked mostly to each other and expected their wives to do the same. While Keith and Andrew reminisced about their good old days at Columbia, Nora struggled to find common ground with Marla, a high-powered television network executive who has no children.

Nora asked her about her job and braced herself for the inevitable "What do you do?" in return. When it came, Marla seemed taken aback that Nora had given up her career for marriage and motherhood.

Nora did her best to spin that decision in a positive way, stressing that it had been the right choice for their family at the time. But the discussion dredged up another unresolved fragment of the past.

Ever since, she's found herself resenting Keith for building a successful career while expecting her to put her own ambitions aside. And yes, she may resent Stacey, too, for being such a difficult child, depleting Nora's energy and ambition.

"Maybe you can get back to horticulture now that your girls are grown," Marla had suggested.

"I'm planning to."

Amid an inopportune lull, Keith overheard. "Planning to what, Nora?"

"Start thinking about my career again."

He'd chuckled and asked Marla about her job, leaving Nora feeling like a little girl who'd been patted on the head and told to run along while the adults talked.

She spent the rest of the evening imagining the conversation they needed to have when they were finally alone together. But during the ride home, he was caught up in a discussion with the driver about a tight ball game unfolding on the car radio. He turned on the TV to watch the end in extra innings, while Nora went upstairs and dipped into her dwindling sleeping pill supply.

Potential quarrel averted, though the strain remains, at least for her.

She's not a shell-shocked twentysomething who needs someone to take care of her. She wants more. She does.

And now, more than ever, Keith wants things to go on just as they have. He wants her to depend on him, wants to keep her at home, the dutiful wife and mother. Because he thinks she had an affair.

This isn't the time to pour peroxide into her wounded marriage. Because if things start to fall apart, if *she* starts to fall apart . . .

No. She won't let that happen.

Triage, Nora.

So, dinner. She's got chicken marinating in buttermilk brine, ready to be roasted with fresh herbs. The basil she'd planted too late in the season had wilted and blackened on the first chilly night, but the other tender plants are still doing fine.

At least they *were*.

Parting the surrounding foliage, she sees that the rosemary, parsley, and thyme continue to thrive, but the sage plant has been reduced to a clump of hacked-off stems.

Stacey

"Girls! Time to eat!"

Hearing her mother call from the foot of the stairs, Stacey hits Save and closes her laptop with a sigh of relief.

It isn't that she's hungry, but she's more than ready to take a break from the college application essay she's been rewriting for the past few hours.

She stretches her burning shoulders, then picks up her phone. She'd set it on Do Not Disturb while she was working, as she often does now that Lennon is in her life. He texts frequently, sometimes just a smiley face emoji with hearts for eyes, or a few letters, like IMY—his shorthand for "I miss you."

The first time, she'd deciphered it and written back, **IMY2**.

He'd responded, **You mean IMYT**. He doesn't approve of abbreviating *2* as *too* any more than he does *U* as *you*. Just one of his little quirks she initially finds endearing, though it occasionally gets on her nerves, as does Lennon.

But that's normal, right? Her parents and Piper get on her nerves, too, and she loves them.

"What about me? Do you love me?" Lennon asks in her head.

He hasn't come out and asked her that in real life. He has, however, told her that he loves her. Every night now, it's the last thing he texts: **Love you**. He's said it in person a few times, too, in parting. *Love you.*

Not "I love you," in which case failing to say it in return would be a blatant omission. But without the *I*, it's much more casual. Not quite as casual as "Luv U," but still . . .

She shouldn't feel uncomfortable for not responding, "Love you, too" . . . right?

Right. No one should ever feel obligated to say they love someone else. The words should be spontaneous, from the heart.

And she shouldn't spend so much time analyzing her relationship with Lennon, but he's . . . *a lot*. He's just a lot.

There are no new messages from him on her phone, but she finds a bunch on the group text with the girls from her lunch table. They're planning to see a movie together at Regal Essex on Friday night.

Who's in? Rebecca asks.

Looks like everyone is. Scrolling through the enthusiastic responses, Stacey is wistful. A movie with a group of girls sounds fun, but she's not sure they meant to invite her.

When Rebecca added her to the group text yesterday, one of the others, Kaitlyn, had questioned the unfamiliar number. When she found out it was Stacey, she'd sent a thumbs-up and smiley face.

Now, though, spotting her own name in a comment from Kaitlyn, Stacey believes for a sickening second that the girls don't realize she's on the thread. What if she's about to read a cruel comment unintended for her own eyes? The electronic equivalent of mean girls talking behind her back.

But no, that's not going to happen to her anymore. Not here, anyway. Not with this group.

Kaitlyn has written, **Stacey? Are you in?**

She heaves a sigh of relief.

Definitely! Thanks!

As soon as she hits Send, she wonders if she should have checked with Lennon first. But they haven't made any weekend plans yet. Not like last week, when he told her in advance about the open mic event—a real date night, and it had been fun.

Until he got up to sing, anyway. She wasn't expecting that. He hadn't even brought his guitar, but he'd borrowed one from another performer.

It wasn't that he wasn't good, because he was. He was fantastic.

But when he took the stage, he said, "This goes out to my girlfriend. It's the song that was playing the night we met, as I was looking out the window literally watching her walk into my life, and it pretty much describes us. Well, *me*. Here's Radiohead's 1993 hit, 'Creep,'" he added, with a self-deprecating smile that got a laugh.

Stacey didn't know the song by title. But as soon as he started strumming, she recognized that it had, indeed, been on in the background when she and her family arrived for dinner that first evening.

And the crazy thing is, she'd actually sensed someone's scrutiny as she walked down the street to his house. She'd been concerned about a man on a neighboring stoop, hidden behind a newspaper. She'd thought she sensed his eyes following her, even wondered if he was the same person she thought she'd seen on the shed roof the night they moved in.

Now Lennon was confessing to a roomful of strangers something he'd never mentioned to her.

He'd spied on her as she walked up to his house?

It wasn't the only time. When he'd materialized in the Edgemont Grind on the first day of school, he'd mentioned that he'd seen her walking Kato in the park before they even met. And what about that first chance meeting in the Grind? Was he there because he'd followed her?

Those were the thoughts racing through her mind at open mic night. She felt trapped, hands clenched in her lap as he fixed her with a penetrating gaze and sang disturbing lyrics about dark, obsessive passion for a girl to whom he felt inferior.

I don't want you getting hurt by some little creep who's not good enough for you, her mother had said the day they'd had their first fight.

When the song was over, the audience went crazy.

Lennon wore a pleased grin when he rejoined her at the table and put his arm around her. "What'd you think?"

"You were amazing," she said, reminding herself that it was just a song. He hadn't written it, and maybe she'd misunderstood the meaning behind it.

Still, the incident bothers her whenever it pokes into her consciousness, so she tries to keep it out, along with disquieting thoughts about the murders, the watcher, the man who'd called her Anna.

This has been a good week so far, with new friends. One of the best weeks she's ever had. No reason to go looking for trouble.

Wondering why Lennon hasn't texted her in the last couple of hours, she opens the Stealth Soldier app to see where he is. The blue heart icon is positioned in Lower Manhattan. Soho. Ah, that's right. A close artist friend of Heather's has a big gallery opening tonight. Lennon is there with his moms and sister.

Stacey pockets the phone, opens her door, and inhales the savory aroma wafting from below. Yeah, maybe she is hungry. It's late, past eight o'clock, their new dinner hour. Dad decided last week that he wants them to eat as a family on weeknights. That means waiting until he gets home from work. By the time they're finished, it's too late for Stacey to go for a walk with Lennon.

"What, you turn into a pumpkin if you leave the house after nine o'clock?" he said when she broke that news.

"I told you, my parents don't want me out at that hour."

"Let me talk to them."

"Yeah, right."

"Then let my moms talk to them. My weeknight curfew is eleven."

"Well, you're a guy, and you've lived here all your life."

"This blows."

"Yeah," she agreed, pasting a suitably bummed expression on her face.

In truth, she doesn't have a curfew, and she'd never asked

her parents about walking later in the evening. She'd welcomed an excuse not to spend quite so much time with Lennon, especially after dark.

She starts down the stairs, and Dad calls from below, "Get your sister, whoever you are!"

"It's me, as usual, Dad. The obedient one who comes when she's summoned!"

"Thank you, obedient one. Please wrangle your disobedient sister."

She backtracks to Piper's closed door. "Hey, it's time to eat, *now*!"

All is silent behind the door.

"Piper!" She knocks.

Still nothing.

Unsettling images storm her brain—the wild-eyed man in the street, the watcher on the roof, Lisa's warning about danger. She turns the knob slowly, bracing herself for . . .

Anything but the sight of her sister sitting cross-legged on the floor with a glass pipe in her mouth, earbuds in her ears, and a cloud of pungent smoke wafting around her.

"Hey! Don't just barge in here!" She pulls out one earbud, and loud music spills from it.

"I knocked. What are you doing?"

"Smoking some excellent weed. Want a hit?"

"No."

"Like you don't do it yourself."

"I don't."

"Oh, please. Don't act all innocent and prissy. I smelled it when I came home the other night, and I saw it in your room."

"That wasn't weed, it was a cigarette."

Piper rolls her eyes, pupils dilated and her expression lazily amused. "That was one funky cigarette, then, all crumbled and sitting in a bowl."

Oh. *That* night. Saturday, when Mom and Dad went out, and Stacey had the house to herself.

But she's not about to tell her sister that what she'd seen wasn't a cigarette or weed. "You're not supposed to be in my room, Piper."

"What a coincidence. You're not supposed to be in mine."

"Whatever. It's time for dinner."

She turns and heads downstairs, deliberately leaving the bedroom door ajar. Her sister slams it after her with a curse.

"I'll tell Dad you're not coming," she calls over her shoulder.

She descends the stairs, glancing at the Williams family portrait.

On Saturday evening, she'd stood here holding a bowl of burning sage leaves and addressed the dead girl directly.

"You need to go. Please. You don't belong here anymore."

She'd gone through the house saying it over and over, to Gertrude Williams and her parents, to the Toska family. Even to the cannonball enshrined in the hallway, in case it was attracting the spirit of a dead Revolutionary War soldier.

As she performed the ritual, she wasn't convinced of paranormal dark energy, and she'd perceived no immediate difference afterward.

Ever since, though, things have been better. She hasn't spotted the watcher since that day on the subway, so maybe he really was a ghost, and she'd banished him.

Overhead, she hears Piper's door creak open.

Her sister appears at the top of the stairs, spots her, and mutters, "Loser."

That hurts.

It shouldn't. She should be used to it. When they weren't being indifferent to each other, they'd bickered their way through the last few years back at home in California. But here, it's been different. Moving away from everything and everyone familiar had forged a bond she hadn't even realized was there.

She remembers how frightened Piper had been the night they'd found out about the murders. Stacey, too, had been scared, but she'd reassured her sister, as if she knew anything about anything.

Piper thought she did.

Stacey reads everything . . . she loves true crime, she hears her saying—bragging, almost—to Courtney and Lennon.

She looks up at her sister now and receives a steely glare in return.

"Don't worry," Stacey whispers. "I'm not telling them."

Piper's blond eyebrows rise but she says nothing, following Stacey down the stairs and into the kitchen.

Dad is at the counter, the sleeves of his dress shirt rolled up as he tosses a salad.

Mom is taking something out of the oven. "Hurry and set the table, please, guys. This is ready."

"Good, I'm starved!" Piper reverts to her usual sunny self as she opens a cabinet and takes out a stack of plates. "It smells great!"

"What is it?" Stacey asks.

"Herb roasted chicken and potatoes . . . sort of."

"*Sort of?*" they echo in unison.

Piper giggles and says, "Jinx," just like when they were little.

Stacey's grin fades when Mom goes on, "I never make herb chicken without sage, but something got into the garden and chomped the entire plant. Just that one. It's the craziest thing."

Stacey takes her time counting four knives and four forks from the silverware drawer, wondering if her mother's comment is a pointed message that she knows exactly what happened to the sage.

Had she sniffed it in the air somehow? Not likely. Saturday evening had been warm and breezy, with all the windows open, and Mom and Dad got home hours later.

Maybe Lennon had mentioned Lisa's suggestion to his moms, and they'd told hers? But Stacey hadn't even told him she'd actually gone through with it, even though she met him right afterward for the open mic night.

Anyway, he's adamant now that Lisa is a fraud. His about-face seems to have nothing to do with what she'd said about warding off dark energy and everything to do with the warnings about someone close to her.

"I feel like she was telling you not to trust *me*," he told Stacey.

"Why? It could be anyone. It's probably *everyone*."

"What do you mean?"

"Just . . . you know. Everyone has secrets."

"I don't. Not from you."

She forced a smile. "Well, great. Then it's everyone *but* you."

"Do you?"

"Do I what?"

"Do you have secrets from me?"

"No," she lied.

Dad and Piper do most of the talking over dinner. That's not unusual.

Mom pokes at her food, lost in thought. Stacey wonders whether she's thinking about the sage, but doubts it. Her mother is often preoccupied lately. So, to be fair, is she.

"How about you, Stacey?"

"What?" She looks up to see her father, fork poised, wearing an expectant look.

"Do you have a ton of homework to do tonight, too?"

"Oh . . . not really. I'm just working on my college essay."

"I thought you finished that a while ago."

The one she'd written in California now feels trite and obsolete. She's doing a new one using the same topic, "overcoming obstacles."

Far more difficult, daunting obstacles.

She shrugs. "If I'm applying to an Ivy League school, it needs to be perfect."

Mom looks up from her plate. "There's no such thing as perfection, Stacey. Don't make yourself crazy."

Seriously? This, from a picture-perfect, surgically altered woman?

"Did you decide, then, on early decision for Columbia?" Dad asks, looking hopeful.

"Early decision somewhere. I'm just not sure which school."

"But an Ivy."

"Yes. Definitely an Ivy."

"I'm going to do an Ivy, too," Piper says. "Whichever ones in California have the best sororities."

Stacey bites back a smile. "They're all in the Northeast."

"Oh. Then I'm not doing an Ivy."

"I thought you love living here, Pipe," Dad says.

"I do, just not for, like, *forever*. It's fine for a year, but I miss my friends and my room and the pool and the beach and my friends . . ."

"You already said your friends."

"Did I? Oops. I guess I miss them twice as much." She gives a loopy laugh before shoveling in more potatoes.

Dad peers at her like he's noticing her bigger-than-usual blue eyes and appetite.

"All I know is that when it's time to go home, I'll be ready," Piper goes on around a mouthful. "Hey, can I have Stacey's car?"

"What? No, you can't have my car!"

"Why not? It's just sitting in the driveway back home. You're not even coming back with us in August because you'll have to go right to college from here," Piper reminds her, piling more potatoes onto her plate.

"Well, you're too young to drive, and I'll probably need it at school."

"Not if you go to Columbia," Dad points out. "Or Harvard. Boston has a great public transportation system, too."

"I'm not applying to Harvard."

"Why not?" Piper asks. "That's where Lennon's going."

"Harvard doesn't offer early decision, and Lennon's still not sure where he's going. Princeton has a better music program. But his grades might not get him into an Ivy anyway."

"Courtney says he's supersmart."

"He is, but . . ." Why, Stacey wonders, are they even talking about him? Or about her, for that matter? Why can't Dad and Piper go back to chatting amongst themselves, and leave her out of it?

She looks at her mother. No longer pretending to eat, Mom is staring into space, wearing a troubled, faraway expression.

Maybe she's just homesick for California. Unlike Dad, who grew up in Kansas and spent part of his college career in New York City, Mom has never lived anywhere but LA.

Or maybe she's still thinking about the sage plant.

Or maybe . . .

Stacey thinks of Jack in *The Shining*, possessed by evil spirits or his own demons, slowly going mad in a place where a family was murdered.

She sets down her fork and asks to be excused.

"In a minute," Dad says. "I think we should plan something fun for this Saturday night. Maybe a nice dinner and a Broadway show? Andrew said Marla might be able to score us tickets to *Hamilton*."

"Yes!" Piper shouts.

"I, uh, already have plans with Lennon," Stacey says. If she doesn't see him the night before, she'll definitely have to—*want* to—see him Saturday.

Piper rolls her dilated eyes. "Geez! You guys are together all the time. Can't you take a freaking break for one night?"

"I'm not even seeing him on Friday because a couple of

girls from school invited me to—you know what? It's none of your business. Can I *please* be excused?"

"What are you doing Friday, Stace?" Mom asks.

"These girls I know invited me to see a movie. I don't have to go, but—"

"No, you should. And we can see the show another time, right, Keith?"

Piper starts to protest, but Dad cuts her off.

"Actually, Pipe, Marla probably can't get the tickets on such short notice anyway. I'll see what I can do for *next* weekend, okay?"

"Sure. Fine."

They clear the table quickly, and head upstairs.

Pausing at the door to her room, Piper turns back. "Stace? Thanks for not saying anything to them about . . . you know. And I'm glad you made new friends at school. That's really good for you."

"Yeah. Just . . . be careful, okay?"

"What do you mean?"

She hesitates. "I don't know. Forget it. Good night."

She closes the door to her own room behind her and opens her laptop again, ready to pick up where she left off. But first, she goes to the window and peeks out, just to be sure . . .

Nope. Still no Peeping Tom.

Most likely he was never there, or if he was, he's moved on. Either way, she's finally starting to breathe a little easier. And she really is looking forward to Friday night.

Not, however, to telling Lennon she's made plans that don't involve him.

Jacob

B aba!"

The voice that slips into Jacob's sleep is his own. He's a child again, calling out to his father . . .

"Baba!"

A sharp poke on his arm yanks him back to reality. He opens his eyes to see his younger son standing over the bed in pajamas. His blond hair spikes straight up over round blue eyes in a wide face. He looks just like Emina, and she's turned him into a little sissy. Jacob does his best to undo the damage, for the boy's own good.

"I miss Mama. When is she coming back?"

It's been nearly a week since Emina's father was rushed to the hospital in an ambulance. He'd had a stroke. Not a massive one, and he's on the mend, but she's been staying with her mother ever since, going back and forth to his bedside.

It had been Jacob's idea, a reprieve from her constant, irritating presence. He'd misjudged how hard it would be to deal with the boys and the household on top of his own work schedule, but it's been worthwhile. He's so tired, and so content to have the bed to himself for a change, that he's been sleeping soundly for the first time in years.

No nightmares about Anna. Not enough waking hours to wonder about her, or follow her around the city.

That's about to change.

"Go back to bed," he orders his son.

"But I miss Mama!"

"She'll be home tomorrow! Now go to bed!"

The boy's face crumples and tears fill his eyes. "You're mean! You're so mean to me!"

"You don't know what mean is," Jacob growls, and turns away, toward the wall. After a moment, he hears his son retreat, back down the hall to his room.

Mean.

As he waits for sleep to overtake him again, he thinks of his own father, and an ominous conversation in the earliest hours of 1994.

Jacob had returned to New York for Christmas when his paternal grandmother passed away. Her husband might have taken the unexpected death in stride, comforted that she'd gone peacefully in her sleep, but her son did not. Baba had always been close to his mother, and she'd doted on him.

Jacob was accustomed to the women in the family wailing at funerals, but his father was inconsolable, howling and leaning so far into the open grave that Jacob half expected him to dive in after the coffin.

"You gave me everything, Nënë!" he cried. "I owe you my life."

Jacob was unnerved, witnessing the blatant anguish of a man who'd always been stoic and in control. In the days that followed, his father's mood swung between depression and fury. He said little, and Jacob gave him a wide berth.

Anna, too, was home with her family on her semester break. They spent as much time together as they could.

She was different here than she had been at school. Troubled by her mother's decline in her absence, Anna told Jacob her mother was begging her not to go back in January.

"You deserve to live your own life. You don't have to be a prisoner in your parents' house. They can't stop you if you want to leave. You're an adult now," he reminded her.

They'd celebrated her eighteenth birthday together in early October, sharing their first kiss beneath a full harvest moon and falling leaves.

"Zemra ime," he'd whispered, staring into her eyes.

"What does that mean?"

"'Heart of mine.' It's what you are. It's what you will always be."

They'd welcomed the New Year with a kiss, too. No moon, no leaves, and they were indoors this time, at a Manhattan restaurant where he knew he'd never run into anyone from the neighborhood.

Just before dawn on New Year's Day, he let himself into the house, assuming his parents were in bed. Still giddy from a romantic, champagne-fueled evening with Anna, he walked into the kitchen to get a glass of water, turned on the light, and cried out.

His father was there, alone in the dark.

"Happy New Year, Baba."

No reply, not even a glance, from the man who sat with his hands clasped on the table before him. His black eyes were shadowed in dark circles, thick black hair gone gray in a week's time.

"Did you just get up, or are you still up?" A sniff of the air and a glance at the stovetop answered the question when his father did not. There was no hint of the strong coffee Baba set to boil first thing every day, nor of his morning smoke. His cigarettes and lighter bulged in the chest pocket of the dress shirt he'd had on yesterday.

At last, he cleared his throat and looked up. "Where were you all night, Granit?"

"Out. It was New Year's Eve."

"I know what night it was. Who were you with?"

"A girl."

"Always a girl. Which girl?"

"You don't know her."

"Oh, but I do."

The words sobered Jacob like a bucket of ice water. He'd been told to keep Anna under surveillance, but clearly, someone was doing the same to him. He forced himself to meet Baba's eyes. How much did he know?

"I trusted you. I believed you were capable of doing what we asked of you."

"I *am* capable!" Jacob protested. "I did exactly as you asked."

"Did you?"

"You said to keep an eye on her. You said to get to know her. Get close to her. Find out what I could about her family."

"And report back to me. You've told me nothing."

"Because she's told me nothing."

"She's told you nothing? Hours and hours, days and days of conversations, of eating and dancing and kissing . . . and she's told you nothing?"

"She doesn't like to talk about her family! She hates them."

"She hates her own mother?"

Seeing the dangerous gleam in Baba's eye, Jacob explained, "It's like she's a prisoner in her own house. In her own body. And her mother . . . there's something wrong with her. She's done cruel, terrible things . . ."

He closed his mouth and shook his head. It felt like a betrayal, repeating the words Anna herself had uttered to him just hours earlier.

"So she does share with you. And what do you tell her in return, about your own father?"

"Nothing at all. Don't worry, Baba. I protect you."

"And what about her? Do you protect her?"

He gave the answer he knew his father expected. "Of course not. She's nothing to me."

"I hope that isn't a lie, my son. If it is, it will soon come to light, and there will be no one to protect you. Not your mother, and not me. In this family, disloyalty carries terrible consequences."

Jacob knew his father spoke not just of the family to which they were connected by blood, but of the clandestine network bound by *besë*.

Even in that moment, weary, bleary with champagne, he'd sensed that he'd reached a pivotal moment in his relationship with Baba; that much was weighing on whatever he said next. But did he grasp that it would determine the direction of his future?

Later, in prison, he endlessly replayed the conversation and the events that unfolded in the weeks that followed. If only he could go back and choose a different response, a different path.

But when he looked at his father's face, branded in the sorrow of that mournful week, Jacob couldn't bear to hurt him further.

"I owe you everything, Baba. I owe you my whole life," he said. "I could never be disloyal to you."

And so his fate was sealed, as was Anna's.

Midway through January, his father announced that Jacob had been assigned the task of executing not just the man now known as Stanley Toska, whose disloyalty had destroyed so much business and so many lives in that distant branch of the organization, but also his wife, and . . .

Anna. Oh, Anna.

Jacob had known it was inevitable, yet hearing the words rendered him speechless. He listened as his father described what he was expected to do, and how, and when.

"Do you understand, Granit?"

At last he found his voice, and it warbled like an injured puppy. "But . . . she didn't harm anyone. She's just a girl. Why her? Why her mother? Why not just the man who betrayed us? Why do they want me to do this?"

Something flashed in his father's expression, and Jacob knew, then. He knew that the order hadn't come from some higher force that Baba couldn't repudiate. It had come from Baba himself, meant to test Jacob's loyalty, like a crude and brutal street gang initiation.

"Do you understand, Granit? Do you?"

This time, Jacob nodded, and he kept his voice steady, and he held that black, black gaze. "Yes, Baba. I understand perfectly."

Part
Five

Stacey

Early October brings the radiant autumn Stacey has anticipated ever since her parents said they were moving to the Northeast. On this Saturday afternoon in the park, a canopy of red and orange boughs blaze fire in the sky and every breeze showers leaves like sparks around the bench where she sits with Lennon.

"*Our* bench," he calls it whenever he texts her about going to the park.

They're unwrapping the sandwiches they'd bought at *their* deli on Edgemont.

He's romantic. It's sweet.

"Look at this. It's gorgeous." She sighs contentedly and leans back, biting into her toasted salt bagel.

"Yeah, they don't skimp on the lox."

She laughs. "I mean the park today! I feel like we're in Paris."

"I've never been to Paris."

"Neither have I."

"Then how do you know this is what it's like?"

"Everyone knows it's beautiful—the City of Light. Brooklyn is beautiful, too. And glowing." She gestures at the luminous foliage and the fountain that shimmers in golden sunshine.

"Yeah, well . . . *'Part of you died each year when the leaves fell from the trees . . .'*"

"What?"

"Haven't you ever read Hemingway?"

"Of course I have."

"Well, that's from *A Moveable Feast*," he says, like he can't believe she didn't know that random quote.

She takes another bite of the bagel that had been perfect a moment before. Now the kosher salt topping burns the inside of her upper lip, and the smoked salmon slimes its way down her throat, oozing too much cream cheese.

This is how things go with Lennon. One minute, it's all great, and the next . . .

"You should read it," he says, "if you want to read about Paris."

"I didn't say I wanted to read about Paris."

"You said you want to go there."

"I didn't say that, either."

Maybe this happens in every relationship. Even her parents, who seem so perfectly suited, have had their ups and downs lately.

Last night, she'd overheard them arguing about Thanksgiving next month. Dad's family is coming from Kansas, and Mom isn't thrilled about it.

"You always said you wished they would visit us, Nora. Now that they are, why are you so—"

"I never said I *wished* they'd visit. I just commented they never did."

"Well, they don't like LA."

"How do they know they like New York if they've never been here?"

The conversation had sounded an awful lot like the one Stacey's having right now with Lennon.

It isn't really about Paris. It's about him putting words into her mouth. About him not listening to her.

She rewraps the bagel in foil and shoves it back into the deli bag.

"What's going on?" he asks, noticing, because he notices everything. Every damned thing, and she's sick of it. "I thought you were famished."

"I never said that."

"Yeah, you did, when we were on our way to the deli."

"I didn't say *famished*. Maybe I said I was hungry, but—"

"No." He's shaking his head. "You said famished. I remember."

"Well, I remember, too."

She doesn't, really. It had been a trite conversation, mostly about the song he'd learned for his guitar lesson later today, and the movie she'd seen the night before with her lunch table friends. He'd interrupted that to talk about the amazing sushi dinner he'd had while she was at the movie.

"We'll go next week," he said.

"Sure, on Saturday."

"The all-you-can-eat special is on Fridays."

"That's okay. How much raw fish can a person eat?" she asked, and laughed.

He didn't. "Why can't you go on Friday?"

"I go to the movies on Fridays. It's, like, a thing. Oh,

hey," she added, seeing his expression, "we need to remember to grab napkins from the deli because remember what happened the other day, when we forgot?"

They'd licked their fingers and then rinsed their hands in the fountain, playfully flicking water at each other as a pair of old ladies scowled at them.

Today, they have napkins. She wipes her hands and asks Lennon if she can bum a smoke.

"Did you forget yours?"

"Yeah," she lies.

The truth is, she'd flushed her last pack down the toilet a few days ago, after Rebecca shared some ugly gossip about a girl in their social studies class.

"I mean, it's not surprising that she has an STD," she hissed as they walked down the hall after class. "She's always been disgusting."

"Disgusting how?"

"You know . . . she shoplifts. And she *smokes*."

"Well, I mean . . . a lot of people do."

"Not smart, classy ones."

The words, and Rebecca's decisive tone, resonated with Stacey. She'd decided she'd better quit the habit before she got addicted, and discovered it was already too late.

Summoning the same willpower that had allowed her to lose so much weight this year, she's managed to get through the last few days without smoking.

So much for that.

Lennon holds out his pack and she puts a cigarette between her lips, avoiding his gaze as he flicks a lighter for her.

"Thanks," she murmurs, inhaling and thinking about

cancer and lung disease and how hard it's been to figure out college while fighting off nicotine cravings.

"What have you been thinking about early decision?" Lennon asks, and for an illogical moment, she wonders if he's read her mind.

Maybe there's an app for that. Virtual Kreskin.

She clears her throat. "So, yeah, what have I been thinking about early decision? I've been thinking that I'm doing it."

"I know, but Thursday, you said you were going to narrow down your list and figure out which schools are—"

"Brown." Until it comes out of her mouth, she hadn't realized she'd made up her mind.

"Brown?" he echoes, like she just announced she's joining the circus.

"Right. That's it. They have an amazing literary arts program."

"I thought you didn't know what you wanted to major in."

"I didn't."

"But now you do?"

"Right."

"So, like, what? You just decided this minute? Brown, and literary arts?"

"No! I've been leaning in that direction."

"Really? When were you going to tell *me*?"

She scowls, taking a deep drag, saying nothing, and not just because her lungs hurt.

Lennon shoves his unfinished bagel into the bag, crumples it, and throws it at a nearby trash can. It's full, and the bag ricochets out. He leaves it lying there among the fallen leaves.

"Lost my appetite," he says, as if she asked what's wrong. Which she didn't because she knows damned well. And she knows, as they sit there in silence, that he's waiting for her to elaborate on the college thing.

Whatever. Let him ask.

He broods. And then he does. "What happened to Columbia?"

"Still there, last I heard."

"Funny."

She shrugs. "I never said I was going to Columbia."

"They have a solid literary arts program, too. And you're a legacy."

"My dad didn't actually *graduate* from there. Anyway, *you're* the one who wants to go to Columbia. Or NYU, Fordham . . ."

"Other places, too."

"You just said the other day that you can't imagine living anywhere other than New York."

"You said the same thing."

"I don't think I did."

"Well, you're wrong," he says flatly.

"I'm wrong about where I want to live? You know better than I do?"

"I'm not talking about what you want, I'm talking about what you said."

"No, Lennon, I think you're talking about what you *heard*. Which is probably whatever you wanted to hear, and not what I actually said!"

"Geez, calm down. Maybe you're right. You don't have to get all—"

"I *am* right."

"*Okay*. Maybe I'll miss you if you're far away. Maybe that's all I'm trying to say."

She says nothing, just sucks toxic smoke into her lungs, thinking about how it's his fault that she ever even started this filthy habit, and how hard it is to quit because it does calm her nerves. There's comfort in the ritual and rhythm of it; in having something to do in difficult moments; in the way it forces you to *breathe*, even if what you're breathing is carcinogenic smoke.

Stupid, she knows. So stupid. But stress can make you forget how to even breathe. Moving across the country, adjusting to an urban lifestyle, her first boyfriend, a new school, a different curriculum, making friends—not to mention worrying about 104 Glover's bloody history and the escaped killer stalking her.

Now that that's all in the past, she has to figure out where she wants to go to college, and whether she'll be admitted, and how to fill out the common app and tweak her essay . . .

Planning for the future is supposed to be exciting, full of promise. Yet she's sick of talking about it, sick of thinking about it.

Or maybe she's just sick of the *present*.

Sick of Lennon.

She shakes her head, staring at the discarded deli bag in the grass.

"What?" he asks.

"So you just . . . what? Throw your garbage on the ground for someone else to pick up?"

"*No*, I don't just throw my garbage on the ground."

"Well, you did."

"Who said I'm not going to pick it up?"

"It doesn't seem like you are."

"I am."

"When?"

She's itching to get up, grab the stupid bag, throw it into the can, and walk away. But she's not going to clean up after him like he's a spoiled emperor.

"Fine." He stalks over to the bag, picks it up, and thrusts it into the can, knocking stuff off the top in the process.

He turns back and catches her pointed stare at the ground, now littered with other people's trash. Growling something unintelligible, he picks it all up and tosses it before stalking back to the bench.

"Okay? Are you happy now?"

She considers the question.

Then she stands and shakes her head. "No. I'm not happy. Not at all. Not with you."

Jacob

For weeks, Jacob has stayed away from Anna.

At first, it was out of necessity, in Emina's absence after her father's stroke. On the day she was due home, the old man was stricken again. He lingered for a few days before passing away.

Jacob had to pack up the boys and spend several days at the wake and funeral, and when he returned, he was forced to work long hours to catch up on all the jobs he'd postponed.

It was for the best—the frenzied ordeal had made it impossible for him to dwell on Anna, attempt to see her, or even dream about her in his deep, exhausted sleep. Having broken the pattern at last, he might have been able to stay away indefinitely, or even for good.

But last night, she'd visited him in a dream.

"She's crazy, Jacob," she told him, weeping.

She was talking about her mother, saying all the things she'd confessed to him that January after his father had assigned him the task of executing Anna and her family.

In life, as in the dream, Anna told him about her mother's belief that 104 Glover had been cursed by the family whose portrait hung on the stair wall. Her mother was obsessed with their tragic story. Eventually, she was delusional, convinced that she was Margaret Williams, and Anna was Gertrude.

"The other day, I was about to walk down the stairs and I heard something behind me and it was my mother, Jacob. She barely gets out of bed most days, but she snuck up and she looked like she was about to push me down the steps. I'm afraid she's trying to kill me. I have to get out of that house. I don't trust her. I don't trust anyone, except you."

Those words drenched him in a cold sweat.

No, Anna. You can't trust me, either. You can't trust anyone . . .

"Kiss me, Jacob," she whispered in the dream, glowing in moonlight, snow falling all around them. *"Zemra ime."*

"'Heart of mine.' You're speaking my language."

"Yes. Please kiss me. It's my birthday."

"No, your birthday is October."

"It's my birthday," she repeated, and the fat white snow-flakes became golden autumn leaves, and the dream morphed into reality. "It's my birthday."

And so it is.

Today is Anna's birthday.

He made his way back to 104 Glover this morning. Just this once, he promised himself. If it didn't happen today—if he didn't find her there, or find her alone at last—he would leave and never return.

She was there, though. And when she emerged, the famil-iar young man was waiting.

Jacob trailed them at a distance along Edgemont to a deli and then the park, just as he used to follow Anna so long ago.

Now he lounges on a bench on the opposite side of the fountain. In his mind's eye, he can still see Anna lost in a book on a hot summer day, or deep in conversation with her friend Ellie. He sees Anna as she'd been, before college liberated her from shapeless clothing, slumped posture, bulky frame.

And he sees Ellie, in flannel and combat boots, smoking cigarettes and drinking beer in a brown paper bag.

On the day Anna was destined to die, his father warned him that if he was too weak to carry out his assignment, someone else would. Either way, she'd be lost to him, Baba said. But if he proved his loyalty to the family, they'd stand by him.

"Choose wisely, Granit. I'm watching. We're all watching."

Jacob made his choice, and he crept into the house to warn Anna. To save her. To take her away.

He was too late.

Days later, he returned home to confront his father. They were all there—Baba, the uncles, the cousins . . .

All there, welcoming him to the fold, telling him he'd passed their test of loyalty. Baba beamed with pride.

If they hadn't carried out the execution, believing he'd failed them . . . then who had?

The answer was clear.

Ellie.

Anna had told him Ellie was shacking up with the low-life dealer who'd introduced her to crack cocaine and now wanted to be her pimp.

"She's desperate, Jacob. I'm afraid for her. She's at the point where she'll do anything for a fix."

Anything . . .

Anna shouldn't have been afraid *for* her. She should have

been afraid *of* her. Afraid that she'd use the hidden key into 104 Glover to rob the Toskas. Afraid that she'd kill them in their sleep.

Enraged, raw, he searched for Ellie in the days, weeks, months that followed. He was going to take her life because she'd stolen Anna's. But she'd disappeared.

Jacob immersed himself in the family business until the feds took them all down, and it was over. Everyone he'd ever known, ever loved, was gone . . .

Until Anna came back.

Sitting on the bench, he pretends to nap, but his eyes are open behind his sunglasses. He sees her here, now, alive. Sees her with the stranger, smiling, eating, talking. Sees her scowling, smoking, arguing. Sees her stand, and walk away, alone.

The young man shouts after her, then he, too, gets to his feet. But he doesn't go after her. He heads in the opposite direction, toward Jacob.

Jacob holds his breath, terrified that he knows, somehow . . .

But then he storms on past.

Now is Jacob's chance. Anna is finally alone. He hurries after her. But as he passes the spot where she'd been sitting, something on the grass beneath the bench catches his eye. He halts in his tracks, staring in disbelief, and then bends to scoop it up.

Nora

With an unobstructed view of Manhattan's iconic cityscape, the urban farm sits high atop a defunct Brooklyn warehouse, built so close to the East River's edge that if you jumped from the roof, you'd land in the water. The sprawling green space is sectioned off into grids and planted with a vast array of crops, many of which have finished producing for the season.

This morning when she'd arrived for her first volunteer shift, Nora had felt like she'd walked into a spectacular party as the band was playing the last song. But it turned out there's plenty to do here even with harvest winding down.

Ricardo Diaz, a middle-aged man with a quick smile and huge heart, is grateful for the help.

"Finally, someone who knows how to tell a ripe squash from one that needs a little more time on the vine," he comments, surveying the bushels she'd filled this afternoon. "Do you know how many times I've told my volunteers to leave the shiny ones alone?"

"Wait, I thought we were *supposed* to pick the shiny ones!" Jules calls, scrubbing her hands at the slop sink.

Ricardo rolls his eyes. "Now you know why I assigned you to manure duty today, *tarada*."

"Something tells me *tarada* doesn't mean 'genius' in Spanish, Ricardo," she shoots back, and he chuckles.

Pulling on her jacket, Nora sees clouds the color of wet cement rolling in on a stiff west wind. "Looks like you won't need to water overnight, Ricardo."

"No, there's a storm coming. Get home safely, *amiga*. See you on Tuesday morning. Oh, if you get here before I do, let yourself in and come right up. The door lock code is 1–2–4–4."

"1–2–4–4," Nora repeats, committing it to memory. "1–2–4–4."

"Don't worry, I've got the same shift. We can come together," Jules tells her. "I'm so glad you liked it enough to come back."

"I loved it. Thanks so much for suggesting that I get involved."

"You mean, for driving you crazy and pushing you into something you really didn't want to do?"

"No, I wanted to do it. I just wasn't sure I was ready to commit."

"Funny, that's exactly what Heather said the first time I proposed. But I can be very persuasive."

Nora laughs. "Understatement of the year. But in this case, I'm glad you are."

If Jules hadn't badgered her about meeting Ricardo this week and signing up for today's shift, she'd be at home, brooding.

"Any other day, that would be okay," Teddy told her on

the phone yesterday. "But not tomorrow. You'll only dwell on things."

"It's not like I'm going to forget what day it is, though, no matter what I do."

"No, but you need to get out of that house."

Not the house. *That* house.

Teddy was right, as usual. Maybe about a lot of things.

Nora and Jules step into the slow-moving freight elevator that will transport them down to the street level.

As the doors close, Jules's phone vibrates. She looks at it and sighs.

"Everything okay?" Nora asks.

"Unknown caller. It must be spam. I'm on more telemarketing lists . . ." She puts it back into her pocket without answering it.

They emerge in an industrial neighborhood that used to be "no-man's-land," according to Jules. Now the warehouses have been converted to restaurants, clubs, shops, and residential lofts. There are no subway stops in the area, so they walk along looking for a cab. The streets are thick with hipsters, graffiti murals, and marijuana smoke.

"Want to stop off and get a happy hour drink?" Jules asks, gesturing at a crowded bar called Lovely 'Ritas, according to a lime-green neon sign shaped like a margarita glass.

"Dressed like this?" Nora's wearing tattered jeans and Jules has on denim overalls.

"Look at this crowd. We fit right in."

"Maybe, if we were twenty years younger. We could be their mothers. Oh, there's a cab. Taxi!" Nora steps to the curb and flags it down before Jules can protest.

The last thing she needs right now is cocktails and conversation. She'd dutifully gotten herself out of *that* house, but now she can't wait to get back.

Marla had come through with a pair of coveted orchestra seats to *Hamilton* for tonight. Keith and Piper should be gone by now.

"Anyway, speaking of our kids . . ." Jules says as they settle into the back seat, and the cab carries them toward Glover Street.

"Were we?"

"You mentioned being mothers, and that reminded me . . . is everything okay with Stacey?"

"What do you mean by okay?"

"Heather took Lennon out to dinner last night at his favorite sushi place to cheer him up."

"Why did he need cheering up?" The moment the question leaves her mouth, Nora is sorry she asked.

"Because Stacey blew him off."

"Last night? She had plans with her friends."

"Well, do you know if she—"

"I have no idea what's going on with them, Jules, and even if I did, I'm really not comfortable talking about it."

"I just figured I'd ask. I hope they're not headed for a bad breakup, like his last one."

Jules had mentioned it once before, but that was when Nora had no personal stake in her son's romantic mishaps.

Now she asks what happened there. "You said they weren't together long, right?"

"A few months, but at that age, well, you know how it goes. He was devastated when she dumped him."

"Why did she?"

"She needed space—code for 'I'm cheating on you,' right?"

"Not necessarily. Some people don't like to feel . . ."

"Loved?"

"Smothered."

Jules smirks. "Yeah, that was exactly the word she used. But he's insecure, deep down inside. And with relationships, he tries so hard, and he falls so hard, and sometimes I wonder if he's too intense for his own good, or anyone else's. I wonder if he smothers people. Why? Did Stacey say something about that?"

"No."

"Good." A pause, and then, "What *has* she said? Never mind, sorry, I know you don't want to talk about this. It's just . . . I worry about my kid. I don't think he'll survive another heartbreak. Anyway, to change the subject . . . Heather and I were thinking of checking out that new Creole fusion place on the boulevard, if you and Keith want to join us?"

"Oh . . . we can't tonight. He took Piper to see *Hamilton*."

"Then why don't you and Stacey come with us? I'm sure Lennon would want to—"

"Thanks, Jules, but I can't make plans for Stacey, and I have a mountain of clean laundry to fold."

"Laundry? Really? On a Saturday night?"

"Yes. And I'm really wiped out from working on the farm all day. All I want to do is take a hot bath and go to bed early."

She'd said almost the same thing to Keith last night, when he had second thoughts about going to the show without her.

"Maybe I should just give Piper both tickets, and she can go with a friend instead."

"I'll be exhausted by the time I get home," Nora had said. "Anyway, you promised her dinner, and we don't want her running around the city at night on her own."

And she wouldn't mind having the house to herself for a change . . . especially tonight.

But of course, Keith has no idea of the date's significance.

Happy birthday, Anna.

Stacey

fter leaving Lennon in the park, Stacey was relieved
that he didn't chase her down to continue the argument, or worse yet, to apologize. She wasn't ready to
forgive him. Maybe she never will be.

Back home, the house was quiet. Kato was dozing, Dad
and Piper were on their way to dinner, and Mom wasn't yet
back from the urban farm. Stacey closed herself into her
room to have a good cry, but she was too angry for tears.
After a while, the anger gave way to numbness and she fell
asleep.

Now she awakens to a dark room and steady rain patter-
ing on the roof. She turns on the lamp, finds her phone, and
remembers she'd turned it off earlier to avoid the inevitable
barrage of texts from Lennon. As it powers up, she braces
herself for the onslaught.

But she finds only one message: **Meet me on our bench.**

He must have sent it earlier, before the weather turned.

But no, it came in a literal minute ago.

She starts typing a response, but thinks better of it. Does
she really want to engage after successfully extracting her-

self? She needs more time to process what happened, and figure out what she wants to do about it.

She notices three dots wobbling in the message window. He's typing on his end.

A single word appears.

Please.

She shakes her head. She'll just ignore it. Maybe go back to sleep.

She leans back, thinking about how nice it had been to escape—and how strange it is that he'd texted her as soon as she woke up, almost as if he'd sensed that she'd stirred back to consciousness.

She opens the Stealth Soldier app. Maybe there's something in the settings that alerted him when her phone powered back on.

But before she can check for that, she spies the blue pulsating heart that indicates Lennon's whereabouts.

It can't be right.

She returns to the text window.

Where are you? she types quickly, and presses Send.

A moment later, he responds, **Bench.**

"In the rain?" she mutters.

More dots. He's typing something else.

It's a heart emoji, followed by the words **of mine.**

She clicks back over to the tracking app.

The blue heart is located over a small rectangle that represents the shed behind the house next door.

She reaches over to turn off the lamp, plunging the room

into darkness. Another text dings the phone in her hand as she walks toward the window on shaky legs.

It says, **RU coming? Waiting 4 U.**

Her own breathing roars in her ears as she lifts the edge of the shade and peers out into the night.

A hooded man stands on the shed roof.

Lennon.

Nora

Nora's phone buzzes.

She'd turned on the alerts for Piper's social media posts, figuring it was only a matter of time before something popped up.

Sure enough, she's posted a selfie.

Intermission! Daddy and me! #Hamilton

They're in their theater seats, turned so that the curtained stage is behind them. Piper is wearing far too much makeup even for the velvet dress she has on, probably with Nora's most expensive and tallest pair of designer heels, conspicuously missing from her closet tonight.

They need to have a little talk about that, and other things. She suspects Piper's growing up too fast, maybe experimenting with things she shouldn't be. She needs more parental guidance than she's been getting lately.

Keith is in a black blazer and white open-collar shirt, his smile revealing perfect white teeth.

So handsome, her husband. It's one of the things that had drawn Nora to him when they met, though his looks weren't the only reason. She's not that shallow, despite the story she'd told Stacey about her old nose.

Yes, she'd had cosmetic rhinoplasty because every damned time she looked in the mirror, that nose anchored her not just to the injury she'd suffered, but to the person she used to be. Altering her physical appearance was her futile attempt at banishing the troubled young woman she'd once been.

Tonight, wearing a baggy old shirt of Keith's, with her colored contacts removed and her hair still damp from the bath, darker than blond . . .

That woman, no longer young, meets Nora's gaze in the bureau mirror.

"*Forget-me-not,*" she whispers, and Nora pivots away.

Keith and Piper won't be home for at least a couple of hours. Stacey is here, but she was sound asleep when Nora peeked into her room.

She sits on the bed with the metal box from the shed, heart hammering in time with the rain on the roof. She'd turned up the thermostat earlier. The old cast-iron radiators are hot to the touch, and she'd sat in a hot bath so long her skin shriveled, yet she shivers as she opens the box.

On top is the thick gold watch that had been wrapped around Stanley Toska's hairy wrist the first time she'd ever seen him. Gaudy, she'd thought. His eyes, though dutifully creased into a smile, were cruel.

She tosses the watch aside like a used tissue, takes out the photo album, and flips pages.

Two weeks; first Christmas; first tooth . . .

First birthday.

The photos, taken forty-four years ago today, have a reddish tint, like all photos from the 1970s. Frightened baby, gaping at a blazing candle on a cupcake. Gleeful baby drooling pink frosting in a high chair. Weary baby surrounded by crumpled wrapping paper.

In the background, a hi-fi console, a brown-and-orange afghan of crocheted granny squares, earth-toned kitchen appliances and vinyl wallpaper . . .

"Everyone had that kitchen," Nora had said the night Keith mentioned that Jules and Heather's retro décor reminded him of his childhood home.

Everyone.

She'd been caught off guard stepping into that room, nearly identical to the old one at 104 Glover Street. Same layout, same knotty pine cabinets, same black iron pulls, same Formica countertops. Everything the same, except for those monkey figurines.

All around the mulberry bush, the monkey chased the weasel . . .

A fragmented image darts into her mind and then back into the shadows. This time, it hovers tantalizingly close. She closes her eyes, straining to grasp it, straining, straining . . .

A shrill scream explodes in the night, and the memory splinters like glass.

Stacey

S tacey! Are you all right?"

Backing into the hallway, clutching her phone, she turns to see her mother rushing out of the master bedroom.

"What happened? Why did you scream?"

"Because he's . . . watching me."

"What? Who—"

"Lennon." She points to her window. "Out there. On the shed roof."

Mom strides past her into the darkened bedroom, lifts the shade, and looks out.

"I don't see anything."

"He's right . . ." Stacey joins her at the window, pressing her forehead close to the rain-spattered pane.

The rooftop is empty.

"He was right there!"

"Okay." Mom's tone is as opaque as her expression.

"You don't believe me! I swear, he was just—"

"Okay! It's okay! If you say you saw him, then . . . you saw him."

Not *If you say you saw him, then he was there.*

Stacey clenches her jaw. "I am *not* crazy!"

"Stacey, no one said—"

"*You* said it. I heard you."

"What are you talking about?"

"Back home, you said I needed a psychiatrist because of my mood swings and my . . . quirky habits!"

She sees the light dawn in Mom's eyes.

With her blue contacts removed, they're a muddy shade of brown, just like Stacey's. In this moment, *she* looks almost like Stacey—like her worst self, tired, uncertain, clothes baggy and hair straggly. Under different circumstances, Stacey might take perverse pleasure in this flawed, human side of the perfect Nora Howell. But right now, she needs her mother's usual self-assurance.

"I . . ." Mom takes a deep breath. "I'm so sorry. I . . . I don't even know what else to say about that. I just . . . you saw Lennon out there?"

"Yes. Out there, and *here*." She holds up her phone. "Look . . . I'll show you."

"You got a picture of him?"

"No." She reopens the Stealth Soldier app. "See that blue heart? That's him."

"You're . . . *tracking* him?"

Translation: *You really are crazy.*

"Only because he's tracking *me*, Mom! He's tracking everyone—his mothers, his sister . . . I thought it was just a thing he did, you know, to keep tabs on people, but . . . now I think there's something seriously wrong with him."

Her mother stares at her, then down at the phone.

The blue heart is inching up Edgemont Boulevard.

"He's on his way to the park. He just texted me to meet him at our bench, by the fountain."

"In this weather?"

"I know. It's crazy. But I haven't heard from him at all since we had this big fight earlier and now I feel like maybe he's . . ." She shakes her head and rakes a hand through her hair. "He's scaring me, Mom."

"Why? Did he threaten you?"

"No!"

"Then did he say anything specific that—"

"No!"

"Stacey . . ."

"He didn't. Not really, just . . . here, see for yourself."

Stacey shows her the texts. Her mother scans them for a long time—too long, like she's looking for something that isn't there, or maybe seeing something that Stacey missed.

"Mom?"

Her mother seems startled, as if she'd forgotten she was even there. She takes a deep breath, lets it out, and says, "Stacey, you're going to be okay. I promise. You've been so stressed lately. Why don't you take a long hot bath?"

"I don't take baths. That's your thing, and Piper's, not mine."

"I know, but you need to calm yourself down, Stacey. Get away from your phone, your room, the windows."

Her mother is right. And the bathroom door is the only one that locks. Maybe she'll feel safe, for a little while.

Five minutes later, she's standing naked over the tub, squirting Piper's fragrant bubble bath beneath the roaring stream of hot water.

She can't stop thinking about Lennon's text, asking her to meet him out there in the park at this hour, in this weather, when he knows . . .

Then it hits her, like a steel beam to the rib cage.

Heart pounding, she reaches over and turns off the tap. For a moment, she stares down at the sudsy inch of water in the tub, thinking it through. Can she possibly be mistaken?

She grabs her phone from the pocket of the sweatshirt she'd hung on the door hook, opens the screen, and double-checks.

No. She's right.

She throws the sweatshirt over her head, pulls on her jeans, and hurries back out into the hall.

"Mom!" she calls.

Her mother's bedroom door is closed. She hurries toward it.

"Hey, Mom, I just realized something . . ." She knocks.

No reply.

She opens the door. The room is dark.

"Mom?" she calls, hurrying down the hall, down the stairs. "Mom! Where are you?"

Nora

A cold rain washes over Nora as she hurries up the boulevard.

The strip isn't quite as busy as usual on this blustery night, but this is New York, and she's far from the only pedestrian on the street. Unlike her, many have umbrellas. But like her, many are wearing dark-colored hooded raincoats. She'd grabbed Stacey's black army parka from the coat tree by the door on her way out.

Twenty-five years ago, at the height of the crack epidemic, the park was crawling with junkies and predators at all hours. Venturing beyond the stone entrance pillars at night would have meant taking her life in her hands. Even by day, she was often uncomfortable here alone—and later, toward the end, even more uncomfortable when she wasn't.

She pushes on through the storm, conversation looping through her brain.

"I'm worried about you, Anna. You need to get out of that house. They're smothering you, and your mother . . . I know what she does to you."

"The same thing your boyfriend does to you, Ellie. He's a jerk. You need to get out, too."

"Where am I supposed to go? The street?"

"There are shelters."

"They're more dangerous than the street."

She rounds a bend in the path and spots the fountain, surrounded by empty benches.

All but one.

A man is there. Waiting. Watching. He, too, wears a dark, hooded coat.

He gets to his feet as she approaches, with an incredulous *"Anna . . . ?"*

She clears her throat. Finds her voice. "Hello, Jacob."

Stacey

Stacey searches the house and finds it silent and deserted.

If this were a true crime novel, her mother would have been abducted. But by whom? Lennon?

No way. He's intense, but he's not a criminal. Besides, when people are being dragged out into the night against their will, they don't take their keys and lock the door after them.

Which Mom did, Stacey confirms back in the front hall.

Noticing the empty coat tree, she's even more perplexed. Where could her mother have gone so urgently that she'd be caught dead in public looking as unkempt as she had a few minutes ago, *and* wearing Stacey's army coat with the ripped lining?

Kato is sleeping in the kitchen, so she didn't take him out.

She dials her mother's cell phone number. It rings in her ear and maybe—though it's hard to tell—somewhere in the house, too?

Yes.

She follows the sound up the stairs and opens her parents' bedroom door.

There's the phone, lit up on the bedside table.

If Mom left it behind, she definitely didn't go far.

Which means she is very likely down the street, telling Heather and Jules that their son's behavior is upsetting her daughter.

Crap.

Lennon hadn't even sent those messages. At least, not the final one, and probably not the others, either. Because Lennon, Stacey had remembered, is as much a stickler for proper grammar as she is, even in texts.

He would never have written **RU Coming? Waiting 4 U.**

No, he'd have written **Are you coming? I'm waiting for you.**

"What the hell is going on?" she mutters, sinking onto the edge of the bed and burying her face in her hands.

Between her splayed fingers, she notices something poking out from under the bed. She bends over and pulls out a flat metal box. It looks old and dusty, shedding dirt crumbs all over the floor where even dust bunnies aren't allowed to linger.

Stacey drops to her knees and lifts the lid.

The first thing she sees is a spiral-bound photo album. She lifts it out and is about to open it when something else catches her eye.

Money.

More money than she's ever seen in her life. Stacks and stacks of cash.

What in the world . . . ?

Her heart rages against her ribs.

Brass candlesticks. An old, embroidered strip of fabric. A man's gold watch. A woman's sapphire necklace. A key. A baby ring engraved with the initial *A.*

A manila envelope. Opening it, she finds a pair of black-and-white photocopied driver's licenses. Both are from Arizona, issued in the 1980s, to a couple named Stanislav and Magdalena Shehu.

She recognizes them from the newspaper archive photos she'd seen about the triple homicide.

Stanley and Lena Toska.

Pulse racing, Stacey seizes the photo album and opens it.

A chubby baby smiles back at her. She has black curls, enormous eyes fringed with thick lashes, and a rosebud mouth. She's familiar. So familiar that Stacey feels as though someone is standing on her chest, squeezing the air out of her lungs. The baby looks familiar, because . . .

That's me.

Jacob

Jacob gapes at the woman standing before him in the relentless downpour. He can't see her face and she's cloaked in black like a specter. But the moment he hears the familiar cadence of his name on her lips, he confirms that it's her.

She's panting as if she's been running.

If she's breathing, then she must be alive.

So it's true, then. He's not crazy. She really has moved back into her house.

But . . .

But he *must* be crazy because she can't be alive because she's dead.

He saw her lying in a blood-spattered room with a gaping hole ripped in the back of her head, and even if someone could survive that, Anna hadn't, because . . .

Because he'd seen her corpse and he'd seen her body carried out of the house and he'd seen them burying her, and he'd read police reports and morgue reports . . .

What the hell? What the hell is going on?

Anna can't be alive.

Yet she isn't dead.

Jacob must be crazy.

Yet he isn't crazy.

He steps toward her.

She steps back.

"Wait!" he says. "I . . . I want you to know . . . I wanted to take you away, get you out of there. I wanted to warn you that you were in danger. That my father, my family, wanted me to—"

"I *know*."

Then, in a voice that's soft, hoarse, deeper than he remembers, she utters the sentence that demolishes everything he'd ever presumed about her. About their relationship. "I always knew exactly what you were, Jacob."

"You . . . *knew* . . . what?"

"Did you think I was stupid? That I didn't realize they'd sent you, and you were watching me? I was aware of everything and everyone around me at every moment. I had to be. Do you think I ever let my guard down for one second, living in that house with that horrible man who was going to get us all killed? With that crazy woman who hurt me from the time I was a little girl, who tried to—"

"*She* hurt you! I didn't. I only wanted to help you, and you . . . you told me you loved me."

"Yes. That's what I told you."

"But . . . why? Why did you let me . . . why didn't you stay away from me?"

"Because . . . you keep your friends close, and your enemies closer."

"I wasn't your enemy. I was trying to help you."

"You were trying to *kill* me."

"No!" He has to make her understand. Why won't she

understand? "I'm the one who . . . I was going to save you, but I got there too late."

The words land in a pause so profound that even the rain seems to cease falling.

Then she speaks, slowly. "What are you talking about?"

"That night . . . the night she . . . I saw you. All of you."

"You saw . . . what?"

"I saw what she did," he whispers.

He closes his eyes, and it's all there, always there—the bodies, the blood . . .

"You saw . . . you were there?"

"Yes."

"You're lying, Jacob."

"No! I was there!"

He needs her to believe him. He needs not just her forgiveness for what he'd done, but also her understanding that he hadn't been responsible for her fate. That in the end, he'd meant to be her savior, not her executioner.

"I was there, but it was too late. I was too late to stop her."

She flinches, but stands her ground, shoulders hunched, hands thrust deep into her pockets, as if she's cold.

Can ghosts feel cold?

Aren't ghosts inherently cold?

He's cold, so cold his teeth chatter around his words. "You didn't deserve what she did to you."

He sees her glance over one shoulder and then the other, edgy. He can't let her go. Not yet. He reaches for her arm.

She moves back. "Don't *touch* me!"

"You don't have to be afraid. Not of me. Only of her. I tried . . . but I couldn't find her afterward. Maybe she ran away. Or maybe . . . maybe she couldn't live with herself after what she did. Maybe in the end she was just another anonymous dead derelict in the park."

She says nothing, but again her head turns, as if to see if anyone is in range.

Not a soul. They're alone out here. Alone at last.

"I'll make this right, I swear to you," he promises.

"What . . . what do you mean?"

"Why do you think I kept coming back to Glover Street? A killer always returns to the scene of a crime, remember? I was waiting for her."

"You were waiting . . . you've been watching the house, watching *her*. With binoculars."

"Yes. And I thought . . ."

He pauses, seeing her take her hand out of her pocket. It isn't transparent even though she's a ghost. She extends it.

He reaches for her, aching to hold her. "I'm going to make it right. I'm going to kill—"

Too late, he sees the glint of something solid and metallic in her hand, an instant before his body explodes in agony on his last word.

"*—Ellie.*"

Nora

The suppressor muffles the shot. Close range, in Jacob's chest.

Her hand trembles as she tucks the gun back into the deep pocket of Stacey's coat, alongside the wad of cash. Just in case, she'd told herself, when she'd taken the money and the gun, leaving behind her phone, and her wallet. Just in case . . .

When Stacey had shown her those texts, she'd realized that the person who'd sent it, the person on the shed roof, the person waiting in the park, was not Lennon.

Lennon didn't have his phone.

Earlier, when she and Jules were in the cab heading home, Jules had received yet another call from an unknown number. That time, thinking it might be important, she'd finally picked it up. It was her son on a borrowed phone, saying that he'd lost his while he and Stacey were in the park.

Lennon was upset, speaking so loudly that Nora could hear his end of the conversation.

"I figured out I must have dropped it, like, two minutes after I walked away," he told his mother. "But when I went back for it, it was already gone. Someone must have seen it and picked it up."

"Okay, calm down, baby. It's okay. I'll help you."

Jules's efforts to placate him got under Nora's skin. He wanted a replacement phone immediately—a better one, as if the phone would never have been lost in the park if it had been the latest, most expensive model. Jules promised to meet him in Manhattan after his guitar lesson and buy it for him, though it sounded like it would be something of a scavenger hunt to find one in stock.

Preoccupied with her own problems, Nora thought it was no wonder the kid expected his relationships to revolve around his own needs. Then she put the missing phone out of her head.

But when she saw those texts, she knew.

The heart emoji, followed by **of mine** . . .

Heart of mine . . .

Jacob.

If Jacob had been following Stacey, watching her, then he could have found that phone and been clever enough to use it to lure Stacey to the park.

Just not clever enough to suspect that someone might be one step ahead of him.

Again.

But then, she hadn't known he was there that January night in 1994, had she? That he'd seen . . .

His last words ring in her ears.

I'm going to kill Ellie.

He thought Stacey was Ellie and he said he was going to kill her, and—

But he won't. Because it's over. Because you did what you had to do to make sure that delusional son of a bitch will never hurt Stacey.

She bends over the crumpled figure at her feet and checks his pockets. Wallet, keys, and sure enough, two cell phones.

Taking everything but his cigarettes, she walks away, and the cold hard rain rinses his blood from her, into the muddy earth.

Stacey

Flipping through the pages, Stacey scrutinizes one snapshot after another, searching for some logical explanation for how her own baby photos came to be pasted in this album.

It takes her longer than it should to grasp that the photos are old—much older than she is. And when she calms down enough to realize that there's writing in the margins, and then manages to actually read the captions, she sees that the handwriting isn't her mother's.

The baby isn't Stacey.

Her name is Anastasia.

Anna.

It makes perfect sense. Not just the photo album, but the other contents of the box as well—the Toska family's belongings, the stacks of cash, the evidence of lives lived in another place, under different identities.

This, then, is why the press accounts of the murders held so few photos of the Toskas, and none at all of Anna. The family was in hiding.

Ties to organized crime, Jules had said. And the murders were presumed to be a professional hit . . .

The box must have been hidden somewhere in the house. That, too, seems logical. The outside is caked in grime, and it smells damp, like wet dirt, as if it had been buried. Maybe it was. Maybe Mom dug it up when she was working in her garden.

It makes sense, now, most of it. Even the wild-eyed man on Edgemont Boulevard who'd called Stacey "Anna." All but one thing:

Why does Anna Toska, a stranger born in 1975, look exactly like Stacey?

Nora

There's a long line of young people waiting in the rain outside Lovely 'Ritas when Nora pays her fare with cash and steps out of the cab.

She steps over the streaming gutter, around a deep puddle, and retraces the path she and Jules had taken earlier.

Neon signs and streetlamps are reflected in shiny pavement and plate glass windows. Music, laughter, conversation, and people spill into the street. Several clubs have long lines; others just a scattering of smokers huddled beneath dripping awnings.

No one pays any attention to her, but even if they glanced in her direction, they'd see nothing out of the ordinary. Just the hooded figure of a woman, walking. No reason to later connect her to the anonymous dead derelict in the park.

She rounds a corner onto a dark, quiet block at the river's edge. The commotion falls behind her as the deserted warehouse looms. From the sidewalk and street, water access is blocked by buildings and security gates.

But not from the roof.

She ducks along an alley to the door she and Jules had

used to access the garden and quickly enters the four-digit code she'd committed to memory: *1–2–4–4* . . .

The lock clicks.

Her footsteps echo along the cavernous corridor. The elevator is waiting on the ground floor. She steps in and presses *R*, for roof.

It jerks into motion, seeming to rise inch by agonizing inch.

She does her best to stay calm. She can't allow panic to overtake her. Not when she's come twenty-five years, thousands of miles, full circle, to make things right.

Memento mori . . .

She thinks of them all—the lost people she'd once loved.

Just a few more minutes, a few more steps, and it will be over.

At last, the doors open. She exits onto the rooftop into a cold, drenching wind and walks to the edge. She looks out at the iconic skyline glittering against a black sky, then down at blacker water far below.

Memento mori.

Remember you must die.

Jacob's words, too, echo in her head.

Maybe she couldn't live with herself after what she did . . .

She takes a deep, shuddering breath.

She reaches into her pocket and takes out the gun.

Memento mori . . .

It lands with a splash far below. The keys follow, and the wallet, one phone, the other phone, and then it's over.

Maybe she couldn't live with herself . . .

And maybe now she can.

Stacey

Stacey put the box back under her parents' bed, but carried the album to her own room. She's just sitting, holding it in her lap, questions twisting her brain every which way, trying to avoid the only answer that could possibly make sense . . .

Because it doesn't.

Sirens wail in the night. More sirens than usual, it seems. Or is it that the rain drowned them out, making them more noticeable now that it's trickled to a steady drip . . . drip . . . drip . . .

Another sound reaches her ears.

Downstairs, the front door opens and closes. Either Mom is home, or Dad and Piper are.

Footsteps.

Just one set, not two.

She waits for her mother to come upstairs. She's going to open Stacey's door, and say . . . what?

Something about Lennon? Had she talked to his moms, or directly to him? Had he denied watching her from the roof next door? And sending the texts . . .

Caught up in the Toska family album, she'd all but forgotten about the messaging shorthand that made her suspect someone else had been responsible. Now she's not even sure about that—about anything—other than that she needs to end the relationship. It doesn't feel like love. It feels like control—his intensity, his all-encompassing need to be with her, to tell her how to be.

It's going to be a messy breakup. But she can get through it, when the time comes. Right now, her more pressing concern is finding answers about the photos she saw.

Below, the footsteps move through the first floor to the back of the house. She hears the distinct creak of the door opening to the basement. After a few minutes, water groans through old pipes—the washing machine.

Mom is doing laundry?

Under ordinary circumstances, it wouldn't surprise Stacey, even at this hour on a Saturday night. Maybe she should take it as a sign that whatever happened down the street wasn't earth-shattering.

Nora

Naked, shivering, and scrubbed clean, Nora steps out of the basement shower stall and wraps herself in a towel. She'd plucked it from a basket of laundry waiting to be folded, and her terry cloth robe from the dryer.

She should have grabbed another towel to use as a bath mat. She wraps herself in the robe and walks barefoot, careful not to slip on the linoleum. It's cracked and ugly, gold with brown flecks, installed by the family that had lived here from the 1960s until 1986.

By then, the Toskas had been in New York for a few years. They had, as WITSEC required, assimilated into their new identities and become self-sufficient. They bought 104 Glover Street in Lena's name. She'd never changed her will after the divorce and remarriage to Stanley. That left her first husband as beneficiary in the event that her only child, Anastasia, didn't survive her.

If not for that unexpected twist in a tragic tale, this house would never have stood empty for twenty-five years. The Howell family would now be living instead in some tiny Manhattan apartment, or perhaps Nora and the girls wouldn't have accompanied Keith after all.

If he'd come to New York alone, their marriage would have been over. They couldn't go on the way they were even under the same roof. With a few thousand miles between them, they'd have become strangers—even more than they already are.

But it's not too late. They still love each other. They just have work to do. Now, at last, she can give their relationship the attention it deserves, and even find a way to build the career she'd sacrificed for her family.

Strange how things worked out, she thinks as she climbs the basement steps.

Kato is waiting for her with an expectant wag of his tail.

"You want a treat, don't you? Okay, boy. You deserve it."

If he hadn't found those binoculars, she wouldn't have realized that a violent, dangerous man had been watching this house, watching her daughter.

She glances at the empty shed roof next door as she turns off the kitchen light.

Should she feel remorse for killing a man who'd been watching her house, stalking her child, seeking vengeance for a crime that in his madness, he thought Stacey—as Ellie—had committed?

No. She should feel only relief. With Jacob gone, her daughter—her family—will be safe.

And so will your secret.

No one will ever know who she really is. She's finally free to heal and move on.

She takes a last satisfied look around the kitchen, taking in the modern appliances, expensive cabinetry, sleek countertops and backsplash.

She'd picked out everything from afar, envisioning how

it would look in a house she hadn't seen in years and at the time, believed she might never see again. That was back in 2012, after Hurricane Sandy had left the house with significant water damage.

"It needs a lot of work," Teddy told her, after flying to New York to inspect it. "What do you say? Is it time to sell?"

"It's your house. I can't stop you, if you want to—"

"It's my house in name only."

Yes. Because Teddy had inherited from her husband, Victor. Because the rightful heir—the daughter he'd had with his first wife—no longer exists.

"This is your decision, my love," Teddy said. "I just worry that hanging on to it makes it impossible for you to fully move on."

"Then do the work and get ready to sell."

But even after the house had been repaired, and renovated, she couldn't let it go. It just sat there like a monument to tragedy.

Forget-me-not . . .

When Keith told her about the move to New York, she instructed Teddy to hire a rental agent.

"But make sure you retain full approval over the new tenant. And I don't want it listed until Keith and I get to New York. I want to be the first to see it."

"Then you're not going to tell him—"

"No! I'll let him think I stumbled across it."

Silence. Then Teddy asked if maybe it was time for her to tell her husband the truth at last. "He already thinks you've been unfaithful. Wouldn't it be best to set him straight about that, and—"

"You mean, tell him that I'm not who he thinks I am? That I've lied to him from the moment we met? How is that best? If I do that now, Teddy, while we're on shaky ground, I'll lose him. Maybe I can tell him the truth someday, but first I have to deal with it and resolve it, just like you said. All I want is to heal without losing anyone else I love."

And now, tonight, at last, she can start.

It's a most fitting birthday gift for the woman who'd been born to Victor and Magdalena Montgomery on this date in 1975.

Anastasia Montgomery—later known as Anna Toska— now known as Nora Howell.

Stacey

tanding at the top of the stairs, Stacey watches her mother ascend.

She's wearing a robe, and her hair is still wet. Or is it wet again? Had Stacey been wrong that she'd left the house? Maybe she'd been here all along.

But something is different about her. The urgency and concern have been lifted; her energy no longer weighted.

"Mom?"

She looks up, startled. Sees Stacey, and then sees the photo album in her hands.

"Where did you get that?" Her voice sounds strangled. She climbs the last few steps slowly.

"I found it in your room. I was looking for you, and I saw it."

A veil descends over her mother's face. What is she hiding?

Maybe Stacey really is adopted, as Lennon had guessed, and Mom had denied. Maybe that explains what she found in the album.

Though, how? It still wouldn't make sense.

The thing that *would* make sense, the absolutely preposterous thing, tries to push its way into her brain. She shoves it back, talking instead of thinking, her tone too bright, the words rushed, a statement and not the intended question.

"Mom, the little girl in these pictures . . . she looks exactly like me."

Her mother opens her mouth, closes it, and looks away.

For a long moment, she stares down at dead Gertrude Williams and her family, hanging on the stair wall.

Then she turns slowly back to Stacey, wearing a peculiar expression.

Stacey thinks of Margaret Williams, and Lizzie Borden. Such nice, respectable, normal women . . .

Until they snapped.

Anna

emento mori.

Ironic, isn't it? The Williams family hadn't outlived their century, but their portrait endures, even surviving the catastrophic hurricane-inflicted water damage to 104 Glover in 2012.

It was hanging on the wall when the Toska family moved into this house in 1986.

Only eleven years old, Anna had already been through so much.

Her parents' divorce had been a devastating blow. Her father lost a fierce custody battle because the judge believed a child belonged with her mother. Even if the mother was battling depression and anxiety. Even if the mother took out her frustrations on her daughter and had destroyed her marriage to a good man by having an affair.

But of course no one, not even Victor, knew about Magdalena's psychiatric problems or Stanislav Shehu's criminal activity.

And so Anna lived with her mother and stepfather, first in Nevada, then Arizona, until his 1983 arrest. After testifying in exchange for immunity and protection, he became

Stanley Toska, her mother became Lena, and she became Anna.

During the first few years of the program, facilitators arranged visits for Anna and Victor. They both had to make several airplane transfers, accompanied by marshals, to meet at remote locations. Every time they parted, they wept. But she couldn't bear to tell him about her mother's mental deterioration and abusive behavior. There was nothing he could do to help her. She knew she could never go back to live with him, because that would bring the constant threat to her own life home to her father's house. She couldn't bear the thought of anything happening to him.

By 1986, when the family had assimilated into their new identities and bought the house, they were essentially cut loose. Once Stanley was in control, there was no further visitation between Anna and her father. The last time she got to see him, she had no idea they were parting for many years to come, but he must have. He gave her a kitten, and told her to take good care of it, and of herself.

The tiny creature was the lone bright spot in her isolating new life. She was forbidden to make friends, participate in activities, couldn't even go to school on class photo day. There were no pictures of her as she grew up, ever. They couldn't risk someone recognizing her as Anastasia Montgomery and figuring out that Stanley Toska was the notorious Stanislav Shehu, marked for death by the transnational crime organization he'd helped to dismantle.

She no longer knew who she was. Even when she looked in the mirror, she saw a stranger whose eyes had seen too much, whose mouth had forgotten how to smile, whose nose had been smashed by her mother's angry fist and left to heal without medical intervention, because there could be no doctors. Not for her, and not for her mother, consumed by depression one moment and rage the next, so volatile that her husband forbade her to leave the house, fearing she'd give them away and get them killed.

Sometimes, Anna wished it would happen.

She was growing up. Her kitten had long since grown up. One stifling summer day, he got underfoot and clawed Lena's bare ankle when she stepped on him. She carried on as if she'd been mauled by a lion. The next morning, he was gone—vanished from Anna's bed where he slept every night.

She searched the house in vain, and later overheard her mother and Stanley laughing behind closed doors, saying that it was a good thing it was trash pickup day, or theirs would really start to stink in this heat. Listening in horror to their conversation, she grasped that they'd destroyed her precious pet and tossed his body away like garbage.

It didn't matter which of them had done the deed. Both found it amusing. Both covered it up.

Both were monsters.

College saved her. She won a full academic scholarship, and she made her escape. She was free . . . until the campus closed for winter break, and she was forced back into that household. Forced to see how her mother had deteriorated.

Lena's silent, bedridden spells and physically abusive rages were increasingly interrupted by terrifying behavior. She'd sneak up behind Anna as if she was going to pounce, then scuttle away in silence.

Her decline culminated in a suicidal, murderous rage over

Anna's "abandonment." She tried to hurtle herself down the stairs and take her daughter with her. Anna managed to grab the rail to save them both, and then fled the house, heading for the park.

That happened on January 16, the day—

"Anastasia."

The name is a ragged whisper in Stacey's throat.

She opens her eyes.

"Mom? Anastasia. Anna-Stacey. I'm named for her?"

Anna-Stacey . . . Anastasia.

Ellie-Nora . . . Eleanor.

"Mom, is this you?" Stacey is holding up the album, open to the final photo.

It isn't on the last page. There are plenty of empty pages, lined with cellophane slots that will never be filled.

The handwritten caption reads *favorite toy.* The photo shows a cherubic little girl with a jack-in-the-box, one chubby hand blurred in motion on the crank handle.

She closes her eyes.

She hears *"All around the mulberry bush . . ."*

She hears Lena telling Victor that she's leaving him.

She hears Victor begging her not to go, not to take his precious Anastasia.

She hears tinkling music as the handle turns faster and faster in an effort to drown out their voices, and the monkey is chasing the weasel, round and round, and—

"Mom?"

Pop!

"Oh, Stacey . . . I'm so sorry."

She reaches for her daughter with the hand that had held a gun, and pulled a trigger.

"Mom? Is it true? Were you . . . *her*?"

The hand settles on Stacey's shoulder.

"Yes. It's true."

It isn't the whole truth. When you love someone as much as a parent loves a child—as much as a child loves a parent—you protect them.

In return for the lies Victor had told to save her, she'd shielded him once again, as she had years earlier from the death threat, and her mother's abusive behavior. Now she was protecting him from her own darkest self. From what had really happened in the house that night.

The first time she'd held that gun, and fired it.

Pop!

First her stepfather . . .

Pop!

Next her mother . . .

Pop!

Finally Ellie, her friend.

Ellie, in her bed, in her room, in her place.

Earlier that evening, Anna had found her in the park in a bad way, shivering on a bench without a coat. She'd had a fight with her boyfriend and he'd thrown her out. Anna brought her to a diner to warm her up and get some food into her, then brought Ellie back to 104 Glover, late, after the lights had gone out in Stanley and Lena's bedroom. She opened the front door with the key she'd hidden in the foundation, closed it without a sound, and fastened the old iron chain lock.

They crept up the stairs in the dark. She gave Ellie a nightgown and toothbrush, and she retreated to the bathroom for such a long time Anna feared she'd passed out. When at last she emerged, they crammed themselves into Anna's twin bed. Ellie was trembling. Anna thought she was cold, or frightened.

"Shh, it's okay. You're safe. I'm here." She wrapped her arms around her friend and drifted off, listening to her breathing. When she woke up in the night, the breathing had stopped. Ellie was gone.

Had the overdose been deliberate? Did it matter?

The horrific shock of awakening with a corpse in her arms remains seared into her memory.

What happened afterward, mercifully, has been lost—her brain protecting her from the overwhelming trauma of what she'd done.

There are snippets.

Finding the gun.

Pop! Pop! Pop!

Watching bloody water swirl into the drain.

Putting on Ellie's clothes.

Burying the gun and key in the box that held fragments of their old lives, their real lives, before they became the Toskas.

She found a pay phone and made a call.

That grounded her again, the sound of her father's voice allowing her to find her own, to convey information, to stifle incrimination.

"They're dead, Daddy. Dead in their beds."

"Your mother? Stanislav?"

"Yes, and my friend . . . Ellie. She was staying with us. They must have thought she was me."

Oh, Ellie.

"Then . . . no one knows you're alive?"

No one would ever know, not even the authorities.

As she made the long bus journey to the West Coast, her father, tethered to the ruse that was her lifeline, flew to New York to identify the bodies. He confirmed that the three victims were Anna, Lena, and Stanislav.

Back in California, he introduced his daughter to his new wife, Teddy.

"Call her Nora. That's what she's chosen."

Ellie . . . Nora.

Forget-me-not . . .

Memento mori . . .

She's spent most of her life remembering death. Remembering that she must die.

That she *did* die.

But until it's her turn to spend eternity in a grave that bears someone else's name, she's going to remember that she must *live*.

Live for the family she'd lost and for the family she's created. Live for the little girl whose life was destroyed and imperiled, for the young woman who'd done what she had to do to survive, and for the daughters who will never look into their own mother's eyes and see murderous madness. Live with the lies she has to keep from the people she loves most and with the truth she can begin to tell at last.

"Mom? Are you . . . were you . . . ?"

"Yes."

She pulls her daughter into a fierce embrace, and she utters the words that have echoed in her mind every day, every moment, for twenty-five years.

Aloud at last; allowed at last.

"I was Anna."